from a

HEAVENLY LAND

Julia's Story

A NOVEL

Cathy Slusser

To Charles + METV,
Thanks for the
promo!
Cathy Slusser

© 2014 by Cathy Slusser
All rights reserved. No portion of this book may be reproduced, stored in a retrieval system, or transmitted in any form or by any means—electronic, mechanical, photocopy, recording, scanning, or other—except for brief quotations in critical reviews or articles, without the prior written permission of the author.

© Cover Image: image copyright, used under license from Shutterstock.com.

To Christina, daughter of my heart.
I am so proud of the woman
you have become.

Julia's Story

We all have our demons. Not the kind in the Bible that came out foaming at the mouth under Jesus' command or even the spirits in fairy tales that planned mischief for the innocent. No, the kind of demons I am talking about are the ones that whisper in your ear that you aren't good enough. The ones that keep you awake in the dead of night when you should be sleeping, terrorizing you with your failures and fears. The memories so horrible you would die before enduring them again. The ones that lead you to think you cannot trust anyone but yourself. That make you desire control over anything else and that keep you isolated from the ones who would love you, including God. Those kinds of demons. We all have them, even those who would pretend they don't. And we all fight them in different ways. This is the story of how I escaped my demons. It took a journey across the ocean and experiences in the wilderness to do it. But, with help, I left them behind. It took years, but I changed from a woman who desired control to one willing to let Someone else be in charge. But, it took time. My name is Julia. *This is my story.*

Introduction

Terra Ceia, Florida 1843

I wake with a start. Bonaparte's barking echoes in the fog. Somewhere outside I hear the sound of bushes rattling. *Who is it?* There are no other settlers near our hut on the north shore of Terra Ceia Bay. The animals should be secure. I last checked at dusk. The cow and calf rest together in their pen made of pine logs. The chickens roost in the big oak tree whose limbs protect the palm thatched roof of our hut. *Perhaps it is just the wind.* I pull the coverlet over me and try to drown out the noise.

My husband, Joseph, left this morning for Fort Brooke. Like a tangled ball of yarn, he tries to unknot the complicated rules and requirements that keep us from filing claim to this land which we were promised. The Armed Occupation Act passed by the United States Congress in 1842 and signed by President John Tyler on August 4, did not discriminate against us, German immigrants not yet citizens of the United States. All it required was that we clear five acres, build a house, live here for five years and serve in the militia. The desire for new settlers in south Florida, who will defend their own land and save the government from paying soldiers to keep the Indians from attacking the established cities in the north, was stronger than any prejudice against nonnative born people. At least in Washington. Here on the frontier, in the Florida wilderness, discrimination is strong but subtle. Joseph's trip to Fort Brooke will likely not prove who continues to make it so difficult for us, but perhaps this time, he will be successful.

A scraping noise against the thatch followed by more barking pulls me back to a more immediate cause for anxiety. *Who is it?* I flash back to the past. Images of hands reaching for me. I curl into a ball. *No, no more. I am safe.* Another noise. *Is it Indians? Do they know I am alone?* Well, not quite alone.

"Mama? Where are you? Mama?" Eliza, my three year old daughter, sits up in her trundle bed beside mine.

Now, I hear the hens squawking and the call of an owl as he signals to his mate. *The hens! An owl is after the chickens!* The need to protect our flock, who supply us with meat and eggs, overcomes any fear. I toss the covers aside and leave my bed. Shushing Eliza, I tell her not to move.

I tiptoe to the entrance of our rudely constructed home. No one told me that moving to the Florida wilderness would require the skill of weaving palm fronds together to make a roof. At least it is better than living in a tent. *Only a little better.* I reach for Joseph's gun which leans against the wall made of palm logs. *Thank God he left it here for us.* My hands shake as I pour gunpowder into the chamber and tamp it down. Stepping outside, I barely see Bonaparte's outline in the soft pale light of the spring moon. I practiced with the gun but never at night.

A large winged shape swoops out of the old spreading oak tree that shelters the hens. It skims over the dog's head. Bonaparte stands bravely between the owl and his next meal. I rush toward them, then, stand firm as I brace the gun against my shoulder. Bonaparte leaps in the air after the owl. I yell at him to get down and pray I don't hit him as I aim and pull the trigger. A tremendous bang echoes through the night air as I fall backwards to the ground. For a moment, I cannot breathe. The impact knocks the wind out of me. My ribs ache. *Have I broken some?*

I hear a scream. *Is it mine?* Eliza runs at me. Stumbling over the hem of her nightgown, she tries to catch herself, but falls on top of me. The pain threatens to knock me out again, but I struggle to sit erect and hold my frantic daughter.

"Mama! Mama!" she cries. I comfort her and then, as a distraction, I ask, "Did I get him?"

"Get who?" Eliza's sobs slow to a shudder. I smooth her hair from her eyes.

"The owl. It was after our chickens."

We both turn towards the direction of Bonaparte's frantic yelps. A large brown owl looks at the dog in disdain. His yellow talons grip the limb of the oak.

"Bonaparte! Leave it alone!" I order. Disappointed, I slowly rise to my knees and then straighten. I gasp with pain.

"I missed."

As if to mock me, the owl turns his wide brown head and blinks at us. Then he hoots and calls to his mate. It sounds as though he says, "Who cooks for you? Who cooks for you?" From the distance, I hear a piercing screech of reply. The owl takes flight flying so close over our heads, I feel the brush of his wings.

I will get you next time, I promise.

"What happened to you, Mama? Did he hurt you?"

"No. I guess I put too much powder in the gun. Your father must have left it loaded, and when I added to it, the charge was more than I could handle." Rubbing my shoulder, I turn towards the hut. "I hope the chickens can hide from him. We cannot afford to lose any of them now."

I tuck Eliza back into bed. Bonaparte guards the door of the hut looking for the owl. Slowly, stiffly, I make my way to bed. *I'll be sore for weeks.* I blow out the candle and ease carefully onto the mattress stuffed with dried Spanish moss, but I cannot sleep. Neither can Eliza.

"When will Papa be home?"

"I don't know. As soon as he can, I expect."

"Where did he go?"

"Eliza, I've answered that question before."

"I forgot, please tell me again."

"Your father went to file papers with the land office. There have been some questions about our claim, and he needs to make sure everyone knows this is our land."

"Why couldn't we go with him?"

"Because someone must stay here to protect our home."

"I'm afraid. I want Papa to come back." Eliza sniffles. I cannot see the tears, but know they stain her pillow. I know because they wet mine as well.

"I want my Papa."

I know child, I miss him, too, I long to confide. *I must be strong for her.* Instead, I say, "Eliza, go to sleep. Papa will be home when he can. In the meantime, we will be fine without him. Bonaparte is here to tell us if anyone comes near, and I have Papa's gun."

Intrigued, Eliza's sobbing stops. "How do you know how to shoot Papa's gun?"

"He showed me how before he left. Now, no more questions. Say your prayers and go to sleep."

Obedient, Eliza is still. I listen as her breathing grows quiet and steady. But, my tears still flow. *Oh, God, how will we survive alone? When will Joseph come home? What have we done? What made us think we could make a life here?*

Chapter One

Bradford, Bavaria 1818

My earliest memories are of Christmas. Even more special to me than simply the day we celebrate Christ's arrival, it is also the day of my birth, a little over a year before Napoleon Bonaparte defeated the Holy Roman Empire and formed the Kingdom of Bavaria. With Napoleon's encouragement, Count Montgelas began modernizing our county, improving roads and communication, and bringing democracy, no matter how fledgling the form, to our world. My parents were thrilled with the changes. Napoleon, despite what others might have thought of him in later years, was a hero to our family.

We began the Christmas season early, on December 6, St. Nicholas' Day, when St. Nicholas distributes nuts and candy to good girls and boys. For days before his arrival, my brothers trembled in fear of St. Nicholas' servant, Ruprecht, who punished bad boys. Though they teased and tormented me all year long, for some reason, Ruprecht never appeared and all of us received treats. I thought it unfair my brothers never once got what they deserved.

From December 6 until Christmas Day, my mother prepared for the celebration honoring Christ's birth. We cleaned the house, striving to make it spotless for the arrival of the Christ Child. My father often laughed at my mother's frantic efforts, saying my birth on Christmas Day in 1807, was hastened by her work. Even as a little girl, I had chores to do—dusting, washing windows, crawling under beds to clear spider webs. I never liked the spiders, though my mother told stories of their industry.

"No spiders under the bed, but they can weave their webs as much as they desire on our Christmas tree." Every year, she told us the tale of the spiders, who desiring to see the Christ Child and honor Him, wove their webs all over a family's Christmas tree. Knowing that the mother of the family would be distraught to see her tree covered in dusty grey webs, on the night of His arrival, the Christ Child turned them into strands of silver and gold. I loved hearing my mother tell stories, but to this day, I do not like spiders.

On Christmas Day morning, we each received a few presents, mostly practical things like clothing, shoes and mittens. On the Christmas of my eighth birthday, my gift was a pair of skates, which I dearly loved. As much as possible, I enjoyed being outside. To have a reason to escape the house in the middle of winter was as much a gift as the skates themselves.

After we opened our presents, we ate Christmas dinner consisting of sausage, potato dumplings, cinnamon cake and spicy Pfeffernusse cookies. Afterwards, we went to church to see elaborate displays recreating the town of Bethlehem. In the evening, we lit the candles on our Christmas tree and sang Christmas hymns like "Come Ye Little Children" and "The Holy Night" before we were scurried off to bed to dream of the next Christmas a whole year away.

We never imagined Christmas would not come or the next year it would be strikingly different, but after eight Christmases celebrated the exact same way, life changed abruptly for me in 1815. The year I received the pair of skates would be the last Christmas I would celebrate for many years.

Bavaria was at peace after the defeat of Napoleon at Waterloo in 1815. Politically, our country moved forward into the modern era, even advancing towards a government that would eventually allow small farmers, like my parents, to participate in elections. But, economically, we suffered. Unusually warm weather, without the customary summer rains, repeated for several summers, created widespread drought.

I remember my father and mother talking in hushed tones at night as I was supposed to be sleeping on my pallet on the floor. Only a curtain separated me from where Father sat with Mother, rubbing his forehead in the dim candlelight and wondering how he could sustain his crops. Each year, the harvest was smaller and smaller. Food prices rose and even those like my family who lived on the land in plenty for many years, could not afford to eat.

"We need rain," he repeated over and over. Along with others in our village, we went to church to pray for rain, but it did not come.

Instead, in 1816 our region, like most of the mountainous portions of Europe, was covered with spreading ash from Asia where a volcanic eruption occurred the previous year. When we finally received the rains we prayed for, it came in such amounts that floods washed away the fertile soil and left only mud and rocks. The rain created standing water where crops should be planted. Perhaps the rain was an omen that farmers should not waste their seed. That year was known as the year without summer as snow blanketed our farm in June and again in July. Ash, rain and snow. What more could God send in perverse response to our prayers?

He sent hunger. My mother baked bread from straw and my father slaughtered our horses in an effort to keep our stomachs filled. Rats sold for a high price in the market and people who could afford them, gladly paid the cost. One by one, I watched first my mother then my brothers, and finally my father die of starvation. Only God knows why my sister and I survived. God knows why the rescuer He sent would only rescue my body, but would do such damage to my mind.

"Monica, hush. Stop crying, he will be here soon, and you do not want him to see you with red eyes. He might not take us." I want to shake my sister, but know that will only make her cry harder. Born in the early years of famine, four year old Monica never knew a life of joyful Christmases, gifts and plentiful food on the table, but only an empty, rumbling stomach and the ache of hunger. Once, the neighbor woman who took us in after our parents' death thought I was not listening and muttered, "Twas that baby who killed her." I understand my mother did all she could to keep us alive, but refuse to think being pregnant without nourishment robbed my mother of her own life. I cannot think that and still love my little sister.

Now we wait for an uncle, my mother's oldest brother, summoned by members of the town council who are not able to feed their own offspring much less care for any orphans. He promised to come and take us to his home in Bessingen. *What will await us there? Would it be anything close to what home once meant? Orphans. We are orphans.* The phrase runs through my mind even as I try to comfort Monica.

Boisterous knocking on the door of the house announces our uncle's arrival. I blink in fear when a large man pushes his way inside. The house is dark and the light behind him prevents me from seeing his face.

"Are these them? I didn't intend to take on a little one," he announces. "I need house help not a nursery."

Rising, I swallow my fear and shelter Monica underneath my arm. *She is so tiny. Will he leave her? That must not happen.*

"She can work. Our mother taught us to work. We can sweep and dust. I will take care of her."

"You?" he sneers. "How can you take care of her? You are barely out of diapers yourself."

"I am eleven. I am big and strong. I can take care of her. I have been taking care of her."

"Food is scarce. I cannot afford to feed someone who does not work."

My stomach growls at the mention of food. I know how precious it is. He must not leave us here alone. I run to him. Looking up, I see my uncle's face clearly for the first time. Do I see some resemblance to my mother there?

"Feed only one of us. We will share. I promised my mother I would not leave her."

At last, a wave of sympathy crosses his face.

"I will take her. But, she will work. And so will you. Come."

I rush back to Monica and take her hand. Nodding to the neighbor, I grab a bundle containing all the belongings we have scavenged from what my father did not sell in an effort to keep food on our table. An extra change of clothing, my family's Bible and buried underneath, my father's pocket watch, a gift from my mother on their wedding day. He wanted to sell it, but Mother would not let him. Even when things were at their bleakest, he could not let it go. It was the only thing he had left of her.

Struggling with my bundle and my reluctant sister who fights back tears, we follow our uncle into the bright sunlight towards our new life.

Bessingen, Bavaria 1830

"Girl, where is my dinner?" In the twelve years since I moved into my uncle's large stone house in the center of Bessingen, he has never called me by my first name. I tried to understand his unwillingness to say it. At first, I thought he did not know who I was and quietly protested, "My name is Julia," when I had the opportunity. I quickly learned speaking my name only earned me a slap across the face. I grew accustomed to responding to "girl." I thought perhaps his grief over my mother's death prevented him from saying her name, which I share, aloud. As time passes, I see that calling me "girl," is his way of keeping me as his slave. If I think of myself as "girl," and not "Julia," I lose my identity. *I will not give in.* His attempt to oppress me keeps my spirit alive, but only in secret.

While I work around the kitchen or clean house, even in my limited free time or before I go to bed, I remember my past and remind myself of who I am and how much my parents loved me. Images of happier times fill my mind like pictures in a book. I hold fast to them and remember a time when things were different. Once, I was cherished. Once, I was a part of a family. I cannot think of my uncle as family. I refuse to even use his name, only calling him "he" in my thoughts. Surely, he cannot be any relation to my sweet, loving mother.

When I address him, he expects to be called, "Sir." I keep my eyes downcast. Any attitude beyond servanthood results in punishment. He learns physical abuse and hunger only rob him of my assistance for if I am hurt or weak, I cannot serve him. His punishments grow stealthy. Locking me in my room, keeping me confined to the house, withholding information. His greatest threat is Monica. Always, he uses her well-being to keep me hostage. The thought she might be harmed is enough to keep me in line.

Early on, he isolates her from me. Contrary to his first warning, instead of expecting her to work, she becomes his plaything. While he treats me as a slave, Monica is his pet. When famine ends, food is plentiful again. He feeds Monica choice foods, brings her fashionable clothes, and pays for her education and music lessons. In public, he introduces her as his niece, but in private, he calls her "Daughter," and expects her to entertain him. Sometimes, she comes to the kitchen to visit with me while he is away from the house, tending to his business and his warehouses. When we are alone, I whisper to my now sixteen year old sister to be cautious of his attention.

"Monica, you must be careful. Stay alert. I fear for your safety."

"Julia, don't be ridiculous. Father would not harm me."

"He is not your father. He is your uncle, and not a kind one."

"How can you say that? You are just jealous. Look at the pretty dress he bought me." She twirls in a pirouette. "If you ask, I am sure he will buy you one, too."

Monica sees the way our uncle treats me, but I think she prefers to ignore it. What if he did the same to her? Perhaps she doesn't want to imagine he would.

"Girl, I said where is my dinner!" His voice booms from the dining room into the kitchen. Quickly, I spread braunschweiger, a soft, spreadable sausage, made from pork, beef, bacon, and garlic on a slice of bread I baked earlier this morning. I add mustard and cheese to his plate. A side of potatoes and cabbage complete the meal. Balancing the plate and a pitcher of beer, I resist the urge to rush into the room. Better not to appear too harried. If only I had known he would come home for the noon meal today, but I expected him to stay away until evening.

"Is this all?"

"Yes, sir, for now. But, there is pie in the oven." *Thank God I bought those apples yesterday.* Now that I am grown, I am allowed to leave the house alone to go to market. It is the brief taste of freedom I relish.

"Pie? What kind of pie?" He rubs his stomach in anticipation.

"Apple."

He nods. "Bring it in as soon as it is done."

I sigh and return to the kitchen. Now he knows there is pie, he will be alright. My uncle has a sweet tooth. I refrain from telling him I made two pies. He will share his with Monica, but the second one will be for me.

The advantage of working in the kitchen is I get to eat as I please. Before the pies are ready, I gobble down two slices of bread with butter and another two with braunschweiger. I eat standing up; always afraid I will be caught, but never so afraid I cannot fill my stomach to overflowing with food. From the girl who never had enough to eat, I have become a young woman always seeking to be full. Sometimes, I eat an entire cake by myself, not even using a fork, just cutting slice after slice and eating them with my hands. Pastries, bread, potatoes, meat. I cook more than is needed for my uncle and Monica. It is good he does not have a wife for she would surely know I buy far more at the market than makes it to his table. Nothing is left over for him to see. I eat it all. Yet, no matter how full my body might be, my heart remains empty.

When my uncle has enjoyed his slice of pie, and I have eaten a whole one, he returns to work. Monica embroiders in her room, and I tie on my bonnet and pick up my basket to go to market. I will need to buy more fruit and flour for tomorrow's dessert. Perhaps I will also get a chicken. A chicken pie would be good for dinner.

I love going to the market. It is my only excuse to leave the house. When my uncle first allowed me to shop alone, I thought about running away. Despite the temptation, I could not leave my sister alone with him. Nor did I know where I might go. Certainly reporting him to the authorities was not an option. It seemed easier to enjoy these times of freedom than to take a chance on angering him and losing the privilege.

Carefully, I cross the cobblestone streets, dodging horses and carts. The air is crisp. Fall is here, and winter will not be far behind. Soon, it will begin to snow. Then, I will not make regular trips to shop. We will rely on the preserves I canned throughout the summer. Only a block away from the market, I focus on my grocery list and remember my mother's admonition to look for a chicken with bright feathers and clear eyes. Oh, how I wish she were here! Thankfully, she insisted on teaching me to cook and clean at a young age, but I miss her so much. How cruel it was that fate took her before the famine ended.

Now, there is more than enough food. Enough to keep a family alive.

I hear the church bells ringing in the distance. I must hurry. There is no time to stop and pray. Since moving to Bessingen, I have not attended church. *Mother would be disappointed. She loved church.* Sometimes, I think I can still hear her voice singing her favorite hymns. I hum a portion of one of them as I walk, "We Plow the Fields and Scatter":

We plow the fields, and scatter the good seed on the land,
But it is fed and watered by God's almighty hand;
He sends the snow in winter, the warmth to swell the grain,
The breezes and the sunshine, and soft refreshing rain.
All good gifts around us
Are sent from heaven above,
Then thank the Lord,
O thank the Lord
For all His love.

I shake my head at the images in the song. I remember the seasons before my parents died. Too much rain. Snow in summer. Failed crops. Death. *If God indeed sent them, how can I thank Him? And even more, how can I trust Him?* Better not to think about it. Better just to do what I can do and depend only on myself. Mother might have thought God to be a loving God, but I have no reason to believe so.

As I turn the corner towards the market, I catch a glimpse of myself in the shop window. I am now my father's height, taller than most women my age. Should I be ashamed of my spreading girth? I am not slim and dainty like Monica. My mind flashes to my mother upon death's door. Boney and frail, she refrained from eating so her children might live. My mother would want me to eat and be strong. When I do, I honor her sacrifice.

In the market, I pick through vegetables and fruit, choosing the ripest and best for my kitchen. I love the colors and smells of the market. Here, I feel free. I do not worry about cutting corners. The vendors charge my purchases to my uncle's accounts. Content with what I prepare, he never complains about the prices. As I consider the freshness of some potatoes, a stabbing pain in my stomach seizes me. I drop my basket and bend over in agony.

"Fraulein," a man reaches for my arm. "Are you alright? Did you drop your basket?"

I shake my head, too sick to speak. He helps me to sit on a crate in his stall. I bend over, arms around my waist and try to catch my breath. Slowly, the pain eases. He occupies himself picking up my purchases and placing them in my basket.

"Do you need me to call a doctor?"

I shake my head again and manage, "No, I will be fine. Thank you for your help. I just needed to rest a moment."

"Are you sure you are alright? Do you need help getting home?"

"I can make it." I stand to go, but my side aches when I try to pick up my basket. He sees me wince in pain.

"Let me help you. Just a moment."

The man crosses to the stall beside his and quietly speaks to another man before coming back to me.

"Come, I will walk you home. Thomas will watch my produce while I am gone."

"No, no. I cannot ask you to do that," I protest. "I will be fine." *What if my uncle sees us?*

"Listen to me, I do not know what is wrong with you, but if you will not let me call a doctor, at least let me make sure you get home safely. Come, I will not rest unless you let me do so." He easily lifts my basket, and I have no choice but to go with him.

The pain lessens, but it is still there. It is all I can do just to walk so I am grateful for his help and more grateful for his silence. I am in no mood to talk. *What is wrong with me? What could cause such pain without any warning? Am I dying like my mother?* Lost in my thoughts I lead the way to my uncle's house.

I do not enter by the front entrance, but go around to the back. My helper follows me. At the kitchen door, I break the silence and reach to take the basket from him.

"How can I say thank you? I appreciate your assistance very much."

"No need for thanks, but you must do me one favor. Tell me your name, Fraulein."

I hesitate, but remembering how he rescued me, I say, "Julia. Julia Hunt."

"I am Joseph Atzeroth, Julia. Take care of yourself." He turns to go, but smiles. "I hope to see you again, soon."

Over time, the attacks continue. I pay attention to what I have eaten or done before they come. I learn the pain reappears whenever I eat too much rich food. I crave the satisfaction of a full belly, the delicious textures and tastes, but when I try to curb my hunger and eat smaller portions, fewer gravies, fat and pastries, I feel better. At least physically. The emotional hunger remains, and whenever anxiety and loneliness push me to eat more than I need, I pay the price. Sometimes, I stand at the kitchen counter, a spoon hovering over a pie tin or a bowl of pudding, and struggle to keep from putting a bite into my mouth. Often I give way to desire, knowing later I will be sick. I am willing to endure it for the moments of pleasure.

One night, I lie in my bed cradling my aching belly unable to sleep for waves of nausea. I know it was fried meat at dinner or perhaps the bread, dripping with butter and jam I ate before bed. If only I could vomit, I might feel better. *Why can't I control my impulses? Why do I eat everything I see without remorse until later when I am sick? I need to stop, but I can't.*

I give way to the nausea and retch into the basin in the corner of my room. Feeling better, I return to bed, but not before reaching into the bottom of my dresser and pulling out a small bag hidden there. My father's pocket watch comforts me as it always does. I wind the clock and listen to its rhythm. Like a heartbeat, it is steady and strong. I rub my fingers along its back. After years of my caresses, the words are almost illegible. I know them by heart. They remind me of my parents and how much they loved each other. "To my husband with love on our wedding day." Would there ever be such a day for me? I think about the man at the market. *Joseph, he said his name was. Does he think of me?* I fall asleep holding my father's watch and wonder if I will ever have such love.

Throughout the long, dark winter, I fall back into the habit of eating whatever I want and however much I want. I learn to force myself to vomit it back up. In this way, I manage to stop the constant nausea and pain. A benefit I do not anticipate is losing weight. By spring, I have taken in all my dresses. Only Monica notices the change in my size and she is complimentary. I do not know if she would praise me if she knew how I achieved this look, so I keep my habits to myself. It must not be so bad, I reason. I still look healthy enough. Just not as large as I was last fall.

On the first day of warmer weather, I return to the market. Now, when I look at my reflection in the shop windows, I see a different woman. I wonder if Joseph will notice as well. Will he even remember me? I have not seen him since we first met. I wonder, as I have for many months, what brought him to the market that day and what will bring him back.

Fresh greens, early peas and rhubarb dominate the sale tables. I could purchase what I need quickly and return home to prepare dinner, but I linger over the produce, moving from stall to stall. I laugh to myself. *How silly I am! Surely I am looking for more than food.* Then, like magic, what I wish for appears as I see

Joseph bent over a display of asparagus. He straightens and his eyes meet mine. He smiles.

"Julia. Are you well?" he asks.

As though the months apart never happened, I smile in return and nod. "Yes, I am well. Thank you for rescuing me."

We begin to talk. I learn he farms outside of town. Only last year did he begin having enough extra produce to sell at the market which explains why he was a stranger that day. We share stories about our lives but I am careful not to tell him too much. Still, I am eager to know more about him. He seems to feel the same way about me.

I come to know his schedule and begin spending as much time with him as I dare without attracting attention to myself or being away from home too long. Our friendship grows over the coming months as he teaches me about his crops and how he farms, and I tell him ways to prepare the food he sells. Sometimes, I bring him samples of my cooking. He says if people could taste the vegetables the way I fix them, they would buy more. We eat together, laughing over a tale about his chickens or a mishap in my kitchen. I wish these stolen moments together could last forever. The look on his face tells me that he does too. We might have remained only friends if something had not happened to change everything.

As Monica nears her seventeenth birthday, my uncle begins bringing a young man named Franz Nicholas home for dinner with him. He rarely brings company so Franz's frequent visits are surprising. At first, I think they must have business to discuss after dinner. Soon, I realize my uncle has more on his mind than work. He plans to arrange a marriage for Monica. She likes the young man's attention and sometimes comes to my room to talk about Franz. I hear in detail what he says and what he does. It is tiresome, but I am glad to see Monica happy. Still, I can't help but wonder what will happen to me if she does marry.

I prepare a lavish meal in honor of my sister's special day. No one remembers my birthday anymore, but I can at least do this for my sister who does not have the same memories of a happier life like I do. I am not invited to join the trio at the table, but that is just as well. I already sampled much of the meal as I cooked it and set aside a heaping plate for myself. I will eat it later after the dishes are done. Two cakes wait on the sideboard in the kitchen. One will be delivered to the dining room for my sister's celebration. The other one is for me. I will take a serving to Joseph at the market tomorrow.

I hover outside the dining room door eager to hear any compliments on the food and wonder if tonight might be the night that Franz makes his proposal. Though I strain to listen, I cannot hear much of the conversation until there is a thump as if something has fallen, followed by Monica's startled scream.

"Father! Father! Are you ill?"

I push through the dining room doors to see my uncle on the floor. His face is bluish grey and he holds his chest. Franz and Monica kneel beside him.

Seeing me, Monica orders, "Julia! Do something!"

I am too late. My uncle takes a last wheezing breath, his head rolls to the side and he is still. Monica places her hands over her face, bows to the floor and begins to cry. "What shall we do? What shall we do?" she wails. I have no answers. *What will happen to us now?*

Franz takes charge. Soon more men enter the house. The doctor pronounces my uncle dead while the undertaker removes his body. I stand just inside the dining room and watch as though it is a play. I feel no emotion for my uncle. I cannot understand Monica's grief. I should go to her and comfort her, but I cannot. All I want to do is go back into the kitchen. *Who will eat the cake?* What an absurd thing to think, but right now, the cake seems most important to me. I turn to leave the room.

"Girl." I start. Has my uncle come back to life then? No, it is Franz speaking. "I am sorry. I do not know your name. Who are you?"

Is he talking to me? Though he looks at me, I turn to see if someone is behind me. No one is there. I look back at him. He nods and leans his head in my direction.

"I am Julia, Monica's sister. He was my uncle." I still cannot speak his name aloud.

"I have been working with your uncle on a business merger. And a proposal."

He walks over to my sister and helps her up off the floor. He places an arm around Monica's shoulders and presses her into his side.

"A proposal," he repeats. "It was to be a surprise for Monica. Tonight, I was going to ask her to marry me."

In her grief, my sister fails to hear his words. Appalled at his lack of manners, I reach for my sister and say, "Perhaps another time, Mr. Nicholas. I think tonight is not a good time to talk of business or of marriage."

I help my sister from the room and into bed as the men leave. *What will happen to us?* When Monica is settled into bed, I drown my fear with food and cake, and spend the night retching into a basin.

Chapter Two

A few days after her birthday and my uncle's death, Monica accepts Franz's marriage proposal. I am glad that she cares for him, because there is really no other choice for her. Neither of us has control of our uncle's property. He left no heirs and two orphaned nieces are not in a position to make a claim. Once again, we are destitute and friendless. Though he had no will, his plans for a business merger with Franz are well known in the community—except to us. When Franz steps in to pay off some of my uncle's debts and complete outstanding business transactions, I see even my uncle's death will not deter his strategy. Used to being petted and cared for, Monica easily falls into the habit of letting Franz make decisions for her. In deference to a period of mourning, it is decided they will marry quietly.

I contemplate my future as I walk to the market. Franz has not said whether he will keep me on as housekeeper once he and Monica marry, and even if he does, I am not sure I could work for him. As a married woman, it will be time for Monica to take charge of her own household. I could seek a job as a housemaid or a cook, but I do not want to work for anyone else. I am twenty four now. Too old for school even if I had the money for tuition. *Could I start a business? A restaurant?* I have no money to do those things. What I need is a fresh start. Desperate, I wish indentured servitude had not been outlawed a few years ago. I would hire myself out in exchange for passage to America. Now, that would be a way out of my troubles!

I hear someone call my name and realize I am already at the market. Joseph! Perhaps he will have an idea.

I am eager to talk to him, but he is busy selling vegetables. I sit and wait for a quiet moment. As soon as we have a chance to talk, my worries spill from me. I tell him about my uncle's death and my sister's impending marriage. I even share my dream of going to America. He frowns when I talk of leaving Bessingen.

Finally, I ask "What do you suggest? Do you know anyone who needs help? I must make a decision soon. The wedding is next week."

Calling Thomas to watch his stall, Joseph beckons for me to follow him to a corner of the market where there is less traffic and noise. Joseph's eyes do not meet mine as he takes my hands in his. He rubs the back of my hand absentmindedly as one would a pet. He swallows hard and meets my gaze.

"Yes, I have an idea. I have had it for a long time, but did not think it was a possibility. I do know someone who needs help if you are willing."

"Who is it? What kind of help do they need? Are they kind?" I recall my uncle's treatment of me. In the beginning, he was cruel, then later, indifferent. I shudder, grateful for the warmth of the shawl draped over my shoulders. *Which would be better? To have someone who is compassionate or someone who lets me do whatever I want? Is it possible to have both? Just not someone mean. Please not someone who treats me harshly.*

"I hope you will think they are kind. It is hard work though. Farm work, not just housekeeping although there will be some cooking and cleaning involved. Have you ever taken care of chickens or goats?"

"Not since I was a little girl, but I am a fast learner. I can do whatever is needed of me." I remember telling my uncle so long ago that I knew how to work. I straighten and raise my head. "I am not afraid of hard work," I add.

"I know you are a hard worker," Joseph teases. "These are hands of a woman who knows how to work."

I pull my hands out of his grasp. I am not sure if that was a compliment. Yes, my hands are rough and worn, but what other choice have I had? No one offered me school or music lessons. I don't expect to be treated like a lady, but I expect to be treated with respect.

"I can see you think this is funny. I don't have time to joke. If you will just tell me who you are talking about and how I can contact them, I will be on my way."

"Don't take offense. The person who needs your help is me!"

"You? What do you mean? You need help with your farm?"

"I wanted time to court you in a proper manner, but time has not allowed that. It is to my advantage now that this has happened to you. Julia, I need more than help. I need a wife. Will you be mine? Will you marry me?"

Marriage!? Never would I have dreamed this day would bring a proposal! I am not sure if I love Joseph, but I like him. He is kind and a good friend. He offers me a way out of my situation. I have not seen his farm, but I know I can work. Maybe I could even take over selling produce at the market. I think I would like that. Monica is marrying for business reasons. *Why shouldn't I?* It takes more than love to make a good match.

My hesitation gives Joseph concern. "Do you need some time to think about it?"

Now it is my turn to tease. "Are there any other applicants for the job?"

He smiles, "No, there is only one I am considering and she does not seem willing."

"Then, I'll take it. Yes, Joseph, I will marry you."

"Good. I was beginning to wonder. At least I know you can cook!"

Laughing, I put my arm through his. "Let's get back to our booth and see if we can make some money. My salary is going to be very expensive!"

We wed quietly at City Hall a few days later. Monica accuses me of abandoning her in her greatest time of need. It tears my heart into pieces to hear her cry, but the time has come for me to leave her. I spent thirteen years caring for her and being treated as a slave. Now, Monica will be the lady of the house. I will be a farmer's wife. I grasp this opportunity for happiness while I can.

We are happy. The moment the clerk hands us our marriage papers, I feel such relief and freedom. I did not realize what a burden I carried until I left my uncle's house. I have no gift to give my husband except my father's pocket watch. In turn, he gives me a house of my own. I love everything about it. Made of stones covered with plaster, the farmhouse is two stories. A chimney rises from the center of the roof supporting two fireplaces downstairs and two upstairs. Large windows light the house in the summer, while shutters keep out the cold in the winter. The kitchen lines the back of the house. From its windows, I see the fields and the livestock. Though our stone floors are cold in the winter, they keep the house cool in the summer. I barter straw from our fields for woven rugs to cover the floors. A barn adjoins the house to shelter our animals in the winter.

For the first time since the death of my parents, I am truly happy. Being the mistress of my own home. Choosing how to arrange the furniture. When to cook a meal. What to plant in my garden. Even small decisions, like whether to use the milk for cheese or cream, are a joy to make. I love feeding the chickens or milking the goats. Sometimes, I just stand and count them and think, *these are mine*. The work is routine to some people, but to me, the freedom is exhilarating. I dare to make plans for our future. A larger herd, a bigger garden, another room added to the farmhouse. Joseph laughs at my enthusiasm sometimes.

"Slow down. We have a lifetime to do those things." He doesn't know what I know. Every day is a gift. You can't take time for granted.

Each week, I look forward to market day. I am proud of the produce my husband and I grow. To take a seed and see it sprout into potatoes, beets, onions and beans is miraculous. People know they can depend upon us for quality goods. We grow fruit trees, too. From lovely blossoms in the spring come pears, cherries and apples. I make jam and dry the fruit adding to the products we sell at market. I discover a gift for growing flowers. Poppies, morning glories, sunflowers, pinks, phlox, nasturtiums and lilies. My flower garden is lush and overflowing. I almost hate to pick them, but I do and sell them in bundles at the market. Where once I was the one bargaining for good prices, now, I am on the other end, negotiating sales that allow us to make the most money from our labor.

"Julia, how did I do it without you? Why, when it was just me, I don't know how I even made a penny. You are a born businesswoman."

Joseph's words of praise just fuel my eagerness to make more profit, and soon, we build a small savings account. The proverb that money cannot buy happiness is wrong in my case. The more we have, the better I feel.

With my marriage comes renewed health. The hard work outdoors, the busy days, Joseph's companionship and the relief of no longer being under my uncle's control, combine to ease my craving for food. With the security of marriage to Joseph, who treats me kindly and as his equal, I no longer feel the urge to vomit after meals nor do I overeat. The emptiness I once felt, alone and afraid, is filled with contentment and surprisingly, love. While I might not have loved my husband as a wife should when we first married, it is not long before I realize I have grown to love him.

I am not sure if I love him more for how he treats me or who he is. I worry over it for a time, but decide to let it go and just enjoy my husband. He loves to tease and though he finds me too serious sometimes, for the first time since I was a child, laughter comes easily. He is a hard worker, but is also a prankster. Once, he hid a baby goat in the outhouse, hoping to surprise me, but the joke was on him when the doe, hearing her kid's cries, knocked the outhouse over to rescue her baby. Another time, while repairing the roof, he made noises down the chimney making me think the house was haunted. He is quick to give praise and encouragement and eager to help no matter what the task. After he works in the fields all day, he surprises me with his willingness to assist with dinner, even with cleanup and dishes. Those are the times I enjoy most. Standing beside my husband doing some small chore and looking up to catch him smiling at me. Steady in times of trouble, he rarely worries or frets. Sometimes, when I am upset, I wish he would stew and churn like I do, but he always sees the good in every situation. I feel calm and loved when I am with him.

Though he doesn't tell me with words, I know he loves me, too. I know because of the way he helps me around the house and by the way he always includes me in making decisions. Even when we disagree, he listens to my opinion. To me, that is more valuable than flowers or gifts. But, gifts he does bring, though mostly practical ones. A new cook pot. A bolt of cloth. Seeds for my flower garden. Just the fact that he doesn't begrudge me time spent on flowers is a rare privilege when we have so many other chores to consume us. Though we did not have time to court, in essence, he courts me now with his service, his gifts, his time and his attention.

I speak of my love to him, for the first time, among the flowers. Several months have passed since we married and while we share everything including the marriage bed, I have been careful to guard my heart. After so many years of servitude, I am still unsure of my position and though my husband daily demonstrates his affection for me, is it my place to be the first to speak of love? I consider our situation one spring evening as I prune some spindly roses and set aside sunflower heads to preserve their seeds for next season. My husband sits nearby smoking his pipe and whittling something out of wood. I move closer to see what it is and find an intricately carved cross. The symbol reminds me of the only difference we now have.

Joseph is a devout follower of Christ. He prays before every meal, giving thanks to God for the food we eat. He praises God for good harvests and expanding flocks. Every Sunday, we attend the Lutheran church. I put on my best dress, sing the hymns and sit through the sermon, but it is only a part I play. On the inside, my mind whirls with thoughts of tasks that need completion or dreams for the future. While I would not say I don't believe in God aloud, it is something I struggle to understand. Thankfully, Joseph assumes I am a believer, too. I sit beside him in church and hear him loudly sing, "May God Bestow Upon Us Grace." As he proclaims,

> May God bestow on us His grace,
> With blessings rich provide us,
> And may the brightness of His face
> To life eternal guide us
> That we His saving health may know,
> His gracious will and pleasure.

The blessings we have are because we work so hard. It is not by God's gracious will that we live, but by the sweat and muscle we provide. Not even Joseph's love can lead me to Christ. My past and the things I have seen and suffered keep me from surrendering to Him no matter how many pious hymns I might sing. If I believe God brings blessings, then I must believe He brings hardship, too. What kind of God allows such suffering and pain?

I concentrate on my flowers, dropping spent blooms into the bucket at my feet. I experiment with making goat's milk soap and want to distill the flower's perfume to add to the mixture. I think it will be another popular item to sell at the market. I smile as I see Joseph watching me. I leave my bucket and approach him. *I suppose I should believe in a God that makes a man so kind and gentle as my husband. But, that same God made my uncle. I am not at all sure I can trust God. Can I trust my husband? Is it time to tell him how I feel?* I decide it is.

"There is something I must tell you."

Joseph pats the bench, and I sit beside him.

"What were you thinking a moment ago? You looked very solemn. Is something wrong?"

"No, on the contrary. Everything is well. I just realized something is all."

Joseph pulls me into his lap. Laughing, I pretend to resist and then, settle into his arms, my head on his shoulder. "So, are you going to keep me in suspense? What did you realize? Do we need more hens?"

"Oh, it is something more important than that."

"More important than chickens? I suppose you are going to nag me into adding more stalls to the barn so you can buy a new herd of cows."

I punch him in the arm. "I don't nag you. I just encourage you."

"Oh, you do, do you? You call that encouragement? I call it nagging!" He turns my face towards his and kisses me. "Now, there's a better form of encouragement."

I struggle to get up. "Joseph, don't tease. I really do have something important to tell you."

"So? Tell."

I hesitate, then, blurt out my feelings. "Joseph, I love you."

His eyes water as he pulls me closer to his chest. "Ah, Julia. I hoped you did. I love you, too."

A few months later, I must have another serious conversation with my husband. This one, I know will be well received. As we lie in bed after Joseph has said prayers for us both, thanking God for all His good gifts, I take his hand.

"Husband?" He turns to face me. "You have one more gift to thank God for."

"Oh, what did I leave out?"

"Your child. You are going to be a father!"

I cannot see his eyes in the dim light, but Joseph's voice breaks as he takes me in his arms and says, "Oh, Julia, I will thank Him right now!"

I stop to see Monica one day when I know Franz will be gone. I try to visit as often as I can but the farm keeps me very busy. I do not want to go back to the house, but for my sister's sake, I do. She looks well and happy. Though she complains about the househelp Franz hired, Monica continues to live a carefree life. I need not have feared about their arranged marriage. Franz treats her kindly, and they attend many parties with his business associates. She already has one child and another on the way. Her daughter is darling. Monica names her Anna. I wonder if I will also have a girl. Monica treats her like a little doll, showing me all the clothes and toys she already has. Her daughter also has a nursemaid. I will not have such luxury, but I don't mind. I can hardly wait to get back to our farmhouse and my husband.

Our son is born in January and baptized when he is a few days old. We name him Joseph, but nickname him Mausi or Little Mouse. My husband is a good father and a great help to me. When he is not working around the farm, Joseph spends as much time with his son as he can. He carves a wooden cradle I can move from our bedroom to wherever I am working. I am grateful we have fireplaces in all the rooms. The winter is very cold, and I move the cradle close to the fire so the baby does not get chilled. I don't even want to take him outside. It gives me a good excuse not to go to church all winter. I confess, I do not miss it. Joseph comes home each Sunday and tells me about the sermon while I pretend to listen. One day, I can tell he is hiding something, so I ask him what is wrong.

"We had some visitors at church this week. Now, I don't want you to get upset. They do not live in our state of Bavaria, but in Prussia. The King of Prussia ruled everyone must worship the same way. There is much turmoil within the church there right now. Some people are even being jailed for refusing to follow the King's orders. Their farms are being seized and they are forced to leave their homes."

I imagine what it would be like to lose my lovely home. I think of our life without our fields or animals. It must be horrible. *But, what does that have to do with us?*

Joseph continues, "Many of the Prussian Lutherans are going to America. They are excited about being able to worship as they please and having more land than they have here. They say in America crops grow with little effort. The ground is so fertile a man can work many more acres than he can here. Look, one of them gave me this flyer."

Joseph hands it to me. He cannot read, so I read it aloud. "It is taken from a book by Gomfried Duden. He visited America and liked it so much, he settled in a place called Missouri. He says, 'There is still room for millions of fine farms along the Missouri River, not to mention the other rivers. The great fertility of the soil, its immense area, the mild climate, the splendid river connections. All these must be considered as the real foundations for the fortunate situation of Americans.'"

"Julia, I have been thinking. We should go to America! We could have a good life there."

What? Is he out of his mind?

"Joseph, once, I too, thought of America as a place where I could go to get away from my problems. Now, we do not need to run away. We have a good life here. We have a farm of our own. No one tells us what to do. We live in Bavaria, not Prussia. We are free to go to church as we like. We do not need to immigrate to America. We are fine right here."

Joseph does not argue with me, but over the next few years, he looks at the pictures in the flyer so often that the edges of the paper begin to wear. Seasons come and go. Our family grows with the arrival of a second son, Julian. Joseph insists on naming him after me. The boys bring us much joy and laughter. Like their father, they love to pull pranks and tell jokes. Early on, we give them chores, no matter how small, to learn the value of hard work and the satisfaction of their labors. They spend time outdoors and grow sturdy and handsome. We live in a country that values education even for its young. Our town has a school and both boys start their education at an early age. Mausi is quite the scholar and though Julian would prefer to be in the fields with his father, he too, excels in school. They attend with Monica's girls. She now has three daughters. The five of them get along well and build a stronger bridge between my sister and me.

We increase our herds of goats and cows and purchase more horses to work the farm and ponies for the boys. Now, when I stand at the kitchen window, our fields stretch as far as I can see. I learn to horseback ride, so I can save time visiting the fields. There is so much to do that we hire two girls to work for us. They help around the house and at the market. I take on more and more responsibility for the business side of the farm while Joseph focuses on agriculture. Joseph defers to my decisions. I enjoy my husband's trust and the negotiating it takes to make sales and contacts within the community. I am well respected in our area. Frau Atzeroth, they call me. People nod in deference as I ride down the street toward the market. I sit taller knowing of their admiration.

We should be content except for the news we hear at church each week. After service, the men gather in the courtyard outside of the building. They exchange information about the community, business successes and prosperous crops. They also share stories of families who have gone to America and tales of how they thrive. One family wrote, "There are many different religions here, German Catholics, English Catholics, Irish Catholics, Lutherans, Evangelicals, Reformed, Jews etc. No one says we have to go to this or that community. Everyone can do what he wants to do in religious or secular matters. Come to America where you will serve God better here and spend the Lord´s day better than in Germany."

Joseph hears other rumors in contrast to the freedom of America. A group called the Ultramontaines now control the Bavarian parliament. They are Catholics, and their goal is to reform the Bavarian Constitution to take away the civil rights of Protestants like us. They also support censorship and want to prohibit political discussions.

"It is just like what happened in Prussia a few years ago. They will not rest until all of us become Catholic! Who are they that they can tell us what we can and cannot do? Or talk about? Don't we have the right to free discourse?" Church is no longer a place of peace for us. Joseph comes home each week worried and afraid about our future.

We no longer have peace at home as well. Once more, Joseph lobbies for a move to America. It angers me he would be so willing to throw away all we have obtained for his God. When he tells me God will bless us in America as He has here, I want to shake him. "Joseph, look around you. We have worked hard for this prosperity. We pushed the plow. We raised the chickens. We built the barns. We are the ones people seek in the market. We. Not God. "

Joseph's face pales. "Julia, do not speak so. We are only God's instruments. All we have comes from His hand. I love you, but you must not speak so of God."

I am too angry to stop now. "I have known poverty and hunger. I have known slavery and punishment. I have also known happiness and love. Can I believe that God was only in the good? Or in the bad? No, if God is in control, if He brings both blessings and curses upon us, then of what benefit is He to me?"

I see from the shock on my husband's face and the way his hands tremble that I have said too much. *Well, perhaps there will be no more talk of America.*

Though I feel Joseph tense the following Sunday when the pastor preaches on pride, I know my husband would not share my thoughts with anyone. The scripture is the First Commandment, "I am the Lord Thy God," and I squirm under the teaching. Pastor says, "There are two parts to this command. The first that we are to praise and trust God alone. The second is we must guard against seeking to be God, to put our trust in ourselves and try to wrest control from God. When we seek to determine our own fate, we show our lack of faith and trust in God." He quotes Martin Luther who said, "The God of this world is riches, pleasure and pride" and closes with the warning, "God will be God so bow before Him now before it is too late." I think about my words to Joseph. *Perhaps I should have been more careful. But, it is what I believe. Should I pretend to change my mind out of fear of retribution? If God truly knows my heart, I have nowhere to hide.*

I consider that choice when the fever comes. I hear rumblings about it in the market one day. A fever that affects both young and old and is accompanied by a rash and a sore throat. Scarlatina, they call it, or Scarlet Fever. It is quick acting and deadly. Pharmacists promote the use of Belladonna to prevent the disease, so I purchase some to take home and decide to keep the boys from school until the epidemic passes. Despite my resolve, I am too late.

When I enter the front door, I find both Mausi and Julian, shivering and complaining of a sore throat. Immediately, I put them to bed and call for the doctor. He orders their heads be shaved and they be covered in cloths soaked in water to reduce their fevers. He leaves me with silver nitrate to brush inside their throats, and tells me to call him right away if the rash should appear. He dismisses my questions about the Belladonna; "There is no proof it will help. In fact, it may make things worse."

When Joseph comes in from the fields, he finds me kneeling in our sons' bedroom, begging God to spare their lives.

"It is my sin, my pride. Do not punish my children. Punish me."

To my husband's credit, he does not blame me. Joseph gently eases me from the floor and comforts me while I weep. Throughout the night, we hold vigil at their bedside. I try to dribble chicken broth into their mouths, but in their delirium they fight me. Joseph restrains them as they scream in pain. The rash appears, but the doctor does not come. He is too busy with other patients. Their stomachs swell, and their breathing is labored. By dawn, both boys are still. The fever has taken them. In less than twenty-four hours, my world is completely undone.

Chapter Three

Only our pastor and his wife attend my boys' funeral. Even Monica fails to appear. Fears of the disease are too great. I am afraid to look the pastor in the eye and wonder if he knows it is my pride that killed my children. His wife pats my hand and tries to console me.

"God must have needed two little angels in Heaven," she says.

I cannot bear the thought of my children at the hands of a God who would strip them from their mother's arms because of her sins. I long for the disease that struck my children to take me as well, but I am strong, if only physically. The fever does not impact our household again. It has done enough damage.

My grief and anger at God create a chasm between me and my husband. I do not voice my emotions aloud, but Joseph knows me well enough to know what I feel. He has no answers for me. I do not have his faith and even he has unasked questions for God. I see it in his hesitancy to go to church each Sunday. A reluctance greater than what my absence would invoke. For I refuse to go back to church. I can no longer listen to the platitudes spoken there. I will have no more of God.

My old eating habits return. I overeat and binge on things unhealthy for me. I seek in vain to fill the emptiness of my heart with food. When the pain and nausea return, I do not care. Perhaps I will die, too. I also pour my anger into my work. We will build the best farm, the best business and we will do it ourselves. But, there is no "we" in my efforts, for instead of teamwork and cooperation, our sons' death has taken away Joseph's enthusiasm for our life here in Bavaria and replaced it with an even stronger resolve to go to America.

"Children die in America, too," I say harshly. I see the look of disappointment in his eyes, but refuse to consider a move until the day I have no other choice.

"I've found a buyer for the farm," he announces one night at dinner. "They will take all the stock and finish planting the fields. I've booked passage to America on a ship leaving from LaHavre. There are freight wagons from the cotton trade to France. I will catch one of those to go overland to the River Seine. From there it is a short journey to LaHavre. I can be in New York in less than four months. Your sister says you can come to live with her if you do not want to go with me. Will you stay or will you go?"

So it has come to this. Even my husband no longer seeks my input. I am reduced to slavery once more. His words are all about what HE will do. Not until he states HIS plans does he ask about me. *Will I stay or will I go?*

"Julia," Joseph says more tenderly. "I bought a ticket for you, too. I want you to go with me."

In the end, it is my pride that propels me to a new life. I do not want people to know this was not my choice. I do not want people to know my husband considers going without me. I begin to pack and say my farewells as though the plans are mine from the beginning. I weep at my sons' gravesite. I will lose even this reminder of them. I beat my hands against the tombstone they share until they are raw and bleeding. My blood stains their names. My sin brought this upon us. *Why, God? Why did you take them and not me?* Joseph leads me home where my sister waits to say good-bye. Monica tries to encourage me.

"Franz wants to come to America, too. In a year or two, we will see you again."

We begin our journey to America in May. Resolutely, I climb into the wagon and refuse to look back.

Our journey is not as easy as Joseph predicted. We encounter hot weather, unscrupulous ticket agents and dismal lodgings; but in a month, we are finally in La Havre. Traveling together, depending on each other and seeing new sights eases some of the discord between my husband and me. Though tempered by our loss, Joseph's enthusiasm for finally seeing America cannot help but be contagious. Soon, we fall back into our old custom of talking about our future. He steps back letting me make decisions again. I see his trust in my instincts never faltered. It was my own unwillingness to listen to his desires that forced Joseph to take the actions he did.

Located on the right bank of the River Seine on the English Channel, LaHavre is a vibrant seaport. LaHavre surprises me with the variety of nationalities living within the city. Germans, English, Swedes, Italians and Poles work side by side on the docks and in the factories. Wood, coal, and wheat from Northern Europe, coffee and cotton from America and wine and oil from the Mediterranean are some of the products that flow through the port. Though the older section, which dates back to its founding three hundred years before our arrival, is surrounded by walls, a newer area spreads out from the city's core which is filled with wealthy merchants, large houses and gas street lamps. There are even seaside baths for travelers from Paris to enjoy. I hope we will stay in the nicer area until our ship is ready to sail, but am disappointed to follow Joseph to another run down rooming house in the neighborhood of Saint Francis.

"Don't worry. We will not be here long. Tomorrow, I will locate our ship and meet the captain. Perhaps, we can move aboard before it sails," Joseph assures me.

Though our room is tiny and smells of its prior occupants, I am grateful to lie down. I have a secret which I am trying to keep from Joseph at least until our ship sails. I am afraid he or the Captain will not let me board the boat if they know. Once again, I am pregnant. I have mixed feelings about this child. The timing could not be worse. If only we were already in America, I might welcome his or her arrival more eagerly. I do not know if

I want to be a mother again. Though I tried to set it aside on our journey, the loss of my boys is still great. I remember how eagerly I looked forward to being a mother when I was pregnant with them. Now, I know what might happen and the fear of another loss is almost more than I can bear. *No, I will keep this news to myself for a little while longer. No reason to delay our travels or alarm Joseph unnecessarily.*

The weather does not cooperate with our plans, however. It is windy and rainy for more than a week. Our ship, *The Sully,* fails to arrive in port on time. Though Joseph goes to the harbor each day, no one goes in or out. The English Channel is too rough to venture out with cargo or passengers. I spend my time in our little room, feeling sicker and sicker each day. I do not know if it is my anxiety, my pregnancy or the return of my old stomach ailments, but in just a few days, I am too ill to get out of bed. Joseph finally convinces me to allow him to call the doctor. I stall as long as possible fearing the doctor will discover my condition, but finally, convinced I am going to die anyway, I give in to his request.

The doctor speaks little German, but after poking and prodding my abdomen and asking a few questions, he spills my secret and urges Joseph to change our lodging.

"This room is too confining. She must be somewhere where she can get some fresh air, exercise and better meals. It may be the pregnancy, but I think it has more to do with being restrained. You are headed for America? I would rethink that journey until after the wee one arrives."

Joseph, stunned by the news, automatically pays the man for his advice and sees him out.

As soon as he reenters the room, he exclaims, "Pregnancy? Julia, how long have you known? When were you going to tell me?" He runs his fingers through his hair and grips a clump in frustration. "A baby! We can't have a baby now! You heard what he said! It's dangerous and you could get sicker! The tickets are already purchased! Julia! What are we going to do?"

"Joseph, this is not my first baby. And you said yourself in four months, we will be in New York. Over a month has already passed. I won't have this baby at sea. We can still go."

My husband is too distraught to listen to me. "No, I will not risk it. I have already lost two sons. I will not take a chance on losing another child. I will not take a chance on losing my wife. We must rethink our plans." He leaves the room, but not before turning and giving me a weak smile. "A baby. Imagine that."

Yes, imagine that. Once again, God has dealt me an unexpected blow.

Joseph's solution is not the same as what I would choose, but he returns to his prior resolute state and refuses to consult me or consider my feelings. He moves us to better, more costly lodging in a different part of town and announces he has sold my ticket to another eager immigrant. He will go on to New York City alone, and I will follow after the baby is born and old enough to travel. I am so angry I cannot speak. Indeed, I say little to him as the weather clears, his ship arrives and he repacks his belongings to board. He will take our furnishings with him, but leaves the cradle that once rocked our sons for the new baby.

"I know you are angry at me, but there is nothing I can do. I spoke to the Captain and even if I felt comfortable with you traveling, he would not allow it. Pregnant women are unlucky aboard ships. I will either come back for you or find a way for you to travel alone. It is better you stay here where there is a doctor until you give birth. I am leaving you with enough money to live comfortably and to travel when you are able. I will send word as soon I arrive in New York."

Pregnant women are unlucky aboard ships. Perhaps my husband has decided I am unlucky all the time. Maybe he will be better off without me.

I refuse to face Joseph or to hug him good bye, and he stands sadly at the entrance to our room. With one hand on the door, he says, "I am sorry, Julia. I love you. We will be together again soon. You will see." I hear the door shut and fight the longing that would propel me to follow and beg my husband not to leave me.

Days creep into weeks, as I adjust to life in a strange city where I do not speak the language. I pick up a little French from interacting with the innkeeper and his family. His wife takes pity on my loneliness and invites me into their rooms, but we have little in common other than she is pregnant, too. Then one day, when I go downstairs for breakfast, I hear a familiar language and turn to see who is speaking my native tongue.

A woman with red hair, half my size, marshals a trio of little girls, equally tiny, into their chairs. She is dressed in the latest fashions from Paris I have come to recognize on my daily walks among the tourists from that city. It is obvious she is used to having her way as she not only commands the attention of the girls, but everyone in the dining room. While I nibble on rolls and drink tea instead of the French-preferred coffee, I watch her with fascination wanting to know her name and everything about her.

Soon, my questions are answered by Margaret Schultz. "Guten Tag. May I join you?" I look up from playing with my food. I would never admit it to Joseph, but sometimes I am glad I am not on board the ship. My stomach feels so queasy in the morning. I am not really hungry, but I do not want to go back to my deserted room. I smile and nod.

"I am Margaret Schultz," she says as she sits beside me. "The innkeeper told me you were also from Germany."

"Yes, from Bessingen. My name is Julia Atzeroth."

"So, Julia. We are two women travelling alone. I am curious to hear your story. Or do you want to hear mine first?" I laugh.

"Oh, you first," I say.

I learn she is from a town near Baden. She is the wife of a mayor's son. Her husband has already immigrated to America. He built a house and opened a store in Pennsylvania and is waiting for his family to join him.

"But I thought I would take my time getting there. I love my husband, but am not sure if his dreams of paradise are the same as mine. America, Pennsylvania sounds a little uncivilized to me."

Margaret draws out the word "Pennsylvania" and it does sound exotic the way she says it. She laughs and winks. "At least all the laws are printed in German in Pennsylvania! A woman like me needs to know how she should behave."

A woman like me. I wonder what kind of a woman she is. As we spend time together, I learn she is a woman of contradictions. Bawdy, flamboyant, outspoken? Yes, these are all words that describe Margaret. But, religious? Not something I would have associated with her at first glance. On the first Sunday she is in LaHavre, Margaret surprises me with an invitation to church. I assume a woman as brash and modern as she would have no use for God, but reason she might just be going out of tradition. Or to show off her finery. We make our way to a small building where a group of Lutheran Germans meet. I feel shy about joining the congregation and hang back, but they are friendly to Margaret and her girls and as a result, to me.

I should have known Margaret would not do anything, even going to church, halfway. When the congregation begins singing "Praise to the Lord, the Almighty," she throws her head back and loudly proclaims:

> Praise to the Lord, the Almighty,
> the King of creation!
> O my soul, praise Him,
> for He is thy health and salvation!
> All ye who hear, now to His temple draw near;

Praise Him in glad adoration.
Praise to the Lord,
Who over all things so wondrously reigneth,
Shelters thee under His wings, yea, so gently sustaineth!
Hast thou not seen how thy desires ever have been
Granted in what He ordaineth?
Praise to the Lord,
O let all that is in me adore Him!
All that hath life and breath,
come now with praises before Him.
Let the Amen sound from His people again,
Gladly for aye we adore Him.

Margaret's voice echoes in my ears. It is as though I never heard that hymn before even though it is one of Joseph's favorites. Perhaps I never heard it sung with such conviction, but my eyes begin to water as I consider the phrase, "Shelters thee under His wings, yea, so gently sustaineth!" *Oh, how I need some shelter from the storms that life keeps sending my way. If only it were as easy to befriend God as it was to befriend Margaret!*

Margaret has a way of drawing things out of a person you can't imagine ever saying aloud to a friend, much less one who was a stranger only a few days before. That afternoon, as I sit beside her on the porch sewing some baby clothes, I hesitate to talk to her about my concerns about God. Thankfully, she brings it up first.

"That was quite a sermon today. I would not want the reverend to know, after all he is more learned than I am, but I think he missed the mark." She frowns as she cuts a piece of thread and runs it through her needle.

The sermon was on Job. The preacher said God punishes us for our sins. The hymn's reminders of a benevolent God vanished as I heard confirmation that everything that has happened to me and to my family was a result of my sin and pride.

Margaret continues, "Sometimes, bad things happen to us just because of the world we live in. Sickness, disease, death." I set my stitching down so I can listen.

"Sometimes, God allows them to happen to us in order to teach us something. To bring us closer to Him or to help us learn a lesson that will serve us in the future. I don't believe bad things happen to punish us. Why, God loves us! He's not the ogre the preacher made Him out to be."

"That is comforting to think about, but I haven't found Him to be that way," I argue. "My mother loved God. She sang hymns while she worked and took us all to church. She even gave us her food so we would live. All I wanted was for my mother to live, too. I held my own two sons while they took their last breath. If God really were in control, surely some of the ones I love would be alive today. What you say sounds good, but it is of little comfort to me when I have lost so much!"

Margaret reaches out to pat my hand. "You have much in common with Job, you know. He lost everything, too. His children. His possessions. His servants. He even was sick himself. His wife told him he might as well just curse God and die. He asked some of the same questions you do. "

I nod. *I know just how Job must have felt.*

Margaret adds "If the preacher today had looked a little deeper, he would have found this is what God told Job: 'Knowest thou the ordinances of heaven? Canst thou set the dominion thereof in the earth? Canst thou lift up thy voice to the clouds, that abundance of waters may cover thee? Canst thou send lightning, that they may go and say unto thee, Here we are?'"

I wrinkle my forehead. *That makes no sense to me.*

She sees my puzzled expression. "Do you want to know what I think that means?" She doesn't wait for my reply. "God controls the heavens and the earth. He is in charge of our world. Sometimes I make decisions for my girls but they don't understand why? You know how it is as a mother."

My heart knots at the thought of being a mother. I was a mother once. I suppose I will be again. If God allows.

Margaret smiles, "Yes, you do know. Look at you. Here in a strange city waiting for your baby when you would rather be on the boat with your husband. You stayed behind because you knew it was best for your child."

Well, not exactly. I did it because my husband made me. But I don't interrupt her.

"We make decisions for our children out of love and experience which helps us know what is best."

I nod. "But that doesn't mean they like it!" *Or me either*!

"I wonder if God feels the same way when we whine and complain. Or reason we must be getting punished for something. Nobody but God knows why He does things the way He does," Margaret says. "We just have to learn to trust He knows best."

Despite Margaret's attempts to reassure me, her answer leaves me more uncertain. It doesn't seem to me God is in control. In fact, the world grows more unpredictable and uncertain every day. How do you learn to trust God when it seems like so many bad things happen?

Our friendship grows as I wait for my child to be born and Margaret for her travel to America which is interrupted by strong winter storms that block passage across the English Channel. I am grateful for her company and selfishly glad she doesn't seem in a hurry to leave France. We continue to visit the Lutheran church, and with Margaret's help, make friends with some of the other women. Perhaps they will assist me when it is time to give birth. As the weather clears, I dread her impending departure.

"As much as I will miss you and France, I expect Frederick is worried by now. There is a ship headed to Philadelphia, 'the City of Brotherly Love'," she rolls her eyes and giggles. How I will miss her jokes and stories! "I had better get the girls packed and moved on board tomorrow or I might miss the boat!"

Tomorrow! I will be alone again tomorrow.

"Julia, I have a surprise for you!"

I try to meet her light mood at least for now. "The last time someone gave me a surprise, I got this!" I rub my expanding stomach to illustrate.

Margaret laughs. "Yes, I know and that is what my surprise is all about. Ada Miller has offered to let you move into their home. You can stay with them until the baby is old enough to travel. No more of this lonely boarding house for you!"

I think of Ada Miller, a woman in the church whose husband works in a cotton warehouse. As kind as she is, I doubt my moving in with her was Ada's idea.

"Margaret, what have you done? Ada doesn't know me well."

"She knows you well enough. She is a sister in Christ and wants to do it. It is all arranged. On Sunday, she and her husband will pick you up after church and take you to their house where you can stay. Please, Julia. I must leave, but I cannot stand to go until I know you will let someone help you!"

That evening, I watch as Margaret packs for her journey. Her girls are already in bed and the two of us stay up late talking. There is urgency to our conversation as time together runs out.

"Julia!"

"Margaret!" We say in unison.

"You go first," I say.

"No, I told my story first on the day we met. Today, it is your turn to talk. Julia, tell me your real story. Tell me what troubles you."

Haltingly, I begin. I tell her of the losses in my life, what it was like to be left an orphan and my uncle's mistreatment. The words come faster as I recall my outburst against God and the death of my sons. I sob as I exclaim, "I killed them! As surely as if I took the knife and stabbed them, I killed them. I defied God and He punished me by taking my children."

Margaret lets me cry until I have no more tears. Then, she says, "Yes, you defied God. More importantly, you failed to trust God. All your life, you have sought control over things that were out of your influence. That has been man's sin since the beginning of time. We want our own way, we want to set our own path and not obey God or trust He knows what is best. This world is full of sin and death. Your children suffered because we live in a world of sin, but they did not suffer because of your sin. Julia, you know how much you loved your sons?"

I nod my head yes. "Well, God had a son, too, and He loved that son more than you loved both your boys combined. But, God knew unless someone stepped in and paid the price for the sin of Adam and of your sin and my sin for that matter, we would all die. The Bible says the wages of sin is death. So He sent His Son, Jesus Christ, to die in our place. Julia, think of it! God loved you so much, He traded His Son's life for yours. How could He do such a thing? How could He love that much?"

I think again of my boys. I cannot imagine God's choice. Knowing the grief of losing my own children, I could not do it.

"God did it because He knew that was the only way for you to truly live. Not just on this earth, but later, after you die, in Heaven. Julia, God wants to be the Father you lost. More than the earthly father who died, but your Heavenly Father. But, that could not happen unless His Son died for you."

I wipe my eyes. It is more than I can imagine. A Father? A Heavenly Father?

"So, what does He want from me?" I ask.

"'All who call on God in true faith, earnestly from the heart, will certainly be heard, and will receive what they have asked and desired.' Martin Luther said that. All God wants is for you to accept His gift of salvation. It is free, nothing is required of you. Just tell him your troubles. Tell him your heart and watch and see what He does."

"Now?"

"Now is as good a time as any. How much lighter my heart would be when I go if I knew I was leaving you with a faith in a God who loves you!"

I am not sure I can. I have too many questions. Why is there so much evil in this world? Why would God love me enough to send His Son to die in my place? But I want to know this God Margaret speaks of so intimately. More than I want answers to my questions.

Margaret sees my hesitation. "Julia, what do you have to lose? Think of all there is to gain. What holds you back?"

I shrug my shoulders and surrender to the longing to have a Heavenly Father. With Margaret's help, I kneel beside her bed and repeat a prayer that could change my life.

"Heavenly Father, I am a sinner. You know how much sorrow and grief I carry. I lay them all at your feet. My sin. My troubles. My fears. Despite them all, I ask you take me to be your child. To comfort me and carry me when I cannot take another step. I need you God. I want to know you. I cannot do this alone. Thank you for sending your son to die in my place. Cleanse me from my sin. Take my life. I want to live for you."

When I rise, I still have my doubts. I am unsure if God is really listening, but I take comfort in Margaret's confidence that God will make Himself known to me.

The next morning, we hug as the wagon waits to take her to her ship.

"I will do my best to get your message to your Joseph," she says. I regret the way I parted from my husband. Even if I wrote a letter of apology, he could not read it. I hope my friend can personally convey the sorrow I send with her.

"Enjoy your time at Ada's," Margaret says. "Remember, now she is truly a sister in Christ. And so are we! I hope to see you in Pennsylvania," she draws out the word the way that it always makes me laugh. "If we do not meet again in America, I will see you one day in Heaven. Read your Bible. And talk to Ada. You will be surprised at how much she knows. I don't think it a coincidence God is placing you in her house. And Julia, pray. You won't have me to talk to, but God is always listening. Don't forget He is there."

My throat closes so I cannot speak. I want to tell her how much her friendship has meant to me, but can only offer a tremulous smile and hug Margaret one more time. I wave as the wagon draws out of sight. For the first time, I understand why I had to stay behind in LaHavre.

Chapter Four

Margaret is right. Ada is not only a kind person, but a wise one as well. Each morning, we begin our day with devotions as Ada teaches me about things in the Bible I never knew. We study Paul's letters, and I read about fighting "the good fight." About how Jesus said there will be difficulty in this world but He came to bring peace and help us to overcome those troubles. I learn the depths of despair Jesus plunged to on my behalf. I find out what is required of a Christian wife. Sometimes I tell Ada I don't think I can do it. I don't think I can be what God wants me to be. She just tells me I need to try and reminds me of how God rewards our obedience. I vow to do all I can to please God. Like when I was a little girl and looked up to my father, I want God to be proud of me. I want to make up for the mistakes I made in the past.

I remember Margaret's encouragement to pray. While Ada's prayers are formal ones spoken aloud asking for blessings or confessing our sins, I learn to pray quietly when I am alone. I think about what I would say to my friend and verbalize my feelings to God instead. I tell Him about my loneliness. How much I miss my husband and my sons. I express my fears for the future, for my baby and the journey ahead of us. I remind Him how much I long for a home and for love. While there are no human arms to hold me or voices to speak of love, when I pray, I feel God's presence. Sometimes I have to smile. For someone who vowed not to believe in God, in the dark night, all alone, I have no doubt He is real and He is there.

The time at Ada's goes by so fast I am surprised when the doctor tells me the baby should come any day. I think I am prepared. I know what to expect. But, how will it be to give birth without Joseph at my side? And how soon after the baby's arrival can I travel to meet my husband and tell him all I truly long to say?

My daughter is born on April 13 in the early hours of the morning. God grants me a quick and easy delivery and a healthy girl. The nurse places her in the cradle Joseph made for our boys. When we loaded it into the wagon to take to America, I never dreamed it would be used so soon. I ache for my husband when I look into her face and see his eyes staring back at me.

I whisper to her. "Your Papa waits for us. Soon, we will see him."

I name my daughter Elizabeth, my mother's middle name. I choose Margaret for her second name in honor of my now dear friend. Elizabeth Margaret Atzeroth. *Grow strong and sturdy, daughter, so I can take you to meet your Papa.*

Three months later, the doctor finally says we can travel. Eliza, as I have nicknamed my daughter, is healthy and nursing well. I have only one problem. No ticket. More and more emigrants seek to leave from La Havre to go to the United States and so, the government now requires them to have a ticket before they leave Germany for the port. All the ships in the harbor are full. Ordinarily, I could purchase a ticket for 150 francs in Germany, but the prices in La Havre are inflated. My only hope lies in some other person, who like me, suddenly becomes unable to travel making their ticket available for purchase.

Ada tells me to pray about it, and we do pray. Her husband scours the docks seeking someone who has a ticket for sale. Finally, he brings word he has found a ship with a space available.

"But, Frau Atzeroth, it is in steerage. I do not think you want it. That is no place for a woman traveling alone with a baby. You should wait until a cabin becomes available."

I am not willing to wait. It has been a year since I last saw my husband, and I coldly turned my back, letting him leave without a kind goodbye. It is already July. If I wait much longer, winter will be upon us and travel more difficult. And what I do not want to tell Ada, for fear of taking any more advantage of them, my money is about to run out. After setting aside a small sum to provide for Eliza and me until I can make contact with Joseph in New York City, steerage is all I can afford anyway.

Despite their protests, I take the ticket and soon, am escorted aboard the ship. I bring with me one locked trunk with all of my belongings and food and clothes for Eliza and myself for eight weeks. I carry a bag of personal items, including my mother's Bible. Ada's husband also carries Eliza's cradle. I pray our journey will be short, but I do not want to have to rely on the ship to provide our meals, as I have heard provisions often run out halfway through the voyage. I pack my bedding separately. I will leave it on board the ship. After eight weeks without washing, I doubt I will want to take it home with me.

My stomach is in knots as I follow a sailor down into the hold of the ship. I am among the last to arrive. Before I left her house, Ada helped me tie a cloth around my chest and shoulders as a sling to hold Eliza leaving my hands free to carry my bag and climb down the ladder into the hold of the ship. I slip the sailor a precious coin and hope he will be honest enough to bring the cradle and my trunk to my bunk.

Once below, I blink until my eyes adjust to the darkness. I almost gag at the stench. The ship has not even left port and already the area smells like human waste, sour food and unwashed humans. It takes every inch of will power within me to stand my ground and not run for escape up the ladder into the sunlight. I weave and bend between the bunks as the sailor points to his left and returns for my trunk. I look up and down, but do not see a spare bed anywhere. *Please God, help me. Help me.* Finally, I see a woman gesturing for me to come her way.

"Frau, we have a space for you. My sister died before we could board. Her husband sold you her ticket. You will share a bunk with him."

Oh, God, no. Share a bunk with another man. What have I done? What does he expect?

The woman sees my confusion and laughs.

"No, nothing like that. We all share bunks. Five in one, don't you know? Put your bag over there. Oh, is that a baby? No one said anything about a baby. I guess one more won't make any difference, now will it?"

I feel the boat shift and then, shake. I fall against the nearest bunk.

"Better get settled then. It looks like we are finally setting sail. I guess we were waiting on you. Captain wouldn't want to leave without every bunk taken, now would he?"

I learn the woman with the odd habit of asking questions of herself is named Meta. Her husband is Werner and the widower with whom I will share a bunk, Ernst. Between them, there are more than a half dozen children, all crying and unkempt. In the dim light, I cannot tell which belong to Meta and Werner and which are the motherless children of Ernst. *It does not matter,* I tell myself. *What is eight weeks? I have waited much longer than eight weeks to finally be going to America.* I want to laugh when I realize that now, I, too, am asking questions of myself.

As the boat exits the harbor, my stomach starts to roll. I brace myself against the pitch and clamber into an empty space in the middle of a three tiered bunk. It is so narrow, I cannot sit up straight. I spread my bedding out as best as I can and dislodge Eliza from the fabric where she hides. She cries and reaches for my breast. I feed my child and pray we will survive this voyage.

Steerage is worse than I ever imagined. The toilets are above us on the deck. In order to reach them, we must climb up the ladders. In rough seas, that becomes impossible and people improvise with buckets and basins around their beds. Not only do they overflow with human waste, but vomit as passengers are overcome with seasickness. I am grateful for the kindness of Meta and her family. Everyone thinks I am a part of their group which gives me a measure of protection. A woman traveling alone in steerage is in a vulnerable position. Several days into the trip, I hear the story of one young woman who is caught alone in her bunk and molested by a fellow passenger. Rather than bear the disgrace, she jumps overboard and dies.

In gratitude for their help, I share my food with Meta and her family. It supplements the oatmeal, rice, flour and tea we are given by the ship, but somehow expected to cook on tiny stoves shared with hundreds of other passengers. Between Meta and me, we manage to cook one hot meal a day for our group. We supplement the other meals with biscuits, crackers and cold tea. My stomach remains unsettled, but I force myself to eat. I am the only source of nourishment for Eliza and cannot allow my milk to weaken and breasts to dry out. Over and over, through the weeks to come, I thank God for His protection in the form of Meta and her family. If ever in my life, I was powerless, it is now. I have no choice but to let God be in control.

Despite His constant provision and surprising peace in the midst of the madhouse around me, about five weeks into our trip, I think I will go insane if I cannot get above deck even for just a minute. The ship heaves and lurches its way across the Atlantic. The cargo doors, once a source of ventilation, are closed due to rain and waves. The overpowering smell of the first part of the voyage has given way to a reek that filters into every pore of my body. Even my baby smells like vomit. Although I am still breastfeeding, my menses begin again, probably from the stress of the voyage. With a knowing look, Meta helps me strip my last clean towel into rags. Cramping and weary, I lie in my bunk and pray. *Oh, God are you there? Wouldn't it be better to die?*

Then, the ship stills. With the incessant darkness, I do not know if it is day or night, but while the other passengers moan and complain in their bunks, I have an overwhelming urge to go outside. Eliza sleeps beside me. I leave her in the bunk and climb over Meta's daughter—or is it Ernst's?

Trying not to call attention to myself, I creep quietly through steerage, slip in some liquid I do not want to know its source, climb up the ladder and onto the deck. It is night. A sweet breeze meets my face. Though I carry the stench of below decks, I imagine I smell salt air and flowers. The sails flap in the slight wind and sing a hymn of peace. The sky is clear, and I see a breathtaking array of stars. So many and so close, I think I could gather a basketful if I reach out my hand. I drink it in like my greedy child sucks at my breast. I must not stay here long, but I want to remember every detail of this moment. It will carry me through the rest of the journey.

I remember a verse in Psalms Ada and I studied. "When I consider thy heavens, the work of thy fingers, the moon and the stars, which thou hast ordained; What is man, that thou art mindful of him?" Here, then, is the answer to my question I just prayed. Though I cannot see Him with my eyes in the squalor of steerage, God is with me.

I make my way to the toilets and relieve myself. I change the rag between my legs. Somehow, I must find a way to wash the old one out. Puzzling over that dilemma, I fail to see the man who has slipped behind me. He grabs my arms and holds them down with one hand. With the other, he reaches for my breasts and then, attempts to pull my skirt up. I scream, but the wind in the sails, once a song, becomes an accomplice in his evil. I doubt anyone will hear and if they do, who is left to care? After surviving this long, will I, too, feel obliged to throw myself overboard? What of the babe who sleeps in my bunk. Thoughts of Eliza give me renewed strength, I fight back and feel the man's hands release their hold. Thank God! Will he give up so easily, then? I turn and see a knife flash in the starlight. Another man has joined us and threatens the first.

"Leave her be. She is not yours to take." *Ernst. My God, Ernst has come to my defense! Thank you, Jesus.*

In the face of the glistening knife, my attacker chooses to run.

"Go back downstairs. I will follow you," Ernst says.

"How can I thank you?"

"Just go; don't do it again. From now on, keep Meta with you. He may try again," he orders.

Trembling, I return to my bunk. I realize I dropped the bloody rag on the deck, but thinking of what else I could have lost, I do not grieve for it. Instead, I thank God once more for his protection. And pray we reach land soon.

Ten days later, earlier than expected with the rough seas, we emerge from the bowels of the ship, blinking in the September sunlight. The noise and confusion of the New York City docks seems quiet compared to the din of excitement below decks when we realize we have made it safely across the Atlantic. Ernst quietly carries my almost empty trunk to the deck. I place my hand on his arm as he shrugs off my thanks.

"I owe you my life, Ernst. I will not forget it."

I hug Meta goodbye and start to shake Werner's hand, but what we have endured makes that gesture meaningless, so I hug him as well. They shepherd their children off the boat leaving me to scan the horizon and wonder how in the world I will find Joseph in such a large city.

Once again, Eliza is bound into a scarf at my waist so I pick up my bag with one hand and drag my trunk with the other. Though the cradle is strapped to its top, the trunk is much lighter than when I arrived on board what seems like years ago. I catch a glimpse of myself in a ship's window. There is much less of me as well. It seems I have been hungry for a long time. My hair is pulled back in a greasy knot. I long for a bath and the opportunity to scrub myself clean. I think it will be months before I erase the smell of the ship from my nose. Yet, dirty as I am, I am happy. I made it. I am about to take my first step onto American soil!

A sailor hoists my bag, the trunk and Eliza's cradle onto the dock, and I quickly follow. *Where should I go first? Who can I trust to help me?* Many voices call out in German and in languages I do not know. They all offer help. For a price. *Who should I listen to?* If the voyage taught me nothing else, it was the power of prayer, so I bow my head and ask the only One who knows the future what I should do. Look up! I feel Him say. So, I raise my head and there standing before me is my husband!

"Julia! Over here! Come, let me help you!"

I think I will faint with relief. I reach for him to steady myself. I am so dirty, and I stink. I hate to even touch him. Is he real?

"How did you know where to find me?"

"We heard a ship from La Havre was making its way into port. Another ship passed you yesterday. I came to see, in hopes you would be on it! Your friend, Margaret, said you would be coming about this time."

Margaret. So she *did* get to talk to Joseph. Did she deliver the rest of my message as well?

He smiles at me and despite my smell, holds me close. Perhaps she did, then. He acts as though he does not bear a grudge. Eliza squirms between us. I pull the folds of fabric aside so he can see.

"Papa, meet your daughter. Elizabeth Margaret."

Joseph looks at our daughter and then, smiles into my face. "A girl? Elizabeth Margaret? Named after a good friend, then." Yes, a dear friend. Margaret must have delivered the message.

Joseph sets my trunk on his shoulder and Eliza's cradle under his arm. He carries my bag in his free hand and I follow him through the bustling streets to Manhattan's Lower East Side. As we walk, the voices become more familiar.

"Welcome to Kleindeutschland," he says. "Little Germany."

Joseph stops in front of a three story brick building. A butcher shop is on the first floor. The butcher and his family live on the second floor and the third floor is divided into apartments. Joseph leads me up three flights of stairs and down a long hallway. The building smells like smoke and sausage. I am out of shape from lying in my bunk for so many weeks. Before we reach our apartment, I gasp for breath and long to put the baby down. He opens the door to what is little more than one room. I ease myself in a chair and look around as I fight not to let the old anger swallow me. Our bed is crammed into what was a closet in our home in Germany. I think of our large farmhouse, the pastures and all our animals and want to cry with homesickness.

"It isn't much, I know," Joseph apologizes. "It was just temporary until you got here. Now that you have arrived, we can move to the country and get our farmland."

We had farmland, I want to snap. I bite my tongue. I have thought about this day for a long time and how my hatefulness was the last thing Joseph remembered about me. *I will do better. God help me, I will do better at being a good wife.*

"I am just glad to be back with you," I manage to smile. "Home is where you are, husband."

Joseph kneels down and hugs me. "I have missed you so. I regretted leaving you like that. I felt I had no other choice. When I watched a woman's baby die and be buried at sea, I knew we had made the right decision, but oh, Julia, how I missed you."

"I am sorry for the way we parted. I should have trusted you. I should have trusted God. I have so much to tell you. So much I have learned."

Joseph buries his head on my shoulder. "We have all the time now."

Eliza fusses in response to her father's embrace.

I laugh. "First, I need to feed her and then, oh, how I would love a bath," I say.

"It will take a while to get the water warm, but I remembered how it felt to get off the ship. I've been hauling water for days hoping you would come soon." Joseph motions to the small metal tub in the corner of the room. As I feed Eliza, I watch him light a fire and heat the water for my bath.

It takes more water than Joseph planned because I wash my hair four times before I think it is clean. I hope I have not brought any vermin from the ship with me. I give him my clothes to be burned. They are almost threadbare, and I cannot bring myself to wear them again. The clothes I wore in Germany, the ones Joseph brought with him, are much too big, but they are at least clean and neat. I bathe Eliza and put her down for a nap in the fresh bedding I placed in her cradle. We are both exhausted. My husband will have to wait to exchange stories about how we passed the time while we were apart. After eating a bowl of soup he provides, I lie down on the bed and despite the unfamiliar noises of the city and our apartment building, I sleep the rest of the day and all through the night.

When I awake, my husband is gone. During his time in New York, while he waited for me and filed his naturalization papers, Joseph found a job working for a building contractor. He is responsible for all the woodworking, cabinets and trim. Though I am eager to leave New York and this tiny apartment, Joseph says we must stay for three more months.

"Herr Mueller has been good to me. I did not know when you would arrive so I promised I would stay through the end of the year. We will finish the job we have. Then, I will be free to leave. I thought we would go to Pennsylvania and see your friend, Margaret. Pennsylvania is supposed to be a good place to live."

I laugh when I think of the way that Margaret said Pennsylvania. Yes, it would be good to see my friend again. I can endure this for a little while. Anything is better than the boat!

But, New York City is not good for me. I start out well. We join St. Matthews Lutheran Church even though the worship services are in English and we do not understand what is said. I do my best to make new friends. It was easy with Margaret. She was so outgoing and vivacious I didn't have to do anything but smile and listen. In New York, not only do even the German women speak English or try to speak English, but they are more competitive. Comparing their homes and husbands' employment, talking of children or social engagements. I do not find them to be very kind. It hurts to think of all I have lost, and I am reluctant to answer questions about my former home or my boys. Despite many social opportunities in Little Germany, beer gardens, sport clubs, libraries, choirs, shooting clubs, theatres and schools, as the weather cools, I chose to stay inside more and more. I would rather be alone than play their catty games. I no longer read my Bible or pray. *If this is what God is like, perhaps I do not need Him.* So, quickly I have forgotten what I learned since Margaret introduced me to her God.

My health declines. With plenty of food available to us, I spend my days cooking and eating. The hunger I felt on the boat is a distant memory as I gorge myself on apple strudel and spatzes, tiny noodles. I eat to make myself feel better, but instead my side hurts and the familiar nausea returns. Under Joseph's watchful eye, I do not feel I can make myself vomit so I endure the pain as stoically as possible. When I am hurting I vow not to overeat again, but at the first opportunity to practice some self control, I go right back to doing what I please. Food comforts. At least for a little while. I no longer feel like going for walks in the public square, the Weisse Garten. The lack of exercise and more food than I need means my clothes from Germany are no longer too big. In fact, they are quite snug. I can imagine what the other women would say about the tight buttons and stretched seams.

Joseph is alarmed by my lethargy. He brings the doctor who prescribes a tonic for my "torpid liver." He lectures me and warns me to eat properly.

"Frau Atzeroth, it is simply a matter of telling yourself no. Just stop eating the wrong things and make better choices." I wish it were as easy as he describes, but with my husband gone all day and being in a new city with no friends, food is my only companion.

The medicine tastes like alcohol and makes me sleepy. Some days, it is a struggle to get out of bed to care for the baby. When I find myself craving the medicine, I decide not to take any more. While it numbs some of my pain, I do not think it will cure this aching need that ails me. Some of it is boredom. But, most of it is homesickness. Every time I prepare a dish like Pflaumenknödel—Plum Dumplings, or Jaegerschnitzel, fried pork with mushroom gravy, I seek a taste of home.

In the market, I compare the produce to what we grew on our farm and find it lacking. The apples are too soft. The cherries too tart. The potatoes, moldy. The beans, not crisp enough. Joseph finds America exhilarating and full of promise. I left all my promises behind in Bessingen.

Compounding my homesickness is my desire to be a good wife to my husband. The memory of how we parted in La Havre still haunts me. I try to overcome how much I hurt him by modeling Ada's teaching about the dutiful Christian wife. In Bavaria, I made business decisions, approved contracts, and set the prices for our produce. Here, my only chore is striving to be meek and compliant. I remember Paul's words in his letter to the Ephesians that I studied with Ada. "Wives submit yourselves to your husbands." If I tell Joseph how unhappy I am, won't it be disrespectful to him? It is not in my nature to be quiet, but I swallow my fears and anxieties, along with my sauerkraut, and hope I will feel better.

Chapter Five

I do not know if it is because my husband works hard or because he is worried about me, but by early November, he finishes his work. We are free to leave! Though it takes me twice as long as it should because I have to stop and rest, I pack in time for us to catch the next boat to Philadelphia. I follow Joseph the two blocks to the docks carrying Eliza. Joseph pushes a hand cart he borrowed from his former employer. It carries our trunks, bed frame, Eliza's cradle and a few other belongings. Joseph has rolled our mattress up and tied it with string. It looks like a long sausage balanced on top of the hand cart. I grit my teeth against the pain in my side and struggle to hold Eliza. At almost seven months, she is getting too big for me to carry.

Reminding myself I am going to see Margaret gives me the determination I need to finish the walk. I sit on a wall and wait while Joseph loads our belongings on a beautiful two masted schooner. A carved and painted woman hangs from her pointed bow. The journey will only take a day or two depending on the winds. If we are lucky, we will be in Philadelphia by morning. Except for the cradle, our belongings are stowed below deck, and we are shown to a large cabin where the other passengers wait. Joseph pulls a chair over into a corner. He gestures for me to sit while he places the cradle beside it.

"Where will you sit?" I ask.

"I want to stay on deck and watch," he says. "Besides, there is a smoking cabin for the men. I can go there if I want to come inside."

I want to stay on deck, too. But, I do not ask. *He expects me to stay here with the baby.*

I angle my chair to face a small window. From my position, I cannot see much, but catch a glimpse of sailors untying ropes and hear their shouts as they raise the sails. We leave port and head to sea. I will not be sorry to see the end of New York City. Joseph told me we will sail south past Long Island and along the coast of New Jersey until we reach the Delaware River. Then, we will follow the river north to Philadelphia.

I wish I could see. I consider taking Eliza outside, but she chooses that moment to begin to cry. The other travelers look at me with frowns. I pick her up, turn away from them and open my blouse to let her nurse. I face the wall. Whatever view of the outdoors I had is no longer visible. For some reason, Eliza will not settle down. Perhaps the motion of the waves reminds her of our long voyage across the Atlantic. I would not want to remember that period either. By the time I get her quiet again, I am afraid to put her in the cradle. I doze in my seat holding her.

A few hours later, Joseph excitedly tells me about all he saw while I slept with the fitful baby. A pod of whales surfacing beside the boat. Seagulls darting overhead. The choreography of the sailors as they work the sails. The coastline as it glides by. It sounds so exciting, but all I have seen is the dingy wallpaper of the salon.

When he asks if I brought something for us to eat, I want to snap at him, but hold my tongue. I unpack some sandwiches and fruit. Perhaps while he is here, I can take a glimpse outside. When I mention it, he frowns and shakes his head.

"The wind is strong, and the boat has picked up speed. I think it is too dangerous for you out there right now." Then, he takes his sandwich and returns outdoors.

Soon after Joseph leaves, I realize I should have asked him to stay with Eliza long enough for me to use the toilet. Forced to take her with me, I huddle into the small room struggling with my skirts and the baby. By the time I finish, I am angry. As luck would have it, I run into my husband on my way back to the waiting room.

"Here, take her," I snarl. He fumbles as he reaches for Eliza, and I push past him, through the cabin and out the door.

Joseph was right. The wind is strong. It howls around me and salt water pelts my face. I hold onto the railing attached to the outside of the cabin wall and struggle to keep my balance. The air cools my temper. I regret acting so harshly. Tears mix with the spray as I realize I have broken my resolve to be a better wife. My nature is not to be quiet and meek. I can't do this! I feel like I am pretending all the time. How can I follow the rules and still be myself?

I ponder that dilemma as the boat turns from the Atlantic and into the Delaware River. The wind calms as we enter a great bay edged by marshes on all sides. Egrets rise from the grass, and seals bob up and down in the water. Their canine faces turn to watch us pass. The water and the shore remind me of the French coastline and La Havre. I wonder what Margaret will say when I ask her what I should do. She will be disappointed I have not spent more time studying my Bible or praying. I remember the love Margaret showed. Margaret was like Christ. I let the women in New York distract me from the real way to live that Margaret taught me. Maybe that is my problem. I pray a swift prayer for patience and kindness before turning back to go inside. I need to apologize to Joseph.

My husband searches my face when I approach and hold out my hands for the baby.

"I am sorry I snapped at you," I say. "She has been very fussy, and I just needed a break. You can go back outside. It is beautiful out there."

"I'm sorry, too. I was so excited about seeing a new part of America I ignored you. Come, let's go outside and watch together. I'll carry her."

I pull the blanket closer around Eliza, and we step outside together. My daughter is as happy to be outdoors, as I am, and gurgles and waves her arms at all she sees. We go to the port side of the boat and watch the sun start to set over the Delaware shore. We should be in Philadelphia by early morning. I hear a shout followed by another.

"What are they saying?" I ask. Joseph frowns and shakes his head. He tilts his head to hear better what they say. A sailor calls down from where he perches near the mast.

"Wave, giant wave. Hold fast."

When he sees Joseph does not understand, he points in front of the ship. We see a tall wave rolling downriver towards the boat.

A giant wave? In the river?

Joseph reaches around me and holds on to the railing. He urges, "Grab on! We don't have time to get back inside!"

The ship rises with the bow of the boat steeply pointed at an angle toward the sky. I feel myself sliding toward the back of the boat and hold on to Joseph with both hands as he struggles to stay upright and shelter Eliza. *What is happening?*

The boat comes down on the other side of the swell and sends a wall of water washing our way. I close my eyes. *Please God, protect us!* We are soaked, but Joseph manages to keep us from washing overboard. We push our backs against the cabin wall. I scream and startle Eliza who also cries.

A sailor slips through the water and helps us back inside.

"Joseph, what was that? That was like something we might see in the Atlantic. I never expected it in the river."

"I don't know." He turns to the sailor and asks. "Does that happen often?"

Thankfully, the sailor speaks a little German. "I never saw such a wave. Not in the Delaware. Are you two alright?"

I begin to tremble and think about what could have happened.

Joseph answers for us, "Yes, we are alright. Just in shock. Thank you for your assistance. I will see about getting my wife a blanket."

Joseph picks up my chair from where it has fallen over in the main cabin and helps me to settle Eliza. The other passengers chatter excitedly about what just occurred. Out of the corner of my eye, I see them huddle over a woman who lies on the floor. Joseph drapes a blanket around Eliza and me, then, stands looking at us with tears in his eyes.

"I almost lost you. Julia, I do not know what I would have done if something had happened to you. I love you."

I think back to the last few months and all we have endured. In my misery and loneliness, I lost my focus on what is most important. *I will do better at being a good wife and taking care of my health.* I must. For all our sakes.

When we dock in Philadelphia the next morning, people are filled with news about the earthquake that shook the city the day before and the rogue wave it spawned. The same wave that hit our ship just before dusk the night before.

We hire a wagon to take us to Margaret's house on the outskirts of the city. Between her excitement over seeing us, finally meeting Eliza and the fears of aftershocks from the earthquake, my exuberant friend is even livelier than I remember her.

"No one was hurt, thank God, but I lost some china when it fell off the table. Who would have thought we would have to fear earthquakes in Philadelphia? Do you want something to eat? What a darling baby. Can I hold her? Come, sit. Tell me about your journey."

Before I can begin, she tells us how Philadelphia has not met their expectations. Riots happen almost daily in the city as Blacks, Irish and Germans clash over what will be taught in the schools, competition for jobs and which religion is best.

"I am afraid to even go to church, much less take the girls to school. And then, there are the abolitionists, constantly stirring up the crowds. Not that I am for slavery mind you, but surely, they could be more delicate in their protests. Whoever named this the City of Brotherly Love was terribly mistaken! There is hatred for one another everywhere you go."

I am exhausted from our travels, but even more so from listening to Margaret talk. I do not think I want to settle in Philadelphia. At bedtime, with Eliza's cradle crammed between us and the wall in Margaret's guest bedroom, Joseph shares what he has learned from Margaret's husband, Frederick. He corroborates all Margaret told me about the problems with race relations in the city and adds, "What upsets me more is the conflict between the Catholics and Protestants. Of all people who should be working towards some kind of peace, you would think it would be the Christians," he exclaims.

I think about my outburst on the boat. *I sympathize with them. It is hard to be a peacemaker!*

Joseph continues, "Frederick says they have a buyer for their house and business. There is a large group of Lutherans here in the city abandoning efforts to make a home here. They are starting over in Missouri. The German Settlement Society of Philadelphia purchased over 11,000 acres of land in a town they call Hermann. They are concerned about our German heritage being lost as our people become Americans. They sent a group of seventeen to settle there three years ago and already they have 450 people living in the city. They constructed over ninety houses, five stores, two hotels and a post office already, but there is still plenty of land left for newcomers. They say the land looks much like the Rhineland. It is near the Missouri River so we can easily get there by traveling up the Mississippi River to St. Louis. Julia, I think we should go with them. I think we can make a home there."

Missouri. More traveling. I had hoped to have a home of my own now. It is fall. Winter is coming. We would not be able to plant even if we purchased a farm in Pennsylvania today. Hermann, Missouri is not a place I thought to live, but after today, I do not want to argue with him. It is more important we stay together as a family. I take Joseph's hand and smile when I think of how Margaret will manage the word, "Mississippi."

If we were not convinced we should keep searching for a place to make our home, the second earthquake in Philadelphia, two days later confirms we should join the group leaving for Missouri. Plans call for us to sail south from Philadelphia, around the peninsula of Florida to New Orleans. From there, we will change boats for a trip up the Mississippi River to St. Louis and then, to Hermann. As much as I dread more boat trips, particularly after our experience on the Delaware, I know it is necessary for us to keep moving until we find what we are looking for in a place to settle.

Joseph and I talk about our wishes a lot. We want a place where there is a Lutheran church that adheres to our beliefs and preaches the Word of God in our native tongue. We want a place where there is a school. Joseph is especially concerned our daughter will learn to read and write since he never had that opportunity. I want a place where there are women who will be friendly and helpful. Having Margaret as part of our traveling group ensures I will have at least one friend and knowing Margaret, we will make more. Most importantly, we want a place where we can farm with land to build a house and make a living. We don't think that is too much to ask from a country as full of bounty and vast spaces as America.

I also look forward to the trip in order to have some time to visit with Margaret. Our stay in Philadelphia is brief and busy as we help the family pack and board the boat. I worry we are leaving at the wrong time of year, but Joseph assures me November is actually the best time to travel south. Not only will the weather be warmer the closer we get to New Orleans, but the summer storm season will have ended. I can't help but remember the wave that almost washed us overboard in the Delaware River and wonder if any travel by sea is safe.

Our ship is called the *Ohio*. A packet ship, named for its scheduled route ensuring regular delivery of mail, the *Ohio* was built at Philadelphia in 1825 and measures more than one hundred feet long. It is smaller than the ship that brought me to America, and though there are twelve families and almost sixty of us in the group crowded on board, Joseph procures for us a small cabin. It is a relief to have our own space, no matter how tiny. After my trip across the Atlantic, I do not think I could tolerate another voyage in steerage.

It takes about five weeks to reach New Orleans. In spite of the length of our voyage down the coast, the trip is a pleasant one. The ship has a cook and though the meals are plain and not always tasty, they are served regularly. Unlike a voyage at sea, the ship stops at ports frequently to deliver mail and take on more provisions so our fruits, meat and vegetables are fresh. There is even milk as some of the families brought herds of dairy goats. Meals are portioned so I no longer battle with oversized servings or between meal snacks. We have little opportunities for exercise, but Margaret and I walk around the deck when we can. The sea air, restricted access to food and most importantly, the presence of my dear friend, improve my health. I am happier than I have been in a long time.

We spend much of our day getting to know the other women and their families. All of us work to learn as much English as we can. The people who lived in Philadelphia help those of us who are newer to the country. Though we will be in a German town, there will be times when we will need to speak English. The ship's crew seems to enjoy teaching us as well. The language is hard to master, but at least we are trying.

"Hello, nice to meet you. Have a good day," we practice.

Margaret and I set aside time for long visits alone. Her girls are eager to play with Eliza so there is no lack of caretakers freeing me from my daughter's constant care. We sit on the deck in the shade when the skies are clear, inside in our cabins when it rains and catch up on our lives. One day, Margaret asks me to tell her about how I located Joseph when I arrived in New York.

"It really was a miracle," I confide. "I did not know where to begin to look and offers of help seemed suspicious. I didn't know who I could trust. So I prayed, and Joseph just appeared before me!"

"Yes," Margaret agrees. "It was a miracle. God is good about answering our prayers when we are all out of our own options!" She looks at me closely. "But, I think that is not the only time He came to your rescue. What was it like on the ship? Ada wrote to tell me you insisted on travelling in steerage."

I tell her the whole story of the journey and about Meta and her family. I do not tell her about my attacker though. I do not want to relive that night.

That evening, lying in bed beside Joseph I remember my talk with Margaret. I ask him again how he knew what day to come to the port.

"I had been coming to the port, whenever I could. I checked to see if your ship had docked. As it drew closer to your arrival, I came every day. When I heard a boat had passed one from La Havre on its way into port, I knew it would be yours."

"Oh, how loved that makes me feel to know you looked for me every day!"

Joseph laughs. "Well, it wasn't as romantic as it sounds. We knew it was an immigrant ship by the smell. It was always clear when the boat was full of travelers from Europe!"

I roll over with my back to him in a huff. I remember how miserable I was on the boat all alone and what would have happened if Ernst had not saved me.

"Julia, I did not mean to insult you. It was just the truth. Come here."

He pulls me into his arms, "I missed you every day you were away from me. Why are you crying? Did you miss me, too?"

Should I tell him? For the first time, I talk about the night Ernst rescued me. I weep as I think about the smell and the cramped conditions, but even more what might have happened if he had not followed me up on the deck.

"Oh, my love. I didn't know it would be so hard for you. I should have stayed with you in France. I wish I could thank that man for doing what I should have been there to do myself."

Even though it was hard, I feel better for having shared the burden of that night. Once more, I am at sea. There is a difference this time. In this cozy cabin with my husband at my side, it is time to put the past behind us and move forward. I hold my husband close and thank God He has brought us this far.

A few days later, I share the story with Margaret. She is equally horrified at what might have happened and thanks God for His protection of me.

"Sometimes, I wonder why He saved me," I confess. "I am not the woman He wants me to be. I don't know I ever can be. I did not deserve to be saved."

"Friend, what troubles you so?" Margaret asks.

I begin to cry as I tell Margaret not only about my struggles with overeating, but about my desperate attempts to be a good wife to my husband.

"My, that is a lot to take on for one person. And you are trying to fix this all yourself?"

I nod. *Well who else is going to help me?*

"Julia, let's take one thing at a time. We need to talk more in the future about what it means to be a good wife, but the first place for us to start is with the understanding you cannot fix your troubles alone. Did you know the Apostle Paul struggled with this same thing?"

I know about the man Margaret refers to as Ada and I spent time studying his writings. *But Paul? The great teacher of the early church? The one who had a personal encounter with Jesus? What can she mean?*

"Paul himself wrote in his letter to the church at Rome, 'For I know that in me (that is, in my flesh,) dwelleth no good thing: for to will is present with me; but how to perform that which is good I find not. For the good that I would I do not: but the evil which I would not, that I do. Now if I do that I would not, it is no more I that do it, but sin that dwelleth in me.' In other words, Paul is saying, 'I want to do good things, but I don't do them, and even though I make a decision not to do bad, I do it anyway.' Paul experienced what it was like to know what was the right thing to do, but to repeatedly do the wrong thing even though he vowed he would not. No matter how much we say we are going to be a better person or do something differently, we almost always fail if we try to do it alone."

"So, are you saying I shouldn't even try?" Now, I am frustrated.

"No. I am saying you can't do it alone. And Paul knew that too. The only way we can change, really change, not just a temporary adjustment of our attitudes, but real life change, is through God's power. He gives that power, not to people who deserve it, but to everyone who calls upon His name. That's what grace is all about. Julia, you don't have to do it alone!"

I shake my head. "Why would God want to help me control my eating or be a better wife?"

"Paul wrote about it in his letter to the Corinthians. He said he asked God the same thing and God replied, 'My grace is sufficient for thee: for my strength is made perfect in weakness. Most gladly therefore will I rather glory in my infirmities, that the power of Christ may rest upon me.' When we let God and His Son, Jesus, make changes in our lives, especially differences that our friends and family notice, and when they hear us say we could not have done it without God's help, then, God is glorified and other people turn to Him for help, too. Julia, when we are weak, then God is the most strong."

"But, I don't like being weak. I would rather be strong. I would rather do it myself."

"You can certainly try, and in fact, you have been trying. How far has it gotten you? You are miserable and sick. You fret and worry. That brings me to my final point. Here's something else I want you to think about. You say you keep giving in to temptation to eat too much. It is too hard for you to say no and eating makes you feel better for a while anyway. It is only a temporary fix. The sin of giving in to temptation is really the sin of a lack of trust. When you take things into your own hands, when you try to control your own life and ignore what God would tell you is better for you, you are really exhibiting your unbelief. If God is Who He says He Is, then He will take care of all the underlying reasons that drive you to food to make yourself feel better. If you really believe He is God and He is in control and has something better for you, then, you will learn to wait on him to provide it."

I struggle with Margaret's words. She has spoken the truth to me before but not so passionately, and not so frankly. I really don't know how to respond to what sounds like accusations.

As if she reads my mind, she says in a softer and gentler tone, "Julia, listen to me. I am speaking to myself, too. I struggle with similar things. Do you really think I want to be on this boat heading to Missouri? When I crossed the Atlantic, I thought I was going to the place where I would live out the rest of my life. I had no idea God would take us hundreds of miles farther away from my original dream. I struggle with trusting He knows what is best for me and my family. Trusting is not an easy lesson to learn! It takes time to truly absorb what it means to trust and its benefits. Every day, my faith grows a little stronger, but believe me when I say, I wish I could just give all my worries to God once and for all. I say I want that, but I keep snatching them back! I love you enough to tell you the truth. You are my best friend. And if I want this for you, think how much more God wants you to live a life free of these struggles."

Ironically, our conversation is interrupted by the sound of the dinner bell. As I eat what is provided to me, I wish God had not given me so many choices. If only I could live where all I had to eat was what was put on my plate by someone else and where I did not have access to my own kitchen. Then, there would be no temptation to eat abnormally. *But, life will not always be like that,* I think. *Soon, I will have my own home again. What will I do then? Will God really help me make better choices?*

Chapter Six

A few days later, Margaret and I continue our discussion. Once again, we are sitting on the deck watching the coast of Florida float by. Already, we have visited the ports of Charleston, Savannah, St. Augustine and Key West. While we do not get off the boat to go into the towns to visit, from what we see of each port, the cities are becoming more and more exotic the farther south we go. Even though it is nearing winter, we see palm trees, some laden with coconuts, flowers of all hues and shrubs of bright green. It is warm enough not to even wear a coat or sweater. At the docks, people sell many different types of fish, octopus, citrus fruits and hats made out of palm fronds.

Now, we head north on the west coast of Florida and stop at Passage Key, in the mouth of Tampa Bay, to load kegs of fresh water onto the boat. While we are anchored, I see a wide river one of the sailors tells me is called the Manatee River. I wonder if the Missouri River, where we will make our home, looks as pretty as that river. Joseph says these lands are not ready for settlers yet. The Federal government still owns all of South Florida and it is reserved for the Indians. Soon, we will be docking at the Cedar Keys, a chain of islands and one of the last ports before reaching New Orleans. Time is running out for me to talk to Margaret about my inability to be a good wife to Joseph.

"You said that you wanted to talk to me more about marriage," I begin.

"Yes, what is it exactly that makes you think you cannot be a good wife to Joseph? Are you faithful to him?"

I feel myself blush. "Of course, I am faithful!"

"Well, then, do you lie to him? Or steal from him?"

"No, no. None of that. It doesn't have anything to do with what I do. It is about who I am. Ada said a good wife is meek and submissive to her husband. But, is not who I am. I have strong opinions. I hear about a problem and quickly make a decision how to solve it. I enjoy negotiating prices and handling money. But, those things are wrong for me to do. I need to focus on my home and leave the business decisions to my husband."

Margaret laughs. She laughs! I am serious, and she laughs at me. I want to get up and walk away, but at that moment a school of dolphin slices through the waves. Their silver fins look like knives cutting through the water. Distracted for a moment, I forget my annoyance with my friend. They are so beautiful!

Margaret speaks. "Who do you think taught those dolphins to jump and leap like they do?"

"God did."

"Do you think he gave them the ability to fish or to swim and then, tells them not to? Do you think he says, 'No more of that, it is time for you to be like the crab and lumber along the bottom of the sea?'"

What does this have to do with me? "No, of course not."

"The abilities you just listed for me, business sense, problem solving, and decision making, God gave you those skills just as surely as he taught the dolphins how to swim. At creation, God made women to be helpers to man. When He paired you with Joseph, He knew Joseph needed someone to help him in those areas. God does not prohibit you from using the abilities He gave you, nor does He say to try and be someone else. Where did you get that notion?"

"Ada showed me where Paul said the wife is to be subservient to her husband. She said we are to be quiet and do what we are told because the husband is the head of the household."

"Ada has a lot of knowledge about the Bible, but either you or she is misinterpreting those scriptures. Letting our husbands lead, does not mean we are to sit on our hands and do or say nothing. It means ultimately the responsibility for our family rests with our husbands. They are the ones who God will look to to lead our families spiritually or even legally since the government includes those rules as part of our laws. But, a husband and a wife are to work together to make decisions and to raise their family. It takes two! That's why God created marriage!"

I feel great relief at Margaret's words. Perhaps I have not been wrong, after all.

"Now, I will temper what I say a bit when I remind you God calls us all, men and women, to be loving, gentle and kind. If you and Joseph disagree about something, you are not to manipulate him to get your way, pout or be angry. That's when sin comes in. You can lovingly express your opinions and tell him why you feel the way you do. The hard part of marriage comes if he still chooses to do things his way. Then, you have a choice about how you will react, and God is clear about behaving in a Christlike manner. What's in your heart shows in how you act. Sometimes love means accepting hard things, but, God made you just the way you are so don't be afraid to be that person. I expect if you talk this over with Joseph, you will find he loves you for who you are and understands he needs your help."

I hope so, but how can I be sure?

Margaret gives me a lot to think about. I do not bring it up to Joseph right away, but consider her words carefully. My first opportunity to talk to him comes while we are in port at Seahorse Key, south of the opening to the Suwannee River, just before the mainland makes a turn to the west forming what people call the Panhandle of Florida. While Seahorse Key might be one of the only ports where ships can pick up provisions between Key West and Pensacola, it is really not a town like some of the other ones we passed. It is a very small army post called Cantonment Morgan or Fort Number Four and is spread out among several islands. Though it consists of just some rustic barracks and a hospital, important business is being conducted at the fort. On Depot Island is the headquarters for the Army of the South where negotiations are being held between the Seminole Indians and the Army. The Federal Government wants to convince the Seminoles to retreat to the Everglades or go to reservations in the western United States. Some of the captured Seminoles are even held prisoner there.

On the night we are in port, a man named Mr. Lewis talks about the Indians. "Why does the United States of America feel the need to negotiate with those savages? Once it is finally a state, Florida is going to be overrun with new settlers. And they will be prosperous. The land is fertile and full of natural resources like timber and turpentine. There is plenty of water for drinking, irrigation and transportation. Even the cattle and horses run wild! All a man has to do is put his brand on them, and he will have a herd of his own. The only thing that keeps this land from growing is the Indians. Get rid of them, I say! Send them off to the Oklahoma territories and give the white man the chance to make something of this place."

The other men nod and smile. I can't believe what I am hearing. Isn't there a place for everyone in this vast wilderness? The Indians were here first after all. I keep my thoughts to myself until we are back in our cabin. Then, I explode.

"Did you hear what he said? How greedy and evil he is! Just because he wants what they have, he would send the Indians away from their home and out west? All I want is a place to call home. I can't imagine the Indians would feel any differently. If they are willing to compromise and share the land, then, why would they be forced out?"

Joseph puts his finger to his lips. "Shush, the walls are very thin. We don't know who might be listening. I am afraid Mr. Lewis' beliefs are shared by many. It will do us no good to start a fight among our own kind."

"Joseph, listen to what you are saying. Among our own kind. I don't want to be associated with someone who has that attitude. Wait! Do you believe what he said is true?"

My husband whispers. "No, I don't, but I am asking you not to make a scene about it. We have enough troubles of our own. Until we find a place to live and become a part of a community, we just need to be cautious is all."

I lower my voice, but his words trigger all the turmoil over what my role is to be in our marriage. I have been confused since my studies with Ada and now, Margaret has a whole different perspective. It is time to find out what my husband expects.

"Are you telling me you don't want me to talk to anyone about this or are you saying I can't talk to you about this? Do you want to hear my opinion or do you expect me to smile and nod and do whatever you tell me when you tell me to do it? Am I just your slave to do your bidding or am I someone whose opinion matters? What do you expect from me?"

Joseph looks confused. "Where did all that come from? Of course I respect your opinion. I depend upon you and your wisdom."

"Then why did you sell our farm without talking to me about it? I worked beside you to make it successful and strong. Yet, you sold it like it only belonged to you! Why did you force me to come here to the United States with you?" I thought all of those hurt feelings were behind me, but they come bubbling up as though we are still back in Bavaria and packing to leave the home I loved.

"Wait. Are you angry? I didn't realize you harbored those feelings. I did what I thought was best for us. You were so distraught over the deaths of the boys. I didn't think you could ever be happy with all the reminders of our sons and thought it was better to get a fresh start. I thought you agreed to move. I am sorry I hurt you so deeply."

"I know you did what you thought was best. What really hurts is that you didn't talk to me about it. I thought we were partners. I thought my opinion was important to you. You just threw it all away with no consideration of what I wanted."

"So, this is not so much about the move as it is about valuing your opinion?"

Yes, that is it exactly. I nod. "I wonder what I mean to you beyond just a companion. Am I someone you depend upon for help and assistance or could you just as easily purchase a slave to serve your needs?"

Joseph's eyes widen. "I would never treat you as a slave. I would never treat anyone as a slave. You know I don't believe in slavery. Whatever have I done to make you feel so strongly? I apologize. I cannot take back the past. What do you expect from me?"

My eyes fill with tears. I did not mean to hurt him with my words. *Is that really how I think? What do I want from my husband?*

"I just want to feel like I have more to offer than my hands to serve and my body to keep you warm at night. I want to know you value what I think and feel. That you respect my opinions and need my wisdom."

"But, I do. There was never any doubt about that. I trust your judgment and look on you as my partner, not my slave."

"Then, why did you tell me to keep my opinions to myself?"

Joseph sighs. "I want to know what you think but sometimes, we have to be careful who we speak to about them. We don't know these people well and don't want to make any enemies. Nor do I know the whole story of what is going on. All I know is what one man said to make himself look more important in front of some other men. I have heard the Indians are not as innocent as you might think. Surely, I don't expect you to just sit back and keep your mouth shut while I fumble through making all the decisions for our family. I'd be lost without you!"

I feel the wedge of anger I didn't know I still carried begin to soften. I am grateful to Margaret for encouraging me to talk to my husband. At least my concerns ease. I still feel sorry for the Indians though.

I feel even sorrier for them at our next port. From Cedar Keys, we cross the Gulf of Mexico in a northwestern direction finally docking in Pensacola which, under the Government of Spain, had been the capitol of West Florida until a new territorial capital was established in Tallahassee in 1824. We enter Pensacola Harbor and pass Fort Pickens and the lighthouse. One of the crew tells us about Michaela Ingraham, the lighthouse keeper's wife who stayed on to serve the lighthouse after her husband's death.

What a brave woman! What would it be like to live alone in this wild country? At least we are going to a civilized town.

Another boat docked in port distracts me from my wondering about what life would be like in Florida. On board are sixty dark skinned men, women and children all clothed in colorful shirts and dresses. They look like patchwork quilts. I ask Joseph about them, and he tells me they are Indians, members of the Mikasuki Tribe led by Coosa Tustenuggee. They are also on their way to New Orleans and will eventually settle on the western lands reserved for them. I squint to look into their faces. They look so solemn and sad. I think about Michaela Ingraham, the lighthouse keeper, and how she works so hard to stay in Florida, and now, these Indians are being forced to leave when they obviously do not want to go. There must be something to Florida I cannot see.

We make the last leg of our voyage to New Orleans. As much as I have enjoyed the time with Margaret and her family, I will be glad to get off the boat even for just a little while. Our group plans to stay in New Orleans for a few weeks until we can board a steamboat that will take us on the Mississippi River to St. Louis. There, we will use a barge for the final leg up the

Missouri River to Hermann. I think about what I have heard the others say about New Orleans. There is a large German settlement twenty five miles north of the city on a lake called Lac des Allemands or Lake of the Germans.

Germans first settled there in 1721 forming the towns of Karlstein, Hoffen, Mariental and Augsburg. They established farms all around the lake, clearing the swamps, braving the bug infested marshes and planting crops in the fertile soil. They were instrumental in keeping the town of New Orleans fed throughout that century and to present day. In fact, in 1803, Napoleon's prefect to Louisiana, Pierre Clement Laussat, stated the Germans were the only people capable of taming the Louisiana wilderness. It makes me proud to know even Napoleon recognized what a contribution we could make to America. Because of the hard work of Germans one hundred years ago, not only do their settlements thrive, but so does the formerly French town of New Orleans.

As we sail into the Port of New Orleans, Margaret and Frederick join Joseph and me. Her daughters scamper around us entertaining Eliza who has begun to stand on her own. They take her hands in theirs and help her to walk.

"Girls, not too close to the edge, please." Margaret says aloud what I am thinking as I reach for my daughter and move her closer to me. She twists away from me reaching for the girls that are now like sisters to her. Joseph picks Eliza up and puts her on his shoulder where she squeals with excitement. *Now I can focus on what is before me.* I gaze ahead as the shoreline of the city comes into view.

Our ship weaves between the sailboats of all sizes, steamboats, barges, flatboats and rowboats fill the river beside the city. Along one side of the river stretches New Orleans with its long rows of tall brick buildings. The spires of St. Louis Cathedral rise above them, and a few blocks away, I see the dome of the St. Charles Hotel. Looking on the other side of the river, I notice a group of Blacks working under the direction of an overseer. Both men and women haul soil from the river's edge in wheel barrows and dump it in piles creating a barrier between the river and the shore.

"Slaves," Margaret says.

Frederick cautions. "Now, Margaret. We are in a different world. We must be careful of what we say and who might overhear."

He sounds like Joseph. I pull my shawl closer around me. The air is chilly, not as cold as I remember Bavaria being, but in the damp air, it feels colder. *Or is it the thought people are watching us and will be asking us to take sides?*

I am reminded of my fears as we disembark the boat. Our belongings are loaded into wagons but we choose to walk to our hotel. It has been so long since we walked on solid ground. My legs feel wobbly and my head light as though we are still dipping along in the waves. As we stroll towards our hotel, I see a poster for an upcoming slave auction.

"Valuable gang of young negroes," it says. "Men and women, field hands. Sold for no fault; with the best city guarantees." I know for certain we are in a different world than Germany or even Philadelphia. *What does that mean? "Sold for no fault?"*

Later, when we can talk alone, I ask Joseph what he thinks it means. "It should have read, sold with no fault. In other words, without blemish or imperfection. But, I think perhaps that sold for no fault is more like it. It is no fault of their own they are enslaved."

I ponder his words as I lie in bed that night. The city is noisy. Horses and carriages replace the sway of the sails, and I hear the laughter of passersby instead of the sailor's night watch. Despite Margaret's teaching and her faith, slavery presents one of the biggest hurdles for me in my struggle to believe in a good God who controls the world. *How can He stand by and watch a blameless people be treated so cruelly? Why did He abandon me at my uncle's?* Sometimes, God seems so near. But, other times, I just cannot understand what He must be thinking to allow such suffering in the world. Despite Margaret's reminders about grace, a part of me still thinks I need to work to earn God's blessing.

I think about the slaves we saw laboring on the shore of the Mississippi. The men and women were neatly dressed. The women wore calico skirts and straw hats. Nothing about their appearance would indicate they were slaves unless you knew their circumstance. They did not bear chains. At least ones we could see. But, they are still slaves.

I am a slave. I am still bound to my past. The burden I carry from the time I spent under my uncle's rule affects me today. Oh, how I want to set aside those ways of thinking. What can truly make me free?

Ironically, the time I felt closest to God and the most peaceful was when I was on the ship crossing the Atlantic Ocean. Then, I knew God was the only One Who could save me. I didn't fight or take charge. I just rested in Him. I had no other choice. *What keeps me from doing the same now? Why do I continue to fight for control?* I fall asleep wishing it was easier to surrender.

Our first Sunday in New Orleans, we attend church at the newly established St. Paul Lutheran Church. There are so many of us in our group, we almost outnumber the members. It seems like the congregation is used to large parties of immigrants coming through the city on their way to new settlements. They welcome us to join them in their worship. The church is decorated for Christmas. As we celebrate advent, I stand between Margaret and Joseph and wonder as we sing, *Savior of the Nations, Come,* how it is they can sing so boldly of Christ's birth and God's salvation through Him?

> Savior of the nations, come,
> Virgin's Son, make here Thy home!

Marvel now, O heaven and earth,
That the Lord chose such a birth.

Wondrous birth! O wondrous Child
Of the Virgin undefiled!
Though by all the world disowned,
Still to be in heaven enthroned.

Praise to God the Father sing,
Praise to God the Son, our King,
Praise to God the Spirit be
Ever and eternally.

Margaret said by not trusting God to care for me, I reject Him. I think about the phrase, "though by all the world disowned." *Is that what I do when I distrust God? What will it take to help me let go and follow my husband and friend's examples?*

Despite the hymn and my longing to be free of this struggle for control, the coming days show me I have far to go. Christmas is a time of gaiety and rejoicing. Margaret's girls are beside themselves with anticipation of Christmas Day. *Next year, Eliza will be excited about Christmas, too.* Awaiting the steamboat that will transport us north to Missouri, we take advantage of the German society that thrives in this riverfront city.

The town may have been founded by the French, but the German influence is strong. Even the music, called "Cajun", part of the culture of the descendants of French colonists forced from Acadia in Canada in the 1700s, uses a German instrument, the accordion. We visit the beer halls that serve as places for families to gather and socialize enjoying a taste of home in not only the brew, but the food. It tastes so good after the weeks of shipboard cooking!

The German bakeries compete to outdo each other. I can't get enough of Baumkuchen, the tree cake. Known as the "king of cakes", it is made by placing a thin spit over a wood fire. The batter is brushed on the spit and baked and then, succeeding layers are added, sometimes as many as 100 "rings" like the rings of a Christmas tree! We eat Stollen, a pastry made with dried fruit like raisins and currents covered in icing and Zimtsterne, frosted star shaped cinnamon cookies. Memories of Christmas flood my mind. I see my mother serving these same foods. Remember how my sons enjoyed them as well. I want those times back. With the tastes on my tongue and my eyes closed, I imagine they are still with me. In my effort to recreate the past, I eat more than I should.

For Christmas dinner, the hotel serves a goose, Christmas pudding and mulled wine. Margaret and Joseph surprise me by turning the meal into a birthday celebration. It has been so long since anyone honored me in that way. I eat until I think I cannot eat anymore but manage to have a second helping of dessert. I think of my mother, my boys and the Christmases of my childhood with every bite. I feel like if I turn around, they will be standing behind me once more.

But by the time Epiphany arrives on January 6, my stomach hurts so badly I am not sure I can even eat a piece of the Three Kings Cake. Made with oranges and spices representing gold, frankincense and myrrh, and decorated with a paper crown, the cake was one of my mother's specialties. As a girl, I looked forward to this day almost as much as Christmas and hoped I might find the piece of cake with the almond hidden inside so I would be chosen queen for the day. I am afraid I have had enough Christmas celebrating. Today, the thought of eating a piece of cake makes me sick. When I refuse a plate, Margaret frowns.

"Are you feeling unwell?" she asks.

I nod, then making excuses, run back to my room to vomit into the basin on the dresser. The next day, the pain is so great I cannot get out of bed. Joseph calls for the German physician, Dr.

Hahn. Despite my discomfort, I cannot help but think his name suits him. Short and stocky, he looks like the bantam rooster his name implies. When he speaks, his arrogance is apparent as well.

"Torpid liver. No food for 24 hours, then, only clear liquids for a week. She must change her diet. No puddings or sweets. She must not travel for at least a month." He leaves abruptly after giving Joseph a bill, a bottle of Sand's Sarsaparilla and some small blue pills I am to take three times a day.

Not travel for a month. But, what about our trip to Missouri? The steamboat will leave any day. Oh, God, what have I done?

Joseph is solemn as he sits beside me on the bed. I wince as he accidently jostles my side. Eliza is with Margaret and her girls. *I keep my husband from his dream and I can't even care for my own child. What use am I?* I wait for my husband to speak, but he says nothing. Finally, I break the silence.

"I am sorry. I should have known better."

"Known better about what? What makes you think that this is your fault?"

"This happens only when I eat too much rich food. I have known the cause since I was a young woman living with my uncle. Remember the first day we met? It was this same sickness and from the same problem."

"I know the doctor in New York told you to change your diet, but when we left the city, you got better. Maybe it is city life that makes you ill. You were never sick on the farm. I think we need to move back to the country. That will make you well."

I grasp at the straw my husband offers me. I do not want to admit to him this is the result of my own failure. Perhaps I will be better in the country.

"What are you proposing?" I ask.

"I know you wanted to go to Missouri with Margaret. We can still do it later on. But, I heard about some farm land to rent outside of the city. Why don't we give that a try for a while until we decide what we want to do?"

My faithful husband. Never quick to blame, always the optimist. Though I know I am the cause of this situation, I allow him to convince me it is not my fault. It just seems easier.

A few days later, when I bid good-bye to Margaret, easier is not the word I would use to describe our parting. My friend is not as gentle as my husband.

Standing beside my bedside, she exclaims, "Friend, what have you done? You've admitted you have a problem, but you refuse to take responsibility for it! Now, look, you are being left behind. What shall we do with you?"

Margaret's harshness dissolves with the realization it will be months before we see each other again. Tears spring to her eyes. She smoothes my hair back on my forehead. I close my eyes. It reminds me of a mother's touch.

"Julia, someday, you are going to find what you are looking for. You are filling your stomach with food, but that is not what will fill your heart. You cannot do this alone and you don't have to. God does not require anything from you except for your willingness to trust Him. You will keep searching, but it will not be until you fully realize Who God is and what He can do for you that you will truly be healed from this disease that plagues you. You cannot change yourself. The only One Who can do that is God. I pray you understand soon. For your sake. And for mine. I will miss you, dear one."

She shuts the door behind her. Joseph takes Eliza with him to the dock to bid the others goodbye leaving me with my shame and guilt. Alone, once more I confess my sins and guilt to God. *Will He ever be tired of me making mistakes and coming back to Him for forgiveness? Is there a limit to His love and grace?*

Chapter Seven

We do not stay in the hotel for long. Joseph finds three acres to lease outside of the city. The property has a farmhouse, a few rows of grapes and a small orchard of apples and pears. Joseph consults with other farmers in the area about what to plant. Even though it is winter, the air is warm and humid. It is already time to prepare the soil. Joseph chooses to start with a mix of crops he knows like beans, peppers and potatoes, and some that are new to us like squash, sweet potatoes, okra and mustard greens. Joseph plants a small area of tobacco, too. Though he has never grown tobacco, he is eager to dry the leaves to smoke in his pipe.

The doctor's warning and Margaret's disappointment keep me on a rigid diet. Soon I am healthy again and able to help Joseph on the farm. Eliza learns to play beside us as we weed and care for our crops. When the produce is ready, we take our excess to the market. I bargain and barter for goods we need as well as cash sales as we stockpile our savings until we are ready to move to a place of our own. At first, we talk a lot about joining our friends in Missouri, but as time goes by, we get used to life in Louisiana. Though we don't own this farm, the fields are already cleared and in some ways, I think it would be better than trying to start fresh in Missouri. Months pass. Eliza's second Christmas arrives. As anticipated, she is excited about the arrival of St. Nicholas. We celebrate in the traditional ways we brought from our homeland, but I am very careful about what I cook and eat. I learned my lesson last Christmas. Before we know it, we have been in New Orleans over a year. I am ashamed to ask if we will be moving. *Is Joseph happy here? Will we stay? Are we just settling for what we have? Do we still dream?*

A letter arrives from Margaret. She tells about their new home and how the girls are enrolled in school.

> I pray for you daily. I pray that you will have peace no matter what the circumstances. The peace that only God can give. I pray that you will be well and whole. As for us, we are content. I feel that I have finally found the place that we longed for for so many years. I enjoy the company of the other families, but I miss you dear friend. When do you think you will come to Missouri?

That night after dinner, we sit at the table talking. Unlike Germany, where we enjoyed spring evenings outdoors with the cool breeze and night sky, in Louisiana, we must stay indoors because of the mosquitoes. I fear the disease of Yellow Fever which creeps up on unsuspecting families like Scarlet Fever did to us. I do not want to risk Eliza's life or Joseph's for that matter. My life is another story. I wonder if I am a weight, holding Joseph back from what he really wants to do. I show Joseph Margaret's letter and read it aloud to him. I do not ask, but he knows what I am thinking.

He shakes his head. "I do not think we should go to Missouri. I know you are probably disappointed but I am concerned about taking you back to a city again. Now that we are living in the country, you are well. The fresh air and farm work do you good. In Missouri, the winters are cold, and we would be confined indoors for several months at a time. I think we are better off living where it is warmer."

I start to argue with him, but stop. I am the reason we are still here in Louisiana and not already established in Missouri with our friends. *Do I have the right to express my opinion?* Once again, my husband knows me too well.

"Now, I am not saying that I don't want to hear what you think. We will discuss this and decide together what is best for us, but listen first. Last week, I heard about a new law the Federal Government passed called the Armed Occupation Act. It became law in August and did not officially take effect until December, but they started giving out land in October. People who are willing to settle in Florida will get 160 acres of land for free. The only requirements are that we clear five acres, build a house, live there for five years and agree to serve in the militia if needed."

Florida again. What is it about that country that has such a hold on my husband? I remember Mr. Lewis' prediction. 'Florida will be overrun with settlers.' Maybe all the land is claimed already.

"I asked Dr. Hahn for his advice." *Without me? He spoke to the doctor about me? How long has he been scheming and making plans without talking to me?*

"Dr Hahn thinks you need to stay in a tropical environment. The cold of Missouri or even Pennsylvania would not be good for you. He thinks Florida is an excellent choice. In fact, he is considering a trip to Florida and is willing to travel with us to help make sure you get there safely. Julia, I think we should move to Florida. Imagine! 160 acres is a lot of land and for free! But, we have to act soon. The offer expires when 200,000 acres have been given away. Some say that will be as early as August."

Dumbstruck, I cannot think of anything to say. Just yesterday, we were talking about what crops to plant for this year and now, he is talking about moving? To Florida! Before I can speak, Joseph continues.

"I know this sounds sudden, but I have been thinking about it for a long time. Ever since we made our trip around the peninsula to come here. Do you remember that island where we stopped for water? Passage Key it was called. Do you remember how beautiful it was? The land near there, south of Tampa Bay is part of what is available. We could live in paradise. And all the crops we grew last year, the warm weather ones like okra, squash and sweet potatoes? I tried them because I knew they would grow well in Florida. I can even grow tobacco there! I know we can make a good living in Florida especially since we will not have to pay for the land. What do you think?"

What do I think? I think I am stunned. All this is such a surprise to me, but I have never seen my husband so excited about anything. While I am angry, he consults the doctor without me, and even angrier that the doctor has convinced my husband we would need a physician to travel with us, my infirmities have held my husband back from pursuing his dreams long enough. As much as I want to say no, I do not have the heart to do so. Still I cannot resist asking more questions.

"Yes, it would be exciting to have our own farm and home, but have you thought about the other things we decided were important? A school for Eliza? Neighbors to share chores and spend time with? A German Lutheran church? What about those?"

"With so much land being given away, I am sure others will respond to the call for settlers. We can make new friends and help to build a church. Eliza will not need a school for a few more years. By then, one will have been built. Julia, this is the chance I have been waiting for." He sees the look on my face and quickly corrects himself. "The chance we have been waiting for."

"This is a big decision, and you been thinking about it for quite a while. May I have some time to consider this idea?"

"Yes, but don't wait too long. We need to tell our landlord, pack and find a ship. Time will run out if we aren't careful."

I do think. In fact, over the course of the next few days, that is all I can do. I wish I could talk to Margaret. Finally, I decide to do what Margaret would do. She would pray. I am not proud that the only time I consult God is when I am desperate, but it is critical we make the right decision, and I am willing to admit I do not have the answers.

Joseph senses my turmoil. That night as we lie in bed together, he reaches for me. "Come here, you are so tense. Let me rub your back. You need to relax. If we make the wrong decision, if it is not the right place for us, we can come back or go to Missouri. Let's just give it a try. We'll never know unless we try!"

His hands rub my neck and shoulders. It feels good just to let go.

"I want to believe you this is the right thing for us to do. This is probably a silly question, but have you asked God for help?"

"All the time. And I ask Him to give you peace about it as well. I will not do what I did in Germany. If you do not want to go, we will stay here. It is up to you."

My decision. Up to me. No, it should not be up to me.

"Joseph, will you pray now for us? For God to give us wisdom?"

"It would be my privilege." Joseph holds my hand and prays. I fall asleep listening to him talk to God like he would talk to a friend.

In the morning, I tell Joseph I am willing to go. I do not know if it is the right choice, but I feel more at peace about the decision. After all, I reason, if it does not work out, we can always move again. Maybe this time, we can follow Margaret and her family to Missouri. Joseph is thrilled I agree to move to Florida, but hesitant about one condition.

"I do not need the doctor. I will be fine. I know exactly what I need to do to stay well and can do it on my own." I think, but refrain from saying, *I do not need a caretaker!*

On this, however, my husband will not budge. Dr. Hahn will travel with us.

"Julia, I gave my word. I believe you when you say you do not need his help, but I said he could go with us and now, he must go. I would never have invited him if I had known how offended you would be."

I remember something Margaret once said to me, "If someone says or does something without intending to offend you, it only becomes an offense, if you chose to make it that way. No offense taken if none intended."

Remembering my husband's love for me, I chose not to be resentful. *But, that does not mean I will be happy about the doctor's company!*

Less than a week later, I stand on the deck of a schooner called the *Essex*. Captain Nathaniel Adams tells us he brought the three masted sailboat to New Orleans on government business. He will be returning to Fort Brooke where his ship is assigned to assist the Army in its work of governing the Florida Territory and keeping peace between the settlers and the Indians. There are a few other families on board who hope to make Florida their home as well. Some will travel farther south and others to the east coast, but Joseph is set upon making our home at Tampa Bay.

As we leave the port of New Orleans and sail down the Mississippi River to the Gulf of Mexico, the pompous doctor stands beside me. I do my best to keep distance between us signifying my disdain, but there will not be much room to stay away from him on the boat. Fortunately, I have Eliza to distract me. While Joseph and the doctor talk excitedly about the future, I keep Eliza contained, too busy to participate in their discussion. In a few months, she will be three years old. *Poor thing has been on the move since she was born. I think she has spent more time on a boat than she has on land. Please God, let this be our last voyage.*

As we sail to Florida's west coast, I learn more from Captain Adams about my new home. We will not be stopping again in the islands that once housed the Army Depot, the place where Mr. Lewis' speech made me so angry.

One night at dinner, Captain Adams explains, "Last fall, a hurricane with a twenty-seven foot high wall of water destroyed Cantonment Morgan and caused much damage on Depot Key. The Seminoles who were there meeting with the Army Officers refuse to return to the area now. Colonel Worth declared the war to be over last year anyway so Depot Key was abandoned by the Army after the hurricane."

A wall of water twenty seven feet high. I try to imagine what that must have been like. Even the giant wave on the Delaware River was tiny compared to that. *Are we right to come here?*

Captain Adams continues, "You know, I do not usually go to New Orleans. Generally, my travels of late take me only between Key West and Cedar Key. But, the Army asked me to make a delivery to New Orleans, and I obliged. I am a seafarer at heart. We sailors do not believe in coincidence. It was not fate that brought us together. I think there is a Divine Hand at work that leads you to Florida." *I surely hope so, Captain.*

Finally, we arrive in Tampa Bay. As we pass between Egmont and Mullet Keys, I wonder again if we made the right decision. The March wind is so strong Joseph warns me not to go up on deck. The small window of our cabin is covered in salt spray and flecks of rain. As the boat twists and turns in the rough sea, our trunks tip over spilling our belongings onto the floor. I try to sit on the bunk and hold Eliza, but the shudder of the ship compels me to move to the floor and brace my back against the bunk. Eliza clings to me and cries. *Have we come so far only to drown? Where is my husband?*

In answer, Joseph staggers into the cabin. The door swings wildly and then, slams shut behind him.

"Are you two alright? The seas are very rough. Captain Adams sent everyone below decks who is nonessential. He says this channel is shallow and always choppy, but he has never seen it this severe. He thinks it has to do with the full moon and a strong tide. The waves are crashing over the deck. The doctor is seasick. I don't want to alarm you, but I think we should pray."

Joseph begins to talk to God. I can barely hear him for the sound of the wind whistling around the boat. I try to pray with him, but my mind wanders. There is some irony in the fact that the doctor is sick. I pull my thoughts back to prayer. I do not want to die.

Despite the distractions, our prayers are answered. Once around the Point of Pines and into the upper section of Tampa Bay, the seas calm. The land protects us from the strong Gulf of Mexico wind and the rush of the tide eases. Even the rain stops. We emerge onto the slippery deck blinking in the sunshine. I watch the coastline slide by. *Where will we build our home?*

Water drips from the sails onto our heads. Captain Adams motions for us to come forward and stand with him. "You see, God is with you, my friends. That was a fierce passage. Any other boat would have been swamped. But, the *Essex,* she is a strong sturdy ship. She has come through worse. You remember this day when times get tough for you. You have come through worse as well."

When times get tough. I sense we have not come through the last gale we will endure.

As we wind our way to the north shore of Tampa Bay, Captain Adams tells me about the establishment of Fort Brooke.

"The fort sits on the Hillsborough River. Our ship cannot navigate through the shallower waters so you will transfer to a smaller boat to finish your journey. The fort was originally called Cantonment Brooke when it was established by Colonels George Mercer Brooke and James Gasden in 1823. A year later, the name was changed to Fort Brooke. They chose the site because of an Indian mound provided a good vantage point for lookouts. There was a hickory tree on top of the mound. Colonel

Brooke had the area cleared of most trees, but left the hickory and some very large oaks standing to provide shade. You will see even in the summer with the breeze from the river and the shelter of the trees, it is not that hot. The soldiers constructed a wooden log fort and support buildings for a guardhouse, barracks, storehouses, a blockhouse, a powder magazine, stables, and a wharf. The fort is sixteen miles square and is the largest and most important fortification on the west coast of Florida."

The ship anchors within sight of the mouth of the Hillsborough River. We spend one more night aboard. The doctor, recovered from his illness at sea, joins us for dinner. Though I have avoided him as much as possible on the trip, I cannot help but ask about his wellbeing. I feel quite healthy and hope he has noticed. The arrogant man refuses to admit he was seasick.

"Just a touch of indigestion," he excuses. "Must have been the fish we had for dinner last night."

In the morning, sailors help us clamber down a rope ladder and into a small sloop for transport to the fort. I watch nervously as Eliza is carried by a sailor and deposited into the boat beside me. She is very shy, and the man's grip of her waist makes her cry. I hold her close to me and comfort her. I understand her nerves. The boat rocks unsteadily as some of our belongings are added to the cargo. Our larger items like furniture and trunks will come separately. Two sailors hoist the sails and their captain maneuvers us away from the schooner. Eliza tentatively waves goodbye. While I know the main transportation routes for this area are by sea, I pray the *Essex* will be the last ship we will have to board for an extended journey.

Despite the captain's description, the ruggedness and the expanse of Fort Brooke surprise me. Compared to New Orleans, the difference is shocking. I knew we were coming to the frontier, but had no idea how rustic it would be. Instead of wide brick streets, the narrow paths are made of sand. The dock is a small rickety wooden platform. I fear it might collapse when I step on it and hurry Eliza onto shore.

In the distance, I see several long buildings made of logs that must be barracks for the soldiers. They are raised about three feet off the ground and have a porch all the way around them. I also see smaller cottages I assume are for the officers. Some of the buildings are whitewashed. They surround a grassy parade ground edged with rows of orange and lime trees. Because it is spring, most of the fruit is already gone, but the blossoms fill the air with a delightful fragrance. I close my eyes and breathe deeply and try to convince myself everything will be as lovely as that smell.

My imagining is interrupted by a sound of someone approaching. I open my eyes and see about a dozen Indians coming toward us. They walk dignified and straight along the riverbank, each carrying a gun. They are taller than I thought they would be and wear moccasins made of deer-skin and a short sleeved tunic that falls to their knees. Two of the men carry a pole to which is lashed the carcass of a deer. One of them breaks from the party and walks over to me.

I freeze with fear. *What does he want?* He stops before us and extends his right hand in greeting. Joseph starts to come our way, but one of the soldiers helping to unload the boat stops him and says, "Maam, it is alright. Don't be afraid. They do this all the time. Return the handsake. He just wants to be friendly."

Hesitantly, I take his hand in mine. The Indian nods, dropping my hand and turning his attention to Eliza. She is fascinated by the beads on his costume and the large silver earrings in his ears. He pats her on the head, then turns to walk away. I let go of my breath which I held the whole time he was before us.

"See, I told you. Nothing to be afraid of" calls the soldier. "At least when you are in the garrison."

We wait in the shade. I fan flies from my face while Eliza fidgets and squirms in my lap. Finally, she goes to sleep. Tiny wasps in the moss draped from the trees overhead drum a lullaby. When a wagon comes to take us to our lodging, Joseph lifts her in beside me. He smiles at me, but I can see the questions in his eyes.

"It is a lot different than New Orleans," he says. "But, think, it won't be long before we finally have our own home."

I try very hard not to think of the home we had in Bavaria. It has been over four years since we started this journey. Though I love my husband more now than I did then, and have finally found a measure of peace with God, this was not at all what I expected when we set out for America. If Fort Brooke is an indication of what is available in Florida, we would have been better to stay in New Orleans. For once, I think Dr. Hahn agrees with me. Eyes wide, he looks around as though an Indian will appear behind the next tree. When we see alligators sunning themselves on the bank of the river, I stifle a grin even though the sight is frightening to me, too. *I think the doctor regrets his decision to join us!*

I suppress my regret as well when I see the only lodging that is available to us. Closer to a shack than an inn, we will share a log house with the doctor and another family. Two bedrooms flank a combination kitchen and living area. The doctor will sleep on a pallet on the floor of the main room while the other family takes one bedroom, and Joseph, Eliza and I stay in a small stuffy room without windows. In the darkness, I light a lamp and watch as the floor comes alive. Cockroaches, three inches long, crawl towards the corners of the room. Some even fly into my hair! I scream and almost drop the lamp which Joseph quickly takes from me. *What kind of a place is this? How can we stay here even one night? What will our own home be like?* I want to run back to the boat and head straight for New Orleans or anywhere else for that matter.

Joseph's hand on my shoulder steadies me.

"Julia, it will be alright. Just for a few days. We will find our own place soon and then you can have the home you have been looking for."

I swallow hard. Just for a few days. I think about the long journey that brought us here including my trip across the Atlantic. Yes, I can do anything for a few days.

Those "few days" turn into weeks as Joseph looks for the land that will become ours. Many other settlers have already staked their claim, so he finds it more difficult than we expected to locate a suitable place that meets our needs. He takes several day trips around the Hillsborough River, but all of the land near the fort has already been claimed. Soon, he is gone overnight on scouting expeditions. He joins with a group of other newly arrived men all eager to find the right place to build a home and farm. They hire a boat and captain to take them around Tampa Bay, but are not satisfied. So, they make plans to be gone for two weeks in order to satisfy their curiosity about what might be available farther south.

"The land is such an interesting mix," Joseph tells me. "It will be important to find just the right place where we can farm and where we can harvest timber. The hammocks or 'hummocks' as some people call them are dense growth of trees like oak, hickory, chestnut, cottonwood and magnolia. Then, there are the pine barrens. The pine trees grow tall and are open to the air and light creating an undergrowth of palmettos and other shrubs. There are also swamps, but I will avoid those as that ground is useless for a farmer."

As much as I want to forbid Joseph not to go with them, I dare not. We have come too far to turn around now. Every day that others claim their land, the territory comes closer to reaching the 200,000 acre limit set by the Armed Occupation Act. With increasing urgency, Joseph prepares to travel along the coast until he finds 160 acres of land that can be ours. The doctor decides to stay behind. He concludes the west coast of Florida is not the place he seeks. He would have left already, but Joseph pressures him to stay with me until we find our home.

The night before Joseph leaves, we lie in bed with the lamp shining in our room. Since I first saw all the roaches, I will not let the light go out. The giant bugs, which the soldiers call "Palmetto Bugs", hide in the corners from the brightness. Though we sleep with mosquito netting draped over us, I cannot rest with the thought of them crawling on me or my daughter. I almost feel sorry for Dr. Hahn when I think about him sleeping on the floor. What must it be like to lie in the midst of all those bugs?

About the doctor's reluctance to stay any longer, Joseph says, "I do not care if he is disappointed in what he found. I gave my word, now he will keep his as well."

The next morning, I kiss my husband good-bye. I am reluctant to see him go, but hope he will find a place for us to settle on this trip. To keep myself busy while Joseph is gone, I take over the cooking responsibilities for our household. The other family is also having difficulty finding a place to settle. Recently, Ed Young went inland to look for land. His wife, Emma, and their two boys have bad coughs. I suspect it is from the pollen that falls like yellow rain from the oak trees surrounding our house. I wish Dr. Hahn would take it upon himself to offer to treat them, but he is not so inclined. He spends most of the day down at the docks talking to the sailors and planning where he will go when he leaves Fort Brooke.

To help Emma rest, I go to the storehouse and purchase supplies to make chicken and dumplings for our group. I am surprised to also find enough flour to make biscuits and a cake. We have grown tired of turtle, fish, deer and turkey. Chicken sounds good for a change. I leave the door of the house open while I cook. I must use the fireplace as there is no stove, but improvise as best as I can. The smell drifts out of the house and soon, a small band of soldiers accumulates in the front yard.

When I go outside to throw out a basin of wash water, one of them is eager to help me. He takes the water and disposes of it.

When he returns the basin, he says, "Ma'am, my name is Andy Wright. What are you cooking that smells so good?"

"Chicken and dumplings, biscuits and raisin cakes," I reply.

"Would you have some to spare? We are starving for some home cooked vittles."

"I don't have enough to go around. There are many of you, and I am feeding my neighbors who are ill."

"If we bring you more supplies, would you cook some for us? Just tell me what you need and we will get it. We will gladly pay you for your help. There used to be a family here that cooked for us, but they have gone off to Manatee to homestead."

Andy and I reach an agreement and before our own food is even done, he is back with enough food to feed an army. Well, maybe not all of the army, but a good portion of it! Word of my cooking skills soon spreads throughout the fort. A day does not pass that at least one and usually more soldiers are waiting on me with supplies to cook for them. It makes the time go by faster and I am eager to show Joseph the money I have made while he is gone. *Maybe we should just stay at the fort. I could make a good living here. Even Emma and her children feel better because of the nourishment I provide. Who needs a doctor when you have access to good food?*

Chapter Eight

The soldiers enjoy entertaining Eliza and though she is shy at first, she plays with Andy who is her favorite. I think they like being around a child almost as much as they do my cooking. Both of them remind the men of home. They confide how much they hate being stationed here and how tedious the hunt for the Seminoles is as they persist in hiding in the Everglades instead of moving to the western reservations. The soldiers often ask me when my husband will be back. I do not think they want us to leave. They cannot pronounce our last name easily so I refer to my husband as Mr. Joe. They begin calling me "Madam Joe." Soon, the other settlers do as well.

One evening, as I am finishing cooking dinner which will feed about twenty hungry soldiers, I look out the front door to see all the men standing at attention. Walking at a brisk pace comes a tall, heavy set man with flaming red hair. I know he is obviously someone in authority, not only by the men's attitudes, but by the way he stands and carries himself. *He is used to people doing what he tells them to do.*

The door is already open to let some air into the house, so he knocks on the doorframe. I smooth my hair and wish my apron was cleaner before I invite him inside.

"Ma'am, I am Colonel Belknap, commander of Fort Brooke," he introduces himself as he takes off his hat. "I came to meet the woman who has created such a stir among my men."

Is he angry? He doesn't look angry, but in the dim light, I might be wrong. But, his voice doesn't sound angry.

"Sir?" I ask hesitantly.

"My men tell me your name is Madam Joe."

"Well, my real name is Julia Atzeroth, but some of the men have trouble pronouncing it. Can I help you, Sir?"

"Where are you from, Mrs. Atzeroth?"

"From Bavaria, by way of New York, Philadelphia and New Orleans. My husband and I hope to make our home here. He is out scouting land now." *What does he want with me?*

I ask again, "Is there something I can do for you Sir?"

"The men cannot stop talking about your cooking. I was hoping you had enough to share this evening. I would love to have something different from what they are serving in the mess tent."

There is enough to share, but it will be good enough for the Colonel? I am sure he has eaten in some fine dining establishments.

I feel as anxious as I did when I knew my uncle waited for his meal, but I set a place at the table for Colonel Belknap and fix him a plate of fried pork, mashed sweet potatoes and cabbage. I add a thick slice of bread with butter.

"Will you join me, Mrs. Atzeroth?"

"No, sir. The men are waiting for their meal. If you don't mind, I will go ahead and serve them as well."

The Colonel does not answer. He is focused on his plate. I hear him sigh as he closes his eyes to bless his food. He takes one bite, and then another. I watch him out of the corner of my eye while I ladle out food for the men from the doorway of the house. The Colonel cleans his plate so I refill it. After he finishes his second helping, I offer a slice of pie which he eats with relish.

He picks up his hat and stands. "Ma'am, that was a mighty fine meal. I appreciate it very much. Should you decide you would rather stay here in Fort Brooke, I think you would do well running a restaurant. How much do I owe you?"

"First meal's on the house, Colonel." I smile. "Come again any time. I know my husband will enjoy meeting you when he comes home."

My nerves turn to excitement as he leaves. *Even the Colonel thinks my idea of staying here is a good one!*

A few days later, Andy arrives holding something behind his back. *He must have more food for me to cook. Maybe it is an animal. He struggles to hold it still.*

"Madam Joe, I have a gift for Eliza. May I give it to her?"

"I don't know. What kind of a gift? Is it something alive? What are you wrestling with behind your back?"

Andy draws his hands forward and in them, he holds a small tan puppy. The dog's ears are bigger than his face. He looks like he is all ears and legs with a long slim tail wagging behind. Eliza claps her hands in excitement. Andy sets the puppy down on the ground, and it runs directly to her. She squeals as it licks her in the face, then shouts when it knocks her to the ground. I rescue my daughter holding her above the leaping puppy.

"Andy, stop him. She will be afraid of dogs!"

My daughter proves me wrong. While Andy restrains the puppy from his jumping, Eliza squirms to get down. She rubs his ears and laughs at the way the puppy wiggles with delight.

"Can she keep him?" Andy asks for Eliza.

"I don't know. A dog is a big responsibility. I don't even know where we are going to live. How can I say yes to a pet?"

"Oh, he will be more than a pet. He will be a big help to you. A family living in the wilderness needs a dog to scare away the wild creatures and protect your chickens and cows. He will be a real asset for you, you will see."

At that moment, the puppy rolls over on his back and puts all four feet in the air. *What kind of animals would such a tiny thing scare away?*

"See? He wants to go with you. Look how nicely he is asking."

"Well, maybe. It will depend on what Mr. Joe says when he gets home."

When Joseph finally returns from his exploration of the countryside, not only have I settled into a routine and made many friends, but the puppy has firmly wormed his way into our hearts. The question of his ownership is settled though I have not decided on a name. Before I can ask Joseph for a suggestion, I need to hear about his trip and tell him my idea of just staying in Fort Brooke.

I do not get a chance. As soon as we are alone, he begins. "Julia, I found it! I found the place where we can settle. I have already started the paperwork for our land claim."

"Are you sure? I have been doing well here while you were gone. I have made quite a lot of money cooking for the soldiers and think maybe we should just stay here."

Once again, I disappoint my husband. His smile fades. "We've come all this way and when I want to tell you about our land, you say you want to stay here?"

I pretend to be interested, but don't want to give up my plans. Perhaps I can talk him out of his. "It was just an idea, but not necessarily a good one. Tell me about our land. Is it far away?"

"No, just on the other side of the bay! In fact, we passed right by it on our trip to New Orleans. It is near Passage Key. I don't know why it has not already been chosen before now. It is on an island. The name is Terra Ceia. Someone told me the name means "Heavenly Land", and it is heavenly! There is a spring for fresh water, and the ground is rich and good. It will be an excellent place to farm and only a day's sail back to Fort Brooke so we can bring our produce to sell here." Joseph describes the land he has chosen. He is so excited that, soon, I forget about the idea of building a business here. I cannot wait to see our land!

Joseph tells me the ship captain who took him south to look for land is willing to sail us to our new home. He wants to leave as soon as possible, so I begin packing right away. The soldiers are disappointed I will no longer be available to cook for them. They try to talk Joseph into staying at Fort Brooke, but I know he has already made up his mind to go.

Surprisingly, Eliza immediately takes to the ship captain, Frederick Tresca. His boat is small enough to sail into the Hillsborough River so we can board at the fort instead of downstream. Captain Tresca invites us to come forward to the wheel where he pretends to need Eliza's help to steer the boat down the river and into the bay.

Captain Tresca tells me the ship is a Bermuda sloop. Originally designed to carry merchandise from that island across the Atlantic, they evolved into being multifaceted and are even used by the Navies of many countries. He brags under a good captain a Bermuda sloop can beat any other sailing vessel even those with more masts and sails. I admire the three triangular sails. They are set at intervals and extend from the mast forward to a long pole stretching from the bow, which the Captain calls the bowsprit. Another larger square shaped sail rises from the back of the mast to the stern of the boat.

Captain Tresca says, "The *Margaret Ann* is made of solid Bermuda cedar. It is deeper than some of the coastal sailing vessels, but gives it more stability."

I can tell he is very proud of his boat and ask him how he became a sailor.

"I grew up in Dankert, France," he replies. "But at age twelve, my father apprenticed me to the master of the ship *Bellerophone*. I served as the cabin boy on that ship when it conveyed Napoleon to Torbay on his way to St. Helena."

I gasp. "You knew Napoleon?"

"Well, can't say that I knew him like a friend, but yes, I served him."

"What was he like?"

"A proud man, though not as proud as he once was. I do not think he truly understood the plot the British had prepared to bring an end to his influence."

I hear our puppy barking at something in the stern of the boat. Probably the chickens we bring with us or the rattle of the sails. He is an alert little fellow. I still have not found a name for him. Then, I think about the man we have just finished discussing. Napoleon will always be a hero to me. Why not name the dog, Bonaparte?

I laugh when I tell Joseph and Captain Tresca my plans. They agree it is a fine name for our dog. Once that is settled, the captain tells us about more of his travels.

As a seaman, he travelled around the world and can speak five languages including German and French, but Captain Tresca tells me he found his happiness in America, particularly in Florida.

"Madam Joe, you will not regret your decision to move to this territory. Yes, it is an untamed country. It will not be easy to build a home there. You will suffer some hardship, I predict. The weather can be temperamental, and Indians are still a problem for those who refuse to treat them with respect—but, the land of Florida has much to give as well. Her nature, her wildness, all combine to bring much beauty and joy in your life. I have lived in Florida for five years now and have seen all of her coastline so I know what I am talking about. I think you will be very happy here."

As we cross the bay and reach land again, Joseph points out the north side of Terra Ceia. "We are on the south shore on a smaller bay called Terra Ceia Bay. We will have to go out into the Gulf to go around the island and reach our land."

We enter the channel between Passage Key and the opening to Terra Ceia Bay. Just to the south is the Manatee River. I think back to the day when I sat on deck with Margaret and watched the sailors draw water to fill the drinking barrels of the *Ohio*. It seems like so long ago. Who knew then we would be back, planning on making our home here? *I did.* I feel a whisper in my heart. *God did.* Despite all we have been through, God has been there. He is in control even when I don't feel like He is there. I remember our journey on the *Essex* into Tampa Bay. I tell Captain Tresca about it.

"March is a fickle month in Florida. You never know one day from the next what the weather will bring. Heat, cold, flooding rain, dry ground, wind or calm. You have to be careful in March. But do you know what March brings? April. April is worth all of March's terrors. Look at this day, is it not gorgeous? April is my favorite month in Florida. The sky is a little bit bluer in April than any other month."

Yes, it is a beautiful day, but I am too anxious to really enjoy its splendor. What will our new home be like? My stomach cramps as we get closer to the island. It is not because of anything I ate, but because of nerves. *Did we make the right decision? Should we have stayed in Fort Brooke or returned to New Orleans? I guess we will soon find out.*

The wind picks up out in the Gulf. I shout to be heard. "Joseph, you did not tell me what our house looks like." Joseph just smiles, and I think perhaps he cannot hear me. *Oh, well, I will find out soon enough.*

We enter Terra Ceia Bay and all I can see on both sides are dense forests of oaks, pine and palm trees. The vegetation is so thick; I wonder how we will farm. I see no houses or signs that anyone else lives on these shores.

Again, I ask, "Joseph, what about the house? Where are our neighbors?"

"Just wait, Julia."

But, I don't want to wait. My stomach hurts even more with fear. I do not see any houses. Not even one small one.

"Joseph, where will we live?"

My husband occupies himself with untangling a line for the Captain. We sail about halfway into the bay along the north shore of the bay. Still, I see no house.

"Joseph?" I ask more demanding.

Captain Tresca calls for the sailors to put down the anchor. There is no house at the place where we have stopped. In fact, the trees and shrubs grow so closely together that I do not know how we will even set foot on land. *Is someone playing a trick on me? This cannot be where we will live. There is no house!*

"Julia, welcome to Terra Ceia. Welcome to your new home."

There is no home! I want to scream.

"Joseph, where do you expect us to live?" Captain Tresca turns away discreetly and orders the men to prepare a rowboat to take us to shore.

"We will build a house. There is plenty of lumber we can cut right here on our own land. In the meantime, I brought a tent. We will live in a tent until we can build the house."

A tent. No, I am not living in a tent.

Aware of our audience, I grit my teeth and manage to say as calmly as I can, "No, we are not living in a tent. You can take me right back to Fort Brooke, and I will live there until you complete the house. I am not living in a tent."

Joseph refuses to listen to my demands, "Come Julia, just come and see this land. You will love it!"

He carries Eliza down the ladder and into the waiting rowboat. The sailors and Captain Tresca all wait to see what I will do. I have no choice but to follow my husband. As we make our way to shore, all I can think about is that I will not stay on this island one night in a tent. The doctor and Captain Tresca join us in the rowboat. After leaving us on the island, Captain Tresca is to take Dr. Hahn to Key West. *He will just have to change his plans and take me back to Fort Brooke.*

As it appeared from the water, the trees are so thick there is not even a place to erect a tent even if I agreed to do so. We find a narrow path through the palmetto shrubs and oaks that passes by a bubbling spring. I am thirsty, so bend down to take a drink. I cup the cool water in my hands and sip, then, spit it out. The water tastes like rotten eggs. It is a sulfur spring! *Will everything about this place disappoint me?*

As we go, the sailors with machetes help Joseph clear a wider path to the place he has chosen to camp. Then, they begin chopping down trees and cutting up palmetto bushes to make a place large enough for the tent. I stand with my arms crossed watching them. Their efforts are fruitless. I will not stay in a tent.

One of the sailors struggles with the grubbing hoe. It is obvious he has never worked a field. I am so angry about our situation. I must do something to keep my hands busy before I strangle my husband. I stalk over to the sailor, wrench the hoe out of his hands and begin to chip away at the bushes. When the hoe is inadequate against the thick roots, I pick up an ax and slice through them. I work with such a furor that I do not see how much progress has been made since we landed. I just keep hacking away at the stubborn bushes. The men work as well.

Soon, someone says something about being hungry, so automatically, I open up some barrels of food and make a meal for us all. While we eat, I look at all that has been done. I cannot explain it, but at once, the anger inside me gives way to delight as I look beyond my disappointment and see the beauty that is around us. I hear blue jays calling in the trees. A large swallowtail butterfly dances among the palmetto blossoms. I smell the sea, and a sweet fragrance I cannot identify.

This is home. I sigh. *I will not return to Fort Brooke. I will sleep in a tent if I have too, but it will not be for long. We will build a house. We will clear this land. This is home.*

I turn to Joseph and smile. The men see I am no longer angry. Although it might have just been the wind in the trees, I imagine there is a collective sigh of relief. As they pick up their tools again, one of the sailors starts to sing a sea song called *One More Day:*

Oh, have you heard the news, me Johnny
One more day
We're homward bound tomorrow
One more day
Only one more day, me Johnny
One more day
Oh, rock and roll me over
One more day

One day at a time, I think. *We'll just take this one day at a time.*

My surrender to life in a tent is short lived. We spend only one night there before I begin begging Joseph to provide a better place for us to sleep. Not only is the tent not much better than being outside and sleeping on the ground, but at dusk, it fills with mosquitoes and a tiny bug no bigger than a piece of ground pepper. These bugs, which we cannot see, bite and crawl inside our clothing. I spend the night with the sound of mosquitoes buzzing in my ears scratching and itching. By morning, I am tired, covered in red bites and angry. The tent represents all of my husband's failures to provide a decent place for us to live. There is no house. No neighbors. No school. No church. What about all the things we vowed to find in our new home? Yes, the island is beautiful and charming, but all that is here is water, vegetation and sky.

And bugs. As I rise early, restless and sore, I prepare to exit the tent in search of a place to relieve myself. I walk right into a thick sticky web and come face to face with the largest spider I have ever faced. With long yellow striped legs, a reddish colored body and white spots on its belly, its web covers the entire opening of the tent like a net. Memories of my childhood flood over me, and I start to scream. Joseph wakes and holds me to ease my trembling. He then, uses the edge of his gun to pull down the web so we can get out of the tent.

I refuse to go back inside. Though I know it makes little sense, I insist we will build a hut.

"I really need to start clearing some land. Seasons in Florida are different. We must be ready to plant by September in order to harvest in the winter. It will take time for me to pull out enough trees to plant a garden. The trees I clear can be used for the house. It makes more sense to stay in the tent until we can build a house."

Not satisfied with his answer, I nag and fuss all the while as I fix breakfast. While he had other plans for the day, Joseph realizes I will not rest until I have a different place to sleep. While still primitive, a hut at least seems more permanent.

"One more day will not hurt your plans. Please Joseph! I will not sleep for thinking about the spider!"

The hut takes longer than a day to build. Neither of us have experience at such construction. Joseph cuts several tall saplings and uses them for a frame. He ties them to nearby trees to give them some stability. One of the soldiers at Fort Brooke told me the Indians cover their houses with palmetto fronds. I experiment with them and finally fashion a mat I think will be sturdy enough for a roof. Though Joseph is concerned for my safety, I climb up on the roof to install the thatch. As soon as the roof is in place, I move out of the tent. The hut is even big enough to set up our bed frame and mattress as well as Eliza's trundle bed. I still feel the need to wave a broom in the doorway every morning before leaving the hut, but at least we are no longer sleeping on the ground.

Over the next few weeks, I work alongside Joseph clearing the land. Every night my muscles scream with pain, but every morning I get up and work some more. As we do, I tell myself every tree cleared is not just space for a garden, but one more section of the wall for our house. The hut proves to be less than ideal. As the palmetto fronds dry, they shrink leaving holes in the roof. During the day, the sun shines through, and when it rains, the water pours through the holes. I make several attempts to rethatch the roof, but continue to have the same problem. Finally, Joseph stretches the tent tarp over the roof and solves the problem.

I wish other difficulties could be solved as easily. In addition to the bugs, the island hosts many snakes. Some are shy and safe like the huge rat snakes we sometimes encounter sunning themselves on the paths we have cleared. One even comes into the hut and twines himself around the frail beams of the roof. His yellow skin reminds me of a ray of sunshine in the darkness of the hut. I briefly consider letting him stay because I know he will keep away rats, but when he loses his grip and falls into the middle of the kitchen table, I shriek and shoo him out the door.

Other snakes like the water moccasin and rattlesnake must be killed. Not only are they aggressive, but their poison will mean sure death in the wilderness. I learn to shoot Joseph's gun with great accuracy, but fear Eliza will come across a snake one day and be attacked. She runs free around the hut and fields with Bonaparte for her constant companion. He scares away a lot of wildlife and has already treed several raccoons and possums, but I am not convinced he will protect my daughter from a snake.

Chapter Nine

Bonaparte proves me wrong one morning just before lunch. Joseph and I labor to push a large log from a pine tree he chopped down. We tie a rope to a tree and pull with all our might hoping to swing the log to the side of the slowly emerging field when we hear Bonaparte's frantic barks. Joseph shouts when I let go of the rope and the tree hits the ground with a thud.

"Where's Eliza?" I ask scanning the cleared area.

"The dog is probably barking at another coon," Joseph exclaims wiping his forehead of sweat. "Why did you let go? One of us could have been killed!"

"Where is Eliza?" I repeat. My voice rises in panic as I follow the dog's barking. *Where is my daughter?*

I rush down a path toward the sound, but I cannot go straight in that direction so I push through palmetto bushes. What I find almost makes my heart stop beating.

Bonaparte leaps and dives in the direction of the largest rattlesnake I have ever seen. It is coiled and striking as the dog darts back and forth in front of it. I see he always keeps himself between Eliza and the snake. One bite from that snake would be enough to kill a man much less my daughter or the dog. I do not want to interfere with the dog's efforts to distract the snake, but need to call for Joseph. Before I can, my husband appears at my side, gun in hand. He takes aim and shoots the snake. It falls, but still writhes and twists before finally lying still.

"Bonaparte, come!" I scream trying to keep the dog from attacking the snake. I know it is lethal even in death.

The dog obeys and comes to my side while Joseph focuses on the snake not trusting it is truly dead. He backs away until he is close enough to Eliza to gather her under his arm. I burst into tears, alternating between praising the dog for his bravery and crying out of fear of what might have been.

Joseph cuddles Eliza who says, "Did you see Boney? He was dancing with that snake. Why did you shoot it Papa?"

I know Joseph does not want to scare our daughter, but if she is to grow up in the wilderness she needs to understand its dangers.

"You must stay away from all snakes! Snakes are bad and can hurt you! When you see a snake, back away from it," I shout.

Eliza frowns at my sharp tone and then, puts her face into her father's neck and cries. I am sorry I made her unhappy, but it had to be done. Later, when Joseph stretches the snake out, it is six foot long.

Fear of more snakes and what might happen to my daughter force me to resort to a desperate measure. With so much work to do and no one but the dog to keep watch on my three year old, I find the only way I know to keep her safe. I take a rope and tie it to a tree. The other end, I wrap around my daughter's waist. I can hardly stand to listen to her cries, but I know no other way to ensure her safety. She runs to the end of the rope flinging her body in my direction and calling my name. I console myself thinking that at least now as I work, I will know where she is and what she is doing, but to confine my daughter like a dog is such terrible treatment. It takes me back to my own childhood losing my own freedom upon entering my uncle's service. I try to drown out the images that flood my mind while I work, but at the end of the morning, when I find my daughter sleeping in the dirt with Bonaparte for a pillow, tears stream down my cheeks.

My sorrow turns to anger that night as I gently strip off Eliza's soiled clothes and bathe her to remove the dirt that streaks her face and hands. I gasp as I look at her waist and see the places rubbed raw by the rope. She is blistered and bruised from her efforts to free herself. I vow I will never do that to my child again. When she is clean and in bed with ointment smeared on her sores, I stay beside her stroking her head until she falls asleep.

Only then do I take my anger out on my husband.

"This is your fault." I emphasize each word as I say it. I want him to hear me clearly, but I dare not raise my voice for fear of waking Eliza. There is no place for us to go to separate ourselves from where she sleeps in her bed beside ours.

"What are you talking about? How is this my fault?"

"Florida. That's all you could think about. All you wanted. Well, Florida is dangerous and disappointing. What about a house? A school? A church? Friends and neighbors? No, you filled your head with the wild and exotic. You would not rest until you brought us here to this desolate place. And now, what do we have to show for it? Bruises and blisters on my baby. Would you build this place upon her back and mine? I cannot stay here. I love you, but I cannot stay with you. I am taking Eliza and going someplace safer. Come and get us when the house is ready. Maybe we will come back."

"You are leaving? Just like that, you are leaving? And how do you propose to go? Have you forgotten? We have no boat. Will you swim then? Across the bay? With the baby? We have no way to get off this island until Captain Tresca comes back to check on us when he returns to Fort Brooke. I am sorry you are angry. Even sorrier Eliza is hurt. But, we're stuck. You're stuck. We have no place to go."

Though I share his bed, I feel lonely and isolated. I lie rigid, hugging the edge, not wanting one inch of me to come in contact with my husband. *How can he be so cruel? Has he ever really loved me? What will I do now?* The thoughts whirl around in my head until exhausted, I finally sleep.

When I wake, Joseph is gone. I poke the broom around the doorway checking for spider webs and step into the sunshine. I do not hear the sound of the ax. I hear nothing but the chickens scratching for food around the house. *At least they like this bug infested place.* I remember his words from last night. *He cannot have gone far. There is nowhere to go.* Eliza calls for me. I return back to the hut and fix our breakfast. I scrape the mold off the inside of the flour bin. *I hate this damp. I hate this place.* I need to conserve what I can. What if we run out before Captain Tresca returns? At least we have eggs. What I wouldn't give for some milk to give Eliza!

Just then, I hear Joseph shout. "Julia, Eliza! Come see what I found."

Eliza goes straight outside to greet her father. I would prefer not to face my husband this morning, but hurry to keep up with her. I never know what trouble might await my daughter. She stops short and so do I when we see Joseph. Using the same rope I desperately used to contain my daughter the day before, Joseph leads a cow. She is thin and scrawny compared to the well fed dairy herd we owned in Germany. A small calf follows calling for her mother. Both are white with red speckles, and the cow has long horns. I wonder how Joseph was able to catch her without getting speared.

My curiosity overcomes my anger at my husband. I grab Eliza's hand to keep her from rushing at the cow.

"Where did you get her?" I ask.

"She was caught in some vines. I was not sure I could untangle her. They were very sharp." He holds up his bloody hands, and I realize some of the speckles on the cow are not her hide, but blood.

"She will need some tending to. I do not know how long she had been there, but I think she was stuck long enough to be subdued. If we pen her up and feed her she will give enough milk for her calf and for us as well."

I close my eyes and open them again. Surprised that the cow still stands there, I wonder, *Is this a joke? As much as this place lacks and then, I ask for milk for Eliza and it appears?* "No, not a joke," I hear the words in my mind as clearly as if someone speaks them aloud. "Not a joke," it repeats. "An answer to prayer. Trust me. Wait on me. I will protect you and provide for you." I rub my ears. *Am I hearing things? Is this God speaking to me?*

My husband grins. "Julia, Florida isn't so bad. Cattle run loose in the woods! This is the beginning of our herd!"

I just shake my head and go back inside. I need to think about what I have seen. I still think Florida is bad, but God is working hard to prove He is not.

Over the next few days, Joseph does as much work as he can alone. I spend my time doing household chores and watching out for Eliza. Her wounds disappear, but the scars on my heart take longer to heal. I am caught between wanting to trust God and being afraid. Joseph and I do not speak unless it is necessary. I see the hurt in his eyes, but cannot bring myself to reach across the breech that divides us. In my anger, I continue to blame my husband for our troubles. This is not what I expected. I am not strong enough to endure these troubles. Even if God provides a thousand cows, I am not cut out for this life.

Captain Tresca arrives the next afternoon. I look around the hut. There is not much for me to pack, just our clothes. I will leave all the household furnishings. There is no need to take them back to Fort Brooke. *I hope our stay there will be brief.* It does not take me long to pack. Soon, two bags wait in the corner of the hut for transport to the boat.

One of the sailors brings me about a dozen small trout he caught in the bay with a net. Joseph has not had much time to fish, and I am eager to cook something different than the dried meat and eggs we eat almost daily. I pan fry the trout, and also cook Salzkartoffeln, potatoes boiled in saltwater, using some water from the bay. It is not much, but all we have to offer until we plant and harvest our garden. Fish and potatoes is a common meal for the sailors so they will not get much variety, but at least I have fresh bread and now that we have a cow, some butter.

Joseph enters the hut with the Captain. He laughs as he tells the story of the cow. He explains he has decided to name her Flower in honor of La Florida, the name that Spanish explorer, Ponce De Leon gave to this land. He arrived on Florida's shores on Easter, the Feast of Flowers. As soon as Joseph's eyes adjust to the darkness of the hut and he sees our bags, his laughter stops. He does not say anything in front of the Captain, but now he knows my intention to leave. I want to tell him I will come back as soon as the house is done. Perhaps it will spur him to work faster, but this is not the time to discuss our problems.

I serve the meal. Our hut is so small, only the captain can eat inside with us. The rest of the food I take outside for the men to divide among themselves.

Coming inside I take my place at the table, Captain Tresca says, "Joseph tells me that you wove the palm fronds for this hut. You are a resourceful woman to make a home like this in the wilderness. You are just the kind of citizen that will take this territory to statehood. It will not be long before Florida is self governing. Florida petitioned for statehood almost five years ago. It is time for the politicians to quit talking and get to work. The number of settlers into the area grows daily."

Joseph asks, "Why the delay?"

Captain Tresca explains, "It's all about slavery. The government is trying to keep the balance of power even between slave and free states. In the Missouri Compromise, passed the year after Florida became a territory of the United States in 1819, it was agreed that every time a slave state is admitted, a free territory gets statehood, too. The powerful men who control our state all support slavery so Florida will be admitted as a slave state. But, there is no territory that meets the criteria of the compromise that is ready for statehood. Why, Florida wrote its state constitution in 1838! Iowa was not even organized as a territory until that year! It is not right that we should be held back just because of some game that the politicians are playing in Washington!"

"When will Iowa be ready for statehood?" I ask.

"Not much longer, Madam Joe. I heard the latest news while I was in Key West. They are working on their constitution now. As soon as they get it voted on, it will be up to Washington. I expect next year, we will finally get our star on the flag."

Maybe that's about the time I will be ready to return to this forsaken island.

"Thank you for the meal, ma'am. I've got to tend to my men and my ship. Joseph, when will you be ready to leave?"

When will Joseph be ready to leave? Is he going with me? Will we be abandoning this place?

"Julia and I have some things to talk over. If you will give me until in the morning, I will be ready to go at first light. "

The Captain nods. "It is too late in the day to make the sail anyway. I will wait." Then, he says, "Oh, Madam Joe, I almost forgot. We crossed paths with a boat from Fort Brooke and I told them I would bring you your mail. You have a letter!"

A letter?

I take it from the Captain and smooth the envelope with my hand. I recognize Margaret's handwriting. Such a precious gift! I long to open it, but Joseph waits to talk to me.

"Were you thinking of leaving then?"

I nod. There is a lump in my throat. I know his feelings will be hurt. But, I cannot stay here.

"Are you leaving me? Or just our land?"

I bow my head. "I cannot stay here any longer. It is not safe for Eliza or for me. But, when the place is settled more, I will come back. I promise you that." My eyes fill with tears. I did not realize this would be so hard.

"Please reconsider. I have something hard to ask of you. I need you to stay here. I need to go to Fort Brooke and I am afraid that if I leave this place unoccupied, someone else will come along and take it."

No, I must have heard wrong. He is going to Fort Brooke and expects me to stay here? Alone? That is completely unreasonable. I am leaving. He can stay.

"I know you hate it here, but Captain Tresca brought word that there is a problem with my homestead papers. I need to go to Fort Brooke and fix them. If you could do it, I would send you, but I must appear because it is my name on the claim. If I do not go, I could lose this land. If someone does not stay here, I could lose it as well. Julia, I am begging you. Please stay here while I go. I will bring back someone to help me with the clearing and farm. I will buy a boat while I am gone and if you still want to go back to Fort Brooke, I can leave the hired hand here and take you."

I cannot do it. I cannot.

"Please Julia. Think about it. I am going to see if some of the Captain's men can help me move some of those logs before dark."

As soon as Joseph leaves, I sit down and put my head on the table. *I would rather die than stay here alone. How would I protect myself? I think of the storm in Tampa Bay. What if Joseph dies? Eliza and I could never survive here by ourselves.* I ball up my fists in anger and hear paper crinkle in my hand. *The letter!*

I open the envelope and read Margaret's letter. She begins by telling me about their new home and how much the girls have grown. Missouri sounds like the kind of place I wish we had chosen. Shops, churches, schools and many settlers. I feel my resentment rising again until I read her conclusion.

You have been on my heart a lot the last few days. When I got your letter that you were leaving New Orleans and going to Florida, it was quite a shock. Florida! Yes, I remember traveling past the Manatee lands, Passage Key and Tampa Bay. It was a lovely place, and I am sure that in time, you will be happy there. I am so disappointed that you will not be our neighbors, but I am proud of you for supporting your husband in this decision. I know it must not have been easy for you. We had such plans, didn't we? And Florida, though beautiful, will be a difficult place to live. But, you are doing the right thing. Remember when we talked about marriage? Your husband will need your help and support. He will need your wisdom in making decisions, but there will be times when you will not understand why he does what he does. You will want your own way and then on occasion (maybe more) you will get very angry. I know this from my own experience! It is hard to let your husband be the leader when we know (or think we know) what is best. This is what we have to remember. When you are unsure if you can trust your husband, when you think he might be making the wrong decision despite your best efforts to help, there is Someone else you can trust. Someone with more knowledge than you and your husband put together. Trust God, Julia. Trust God when you don't think you can trust your husband because God really is all powerful, all knowing and always there. He loves you and wants the best for you. So, let God be in charge of your marriage. Let God be in charge of your husband. That's the only way to make it work. I love and miss you. I hope we see each other again soon, but if not, know your friend in Missouri prays for you every day. Give Eliza a hug from me and the girls. Love, Margaret

By the time I finish Margaret's letter, I want to cry. How ashamed I am for my behavior! How did she know exactly what I needed to hear today? I feel as though God says, "I told her." *Oh, God. If this really is a message from you, then, that means I must stay here. I do not want to stay here. I want to go. I want to go anywhere, but here. Why can't we go to Missouri?* "Because I want you to be here. Trust me, Julia." *I can't God.* "Yes, you can. Start now."

When Joseph comes back to the house, it is very dark, but he feels good about all he and the men accomplished. "It will be easier when I have a hired man," he says. "There is more than you and I can do alone."

He grows quiet and looks at me. "That is, if you will stay."

Start now. "Yes, I will stay. I do not want to, but for you, I will stay."

He hugs me and whispers. "Thank you, Julia. Thank you, God."

Joseph leaves at first light. "The sooner I get to Fort Brooke, the sooner I will be home. I do not know how long it will take to get my papers straightened out, hire a man and buy a boat, but I will be back as fast as I can."

I hand him a list of supplies to purchase. He cannot read it so will have to give it to the shopkeeper to fill. I hope they have everything I need. As I watch him walk down the path to the bay, the thought occurs to me. *Does my husband even know how to sail a boat?*

The days drag by. I try to keep busy. Every morning, I get up and milk the cow. She is ornery and strong. The hardest part about milking her is catching her to tie her to the bars of the pen. And to dodge her hooves which are quick to catch me in the side if I do not position myself just right. After milking, I prepare breakfast for Eliza and me. My fear tempts me to eat more than I should, but I must stay healthy for my daughter. Who knows when my husband will return? I cook very small meals with no extras. Our supply of sugar is low anyway, so I resolve not to waste it cooking sweets. After breakfast, I do the dishes, make the bed and straighten the hut. Sometimes, there is laundry to do or bread to bake. None of it takes very long. Every day, I spend some time practicing loading and shooting the gun, but I do not want to use too much ammunition. I might need it before Joseph returns.

While he is gone, I do not sleep well. Noises that did not bother me while he was here wake me up several times each night. I do not think Eliza sleeps well either. My tossing and turning and occasional forays outside to chase away a wild animal keep her awake. She misses her father and is irritable and contrary. One day, to amuse her, we walk down to the bay. Secretly, I hope to see a boat that will signal Joseph's return, but think it is probably too early for him to come back yet. I wish I knew when he will return home, but then, that is part of learning to trust. Still, I think this is the longest week of my life.

Bonaparte follows us to the water's edge. He picks up a stick and dances around me. He loves to swim in the water and retrieve so I throw it for him. Eliza loves the game, too, and claps whenever Bonaparte brings the stick back and drops it at my feet. She laughs when he shakes water all over us. Glad to have something that makes her happy, I throw the stick until my arm aches.

"No more, Boney. That's enough." The dog persists, even bumping my legs with the stick to get my attention.

"Alright, one more time." He heads back into the water in anticipation of the throw. But, a few yards from shore, I spy a long thick shape under the water tracking Bonaparte as he swims.

"Bonaparte! Come! Come here now!" Frantically, I wave the stick over my head to get his attention.

"What is it Mama?" Eliza asks.

"Eliza, help me get his attention."

She joins me in calling the dog. "Boney, come here."

I can see the form clearly now. It is a grey colored shark about seven feet long! Finally, Bonaparte realizes I am not going to throw the stick and turns for shore. The shark also turns its bluntly rounded snout, changes course and follows the dog. Bonaparte thrashes towards us reaching shallow water, just as the shark comes inches from snatching him in its open jaws. The shark veers back into deeper water as Bonaparte races up the bank towards us.

I collapse on the sand as Bonaparte licks Eliza's face and nudges me with his head. *Oh, God. Oh, God. Not my dog! Would you take him, too? I cannot bear it. There is so much to fear. Why do You leave me here all alone?*

"You are not alone. I am here. Don't be afraid." There is that voice again, echoing in my heart. I listen to God, but it is a long while before I have the strength to stand.

Chapter Ten

It was optimistic to think Joseph might be home in a week. He does not appear for ten days. When he arrives, he brings with him a young man named Ben who steers a sailboat to shore. The boat is small, only about eighteen feet long with a single mast and one sail. Joseph rubs his hand along the gunwale. The top edge of the boat is smooth polished wood. It is a beautiful little boat. He grins.

"Never thought I would be a boat owner," he says. "Horses and wagons, yes. But, whoever could have imagined we would live in a place where we needed a boat to get around?"

There he goes again. How he loves this place! I bite my tongue. I don't think I could say anything nice after the past week.

Joseph introduces me to Ben. "He came to settle in Florida, but the Armed Occupation Act is closed. All the land that was to be given away is gone. We got here just in time! There is some land to be sold, but Ben needs to earn some money to buy his portion. He'll learn about Florida and farming while he works for us. Then, when he has a place of his own, he will know just what to do." He smiles as he goes to help Ben set up a small tent where he will sleep. *Men. Always looking for an adventure!*

Having Ben is a tremendous help for Joseph. The two of them clear the land much faster than Joseph and I did alone. Even with the delay caused by his trip to Fort Brooke, the garden is ready to plant by mid August. Even Eliza helps. I let her drop the seeds into the holes I poke into the ground with a stick. I want to laugh when I see her go back and dig them up, but fuss at her to make her stop. She is worse than the ants and birds. Eliza enjoys helping me build a scarecrow to keep the birds away. Once the seeds begin to sprout, there is endless weeding to be done to give them room to grow. If it does not rain, I haul buckets from the spring to keep them watered. I am determined our crops will blossom. And even more determined to help Joseph so he and Ben will have time to start working on our house.

Finally, the day arrives. Joseph announces at breakfast that he and Ben will begin laying the foundation for our cabin. All the while they were clearing the land for the garden, they set aside the rocks they found buried in the ground. The rocks are a unique shape and texture. Not quite round, but not flat either, they have the imprints of sea creatures in them. Joseph tells me Florida was once underwater and the pressure of the ocean formed the rocks.

I watch anxiously as the men place the rocks in a rectangular shape. Joseph and I talked of this day for many months. To begin with, our cabin will have two rooms separated by a wide hallway. One room will be our main living area with a fireplace for cooking. The other will be a bedroom. Joseph will create the space for a second floor and someday, we will finish that portion of the house for extra bedrooms. But, for now, two rooms will be enough. The cabin will face south and the bay with porches on the north and south sides. The hall will have doors at each end, but most of time we will leave them open for air circulation. Ben is from Georgia and tells us that in his state, they call this type of construction, "dog trot." I chuckle when I think about Bonaparte running through the hallway.

When the foundation is complete, Joseph and Ben begin placing the logs that will form the framework of the house. They use pine logs stripped of the exterior bark. The work takes time. The logs must be fitted just right, notched and held into place with wedges of wood. As days pass, it is clear Joseph and Ben alone will not be strong enough to lift the logs into place as the walls rise higher.

"We are going to need some help," Joseph says one evening at dinner. "I think tomorrow, I will leave Ben here to do some weeding and watering while I sail over to Manatee and see if I can get some of the other settlers to come and help me set the upper logs. I will likely need help for the roof, too. Manatee is closer than Fort Brooke. We can get there in a few hours. Do you want to go with me? It is Sunday. Perhaps we can find a church to attend while we are in town."

Sunday? The days all blur together for me. In the endless cycle of farm and household chores, I have no need to know what day it is.

"I don't know Joseph. Eliza and I really don't have anything to wear. Everything we own is worn and faded from washing. Maybe you should just leave us here."

"I'd like for you to go with me. Why don't you dig deep into the trunk? I bet you have something nice stored there. You have lost so much weight that some of your clothes from Germany, the ones you haven't worn in a long time will probably suit you."

It is true. I have lost a lot of weight. We ran out of sugar a long time ago, and a steady diet of fish and vegetables combined with the exercise of farm work slimmed me down. I rummage in the trunk that has travelled so many miles with me and find a skirt and a blouse unworn since we arrived in Florida. I also find my mother's Bible. In the day to day demands of homesteading, I do not read it like I should. I set it aside and look for something for Eliza. A dress handed down from Margaret's daughters will fit her. She has grown so much since we left New Orleans. She has no shoes, but if Joseph carries her, perhaps no one will notice.

Joseph draws water for a bath while I heat the iron in the fire to press our clothes. I take care to wash my hair and let it dry while I iron. With each run of the iron across the table, which serves as a makeshift ironing board, I feel my anxieties grow.

What if the women are not friendly? What if they make fun of our clothes? I wish I had a hat to wear. My sunbonnet is so ragged. What if Eliza is afraid? What if no one will help us? What will the church be like? Oh, I wish we had something sweet to eat. A cookie would taste so good right now. Or a piece of cake. Maybe we can find someone who will sell us some sugar. Even molasses would do.

"Julia."

I jump at the sound of my husband's voice.

"You are worrying. Stop worrying. It will be fine. Maybe we will even meet some neighbors."

Joseph takes the iron from my hand and sets it down on the cloth I used to protect the table. "Come here," he says as he hugs me. He rubs my back. "It will be fine."

Despite my husband's assurances, I can't fall asleep. I toss and turn on our mattress stuffed with the Spanish moss that hangs from the oak trees around the house. Though I took care to dry it and make sure it was insect free, my skin crawls as though insects attack me. *Nerves again,* I think. I ease out of bed trying not to wake Joseph and sit by the cooling fire. I can see only a little, but I pick up my Bible in the dim light. I think about how much my mother loved to read scripture and the comfort it gave her. Perhaps it will do the same for me. I stroke the leather cover imagining her hands once did the same, and then, open it at a random spot. Or perhaps it is not coincidence at all for when I squint to see in the flickering firelight, I read Psalm 63:

> O God, thou art my God; early will I seek thee: my soul thirsteth for thee, my flesh longeth for thee in a dry and thirsty land, where no water is; To see thy power and thy glory, so as I have seen thee in the sanctuary. Because thy loving-kindness is better than life, my lips shall praise thee. Thus will I bless thee while I live: I will lift up my hands in thy name. My soul shall be satis-

> fied as with marrow and fatness; and my mouth shall praise thee with joyful lips: When I remember thee upon my bed, and meditate on thee in the night watches. Because thou hast been my help, therefore in the shadow of thy wings will I rejoice. My soul followeth hard after thee: thy right hand upholdeth me.

"When I remember thee upon my bed, and meditate on thee in the night watches." That is certainly appropriate for my situation. Instead of lying here worrying, I need to think about Who God is and what He can do for us. I read the passage again, and notice something else, equally important. *"My soul shall be satisfied as with marrow and fatness; and my mouth shall praise thee with joyful lips."* I remember earlier in the midst of my fretting, I longed for something sweet. That is always my first impulse. Eat my troubles away. If there had been a cake in my kitchen, I would have devoured the whole thing in fear and frustration. *These verses say that my soul can be satisfied just as if I have eaten a good meal.* I look at the sentences above that phrase. What could satisfy my soul? *"Thy loving-kindness is better than life. My lips will praise thee." What do I have to praise God for? So many troubles?*

As though a voice speaks aloud, I hear my name. "Julia." I look at Joseph to see if he wakes. Can he hear it? Again, I hear. "Julia, what troubles you?"

I think about my earlier worries. *What will tomorrow bring?*

"Can you trust me with tomorrow?" There's the problem. Can I trust God? I am not sure I can. "Just try. Give me your troubles and let me take care of them. I don't promise it won't still be hard, but I promise I will be with you."

I put the Bible away and lie down once more. The words I read and heard echo in my mind. *This is a dry and thirsty land if there ever was one. Hardships at every turn. No one to share my heart-aches with. When have I seen God's power and glory at work in my life? The Bible says God's kindness to me should be enough. I don't have to fill myself up with food to be satisfied. Instead of worrying, I can praise God. About what?* I think for a while. Though our life on the island is difficult, there are still some reasons to be thankful. My husband, who loves and cares for me, understands me and listens to my fears. My daughter, happy and healthy. A roof over our heads. Even though it is temporary, it keeps out the rain. A house under construction. The garden. My dog. A boat. God Himself. I drift off to sleep making a list of blessings.

The next morning, I focus on that list as I sit beside Eliza in the boat as we sail west, then south out of the mouth of Terra Ceia Bay. The wind rocks the small sailboat as we make the turn into Tampa Bay. I grab onto the wooden bench where I sit to steady myself with one hand and pull Eliza tightly to me. For a moment I am frightened. *What if the boat tips? I do not know how to swim, and in this skirt, I would surely drown before anyone could rescue me.* I take a deep breath and try to remain calm. Eliza loves the boat and the excitement of sailing. I cannot hear her over the wind, but her lips move so I know she is chattering to herself about something. I see Passage Key in the distance and remember the first time I saw it. How far we have come! And where did my husband learn to handle a boat? He adjusts the sails and we turn into the Manatee River. We head to the Village of Manatee.

I think about what Captain Tresca told us. He said the old maps spelled the name of the Manatee wrong so it has been corrected now. When we first saw this land, it would have been called "Manitee" with an 'i'. Now, it is spelled with an "a". I wonder what the people will be like who have enough power they can change place names on long established maps.

We sail past the wide beaches lined with pine and oak forests interspersed with white piles of shells that gleam like snow. The wind and waves are calmer in the river, so we can talk.

Eliza asks her favorite question, "What's that?"

Joseph talks to her like she is an adult and tells her the mounds are the remains of Indian villages from many years ago. We travel for miles without seeing any sign of inhabitants until plumes of smoke marking the Village of Manatee finally appear. I rub my hands over my skirt. It is a navy velvet and too heavy and hot for this climate.

I remember the voice. "Don't worry. I will be with you." *Oh, God. I hope so.*

Joseph navigates the boat to a wharf made of stones and shell on the south shore of the river. Tabby, he calls it. He ties the boat in place and helps us onto the walkway. I wait for him before moving toward the shore. For once, I do not want to be first. I follow my husband along the dirt path that serves as the main thoroughfare for the Village of Manatee. My skirt drags on the ground creating a plume of dust around my feet. It is not much of a village. Just a scattering of wooden buildings all of them built of logs just like our house will be. My hopes rise. Someone here must be able to help us.

A man lounges under the shade of an oak tree. He spits a stream of tobacco in our direction. Joseph hesitates to approach him and stays on the path holding Eliza. I remain in his shadow.

"Good afternoon," he calls. "I wonder if you can tell us if there are church services today."

The man spits again. "Where're you from?" he asks.

"Terra Ceia," Joseph replies. "We are newly arrived and looking for a church."

"What country you from?" the man asks again.

"Bavaria, originally. But this is our home now."

"We don't need any Catholics here. Or dumb Dutch for that matter. Get on with you."

I want to cry, and tug on Joseph's arm. *We are not welcome here.* My husband persists in pleasantries.

"Good day." He turns to follow the path farther inland.

"Joseph, let's just go. I'm scared." I hear a sound of people singing ahead as my husband continues to move forward.

"That was just one man. And I am not sure he was sober. Let's see who else we can find."

"Why did he think we were Catholic? Or Dutch?"

Joseph just shakes his head.

We enter a clearing of trees. In its center is a tall fence made of tree trunks. The gate is open so we walk through and see several wooden buildings clustered within the enclosure. The singing comes from one of the buildings, a log house like the others we have seen. I try to hold Joseph back, but he marches resolutely to the front door and knocks. He still carries Eliza so I follow.

The singing quiets. A man comes to the door. "May I help you?"

"My name is Joseph Atzeroth. I came to see if there was a church in the village. My wife and I would like to find a place to worship."

"I am Ed O'Connell," the man answers. I see wariness in his eyes. He does not smile. "This is my home. Are you Catholics?"

I tighten my grip on Joseph's arm. *We need to go.*

"No, Mr. O'Connell. We are Lutherans. But, above all we are Christians. May we join your meeting?"

O'Connell hesitates, but opens the door to let us in. I see the women's eyes upon me and run my hand down my skirt to smooth it as best I can. All the seats are taken. There is no place for us to sit down. Finally, a black man sitting on the floor in the corner of the room exits and returns with chairs for us. We sit down, but I think we would be better just to leave. Joseph balances Eliza on his knee exposing her bare feet. I reach to pull her skirt down, but am relieved to see the other children are also barefoot.

Another man who they call Ezekiel, leads us in a short devotion on Philippians 4. I pay attention to the scriptures as they are read:

> Be careful for nothing; but in everything by prayer and supplication with thanksgiving let your requests be made known unto God. And the peace of God, which passeth all understanding, shall keep your hearts and minds through Christ Jesus. Finally, brethren, whatsoever things are true, whatsoever things are honest, whatsoever things are just, whatsoever things are pure, whatsoever things are lovely, whatsoever things are of good report; if there be any virtue, and if there be any praise, think on these things.

I know these words are meant for me. Prayer will bring peace. Worrying will not. I shouldn't focus on the things that trouble me, but think about things that are honest, just and pure, and instead of complaining, praise God. I feel myself relax. When the man is done speaking, another hymn is sung and the meeting closes with prayer. My moment of quiet is short lived. The man's prayer brings me to alert again as he prays for God's blessings on the village and for protection from the enemy.

He asks "Bring more like-minded people such as ourselves to tame this country and bring civilization to this wilderness. Bring unity to our congregation."

Like-minded people such as ourselves? What does he mean by that?

When the meeting dismisses, I take Eliza from Joseph and stand alone while he joins the men outside. The other women all turn their backs to me and talk among themselves. From across the room, I note their pretty calico dresses trimmed with lace and fancy stitching. My clothes are outdated and unsuitable for Florida.

I turn to go, but finally, one woman leaves the group and comes over to me. "So, you are Lutheran then? Not Catholic?

Not that I have a problem with Catholics, but you will fit in better here if you are Protestant."

Stunned by her rudeness, I can only nod. She continues, "So where are you from? Are you Dutch?"

"No, we are from Bavaria. We were going to settle in Pennsylvania, but my husband wanted to come to Florida."

"Oh, Pennsylvania." I think about how Margaret pronounced that name and want to smile. But, the woman's next words stop me.

"We are all Southerners. Well, except Ezekiel and Abigail and a couple of others. I guess every town has to have at least a few token Yankees."

The other women laugh. I feel flushed. *Is it hot in here? I need some air.* I try not to show my panic, nod and excuse myself.

As I exit, I overhear Joseph's conversation with Ed O'Connell.

"What did you say your name was again?"

"Joseph Atzeroth, but you can call me Joe."

"Well, Mr. Joe, I'd be happy to hire out one of my people. If you want to follow me, I will call them out so you can look them over. King or Jacob would do for you. Or if you want the job faster, you can rent them both."

Joseph stammers. I know what he is thinking. In good conscience, how could he use someone's slaves?

Finally, he says, "No thanks, Mr. O'Connell. I was hoping to find someone willing to trade work with me. If you know of someone who needs a hand and would work on my house, in exchange, I would come and work on theirs."

Mr. O'Connell frowns. "It'd just be easier to get yourself some slaves. Man can't do it all himself. No harm in it. They do what they are told and get the work done in good fashion."

"Thanks, but no. Please spread the word that I am looking for some help if anyone is able." Joseph changes the subject. "Do you meet regularly for church then?"

O'Connell nods. "Every Sunday. The Circuit Rider comes about once a month and then, the whole village gathers for worship. Don't know of any Lutherans in the area, but I suppose you are welcome to join us, but I wouldn't spread the word that you are adverse to slavery. Not a sentiment that our people share and it would make you even more of an outsider than you already are."

I've heard enough. "Joseph, Eliza is getting fretful. I think it is time for us to go."

As we leave, O'Connell calls to us, "Haven't seen any Indians out your way, have you? I'd keep my eyes peeled. You never know when you might get visitors that don't have your best wishes at heart."

Was that a threat? Was he warning us?

We walk back to the boat in silence. Sweat drips down my back. Whether it is from the heat or fear, I do not know. I walk as fast as I can with my skirt dragging in the dirt. I am not one to waste anything, but if I could, I would throw this outfit away. I will think of the way we were treated when I wear it again. I cannot reconcile the words I heard preached this morning with the attitudes that were expressed after service. *Is this how Christians are to live? And God, where are you now? Didn't you promise that if I would trust you, you would take care of us? Is this how you do that? Setting us in the midst of people who hate us already? And for things we have no control over like our clothes and our nationality?*

I wait until we are away from the land before I voice my concerns.

"Joseph, was he threatening us? Do you think that they would hurt us? Why would they hate us so? And what difference would it make if we were Catholic? Why did you have to tell them that we do not want slaves?"

"Julia, stay calm. He was just trying to make himself look better than me. God will provide for us."

"I am not so sure. Do you think that they have something to do with our land claim problems?"

"Why would they concern themselves with us? There is plenty of land to go around. We are far enough distant we can stay out of their way. We will just do business in Fort Brooke from now on. You'll see. Everything will be fine. Trust God."

I clinch my fists in frustration. I want some answers to my questions. To be told simply to trust is not enough. *How can my husband be so faithful? "Trust me," God said. "Trust God," Joseph says. If this morning is an indication of what happens when I trust, I don't think I can do it anymore.* The closeness I felt to God last night is lost in my memory of how "His people" acted toward us.

We board our boat to head home. My thoughts swirl around me so I don't notice another boat follows us into Terra Ceia Bay until Joseph points to it. It comes from the direction of Fort Brooke.

Joseph shouts over the wind, "Captain Tresca! See Julia, God sent us help after all."

Whether or not God sent the good Captain, I don't know. But, we are grateful when he anchors offshore and unloads his boat of men and provisions. I was so upset when we left Manatee I forgot to ask about a store. Thankfully, Captain Tresca brings not only sugar, but more flour, fruit, spices and beef.

"I thought perhaps I might trade you labor for some of your good cooking. My men and I are sure tired of fish and potatoes."

"I know just what to do with this," I laugh. "We are grateful for your offer of help, Captain."

Over the next few days, the sailors help Joseph and Ben finish erecting the walls and frame the roof. They also lay split logs for the downstairs floor and more to form the floor of the upstairs which will also serve as the downstairs' ceiling. I keep the men fed, hoping if they are well nourished they will get more work done. I even sacrifice one of the hens to make chicken and dumplings. It is worth it to see the walls get taller and taller.

At meals, I listen to the men talk. It is hard not to participate, but I don't think Joseph would appreciate what I have to say. Particularly when it comes to the situation with the settlers in Manatee.

Captain Tresca explains. "Only a few of them actually own slaves. Gamble and Braden have sugar plantations and need a lot of labor. Gates has five or six to help on his farm, too. It is not like some places where there are hundreds of slaves. But, they all like to think they are big landowners. One day they might need the labor, so they support slavery even if they don't own any now."

I struggle with the belief that one man should own another, but keep my mouth shut. I do not know on what side of the fence Captain Tresca sits. On their last night with us, I am disappointed to learn Ben will be leaving with Captain Tresca.

"I hoped he would stay longer," I complain to Joseph as we prepare for bed. "There is still so much to do on the cabin."

"I know, but we must be grateful for how hard he worked on the garden and the house. We would not be this far along without his help. Captain Tresca told him some settlers in Punta Rassa might have land for sale. I can't hold the boy back from his dreams, Julia."

"It would sure be a lot easier if we believed in slavery," I sigh.

"Julia! I can't believe you said that."

"I am not saying that I do, just that it would be easier to have some help that didn't run off at the first chance."

Joseph just shakes his head. "Count your blessings, Julia. The house is almost finished. All that needs to be done now can be done with the two of us. The crops are about ready to harvest. Before winter comes, we will be snug in our cabin and have enough food for ourselves and some to sell."

The work is not as easy as Joseph predicted. It makes me very nervous to see him up so high, stepping from rafter to rafter putting up thin strips of wood that will be used to nail the shingles in place. I convince him to tie a rope around his waist and attach it to one of the big trees that overhang the cabin.

"What would I do if you were injured or worse, dead? Who would help me? How would we live without you? Take better care of yourself for Eliza's sake."

Though he complains about the restrictions, I am thankful for the precaution the day I hear a shout and see my husband swinging from the tree. The rope is the only thing that keeps him from falling. I don't know whether to weep with relief or yell in anger.

While he won't let me on the roof, I help Joseph with the rest of the house. We chink between the logs with moss and mud. Even Eliza enjoys stuffing the cracks with the mixture. She is filthy, but at least I don't have to worry about what she is doing and can focus on my work. We build the chimney out of mud and sticks. I wish we had some bricks, but Joseph says this will do until we can get some. Neither do we have glass for the windows, but Joseph builds shutters that we can close at night. At least the openings allow sunlight inside and air to circulate through the house unlike the stuffy, dark hut. On the day that he finishes the front and back doors, we stand arm in arm and admire our work.

"See how much prouder we are because we did it ourselves?" he asks. I roll my eyes. He is right, but I prefer not to admit it.

We spend one last night in the hut. I wake early before the sun comes up eager to begin our moving day. Perhaps it is my elation or relief at finally getting a house, but I feel the urge to pray. I haven't been speaking all that often to God since our experience in Manatee. While he did answer our prayers by sending the sailors to help us and keeping Joseph safe while he climbed up on the roof, the way we were treated in Manatee makes me reluctant to approach God. If His followers could be so negative, how can I expect kindness from Him? Still, we have much to be grateful for and my husband is quick to give credit to God. For a few minutes, I whisper my thanks as well. Then, I poke Joseph awake and urge him out of bed so he can begin moving our belongings to the house.

By the end of the day, everything is put away. The kitchen is arranged, our bedroom in order and dinner bubbles in a pot hanging in the fireplace. As I pat biscuits into shape with my hands, I am glad that I started the day with a prayer. Maybe now that we are in our own home, life will be easier and I will remember to pray and read my Bible more often. Whether it is the house or the prayer, I don't know, but I feel more at peace already. Despite the way we were received in Manatee or maybe because of it, Terra Ceia is starting to feel like home.

Chapter Eleven

Despite my joy at having a real roof over our heads, Eliza and I are often left alone. Joseph travels back and forth to Fort Brooke. Sometimes, he delivers vegetables to the market there. Other times, he is required to appear to file more paperwork about our claim. He is puzzled. Other settlers don't seem to be having as much trouble as we are. I think I know the reason, but he is quick to dismiss my concerns.

Not that I can understand why anyone would want to live on the island. While it is beautiful with the wide spreading oaks and tropical flowers, it is still wild and untamed. Keeping the landscape under control is hard work. I often sleep poorly, disturbed by animal noises like the screams of the panther which sound like someone is torturing a child. At first, I get up and check to see if Eliza is still in bed. Now I know, but it still does not help me rest easy.

One morning, I am particularly cranky and out of sorts. Eliza stands on a stool beside the butter churn. At four, she is still small for her age. I probably ask too much of her to expect her to do the churning. Joseph is in Fort Brooke, delivering vegetables and I need whatever help I can find. She rubs her elbow.

"Mama, I'm tired," she whines. "Can I stop now?" Hopping in place to ease the cramping in her legs, Eliza loses her balance and falls off the stool.

"Is the butter made?" I ask.

Eliza lifts the wooden lid from the glazed pottery jar and peeks inside. I look as well. At the bottom of the tall container are flakes of pale yellow beginning to show as the cream separates. It will take more time for a round ball of butter to emerge from the cream. I know she wants to go and play. Fickle spring turns bright sunny days to dark, gloomy ones as rain soaks the island.

Eliza and I have been stuck inside this cabin for four days. How grateful I am for the snug log cabin instead of the palmetto thatched hut of just a few months ago. But, inside the shuttered cabin with its cedar shake roof, time seems to run together. Eliza is restless. Joseph's absence combined with the poor weather makes me irritable, too. I should let her stop and play, but life is not about play. The sooner she learns hard work is what is expected of a frontier woman, the better. Eliza knows not to ask a second time. She sighs, covers the churn and begins to beat the cream again.

With each thud of the wooden beater against the crock, I think, "If only." If only…the rain would stop so I could work in the garden. The potatoes will rot and the corn mold from all this weather. If only…I could hang the sheets on the line. I am tired of damp smelling linens. If only…I had a neighbor nearby. Someone to have tea with in front of the fire and share a recipe or story. If only…we had stayed in New Orleans or even Fort Brooke. If only…Joseph would come home. Yes, that was the problem. If only…Joseph would come home. I force myself to change my thoughts. If only, will not help. Maybe I will make a pie. No, I will not start that again.

I remember Philippians 4:8. Though I did not find the people of Manatee to be welcoming, the scripture I learned that day stays with me.

> Finally, brethren, whatsoever things are true, whatsoever things are honest, whatsoever things are just, whatsoever things are pure, whatsoever things are lovely, whatsoever things are of good report; if there be any virtue, and if there be any praise, think on these things.

"Think on these things." I walk over to Eliza again and stand behind her. I reach around and take her small hands into mine and together, we make the butter.

"Aren't we lucky to have such a nice sturdy house to keep the rain off of us while we work?" I encourage my daughter to talk to pass the time. I don't have a neighbor, but here is someone, even if she is a child, that I can talk to.

Eliza smiles. "I helped make it, didn't I? I'm little, but I helped. We chopped down the trees and cleared the land. My favorite part was putting the mud and moss between the logs. I liked playing in the mud, the best."

"Yes, you were a big help," I agree. "And you are a help when we plant the seeds and weed the garden plants, too. I wonder if Papa got a good price for the vegetables at Fort Brooke. What do you think he will do with the money he makes?"

"Do you think he will bring me a present?"

"I don't know." I laugh. "What would you like Papa to bring?" *Probably candy or a doll.*

Eliza's answer surprises me. "I would like some windows," she says. "I would like to see outside when we are in the house."

Yes, windows. How nice it would be to have light even on a stormy day. That would make us all feel better.

"Papa promises someday we will have glass windows, but the panes come all the way from New Orleans and are hard to find. Don't get your hopes up this trip. Look there, what's in the churn now?"

"It's done! And listen, the rain is over. Can I go outside? Please Mama?"

"Yes, you may go outside, but stay on the porch. It's too wet to play in the yard."

Eliza bolts for the door. I shake my head at my daughter. She is so much like me when I was her age. Her father loves to be outside, too. Joseph loves this land. I frown. He has been gone for so long. Something must be wrong. Nothing else would keep him from the farm for so long.

I thrust my negative thoughts away and cross from the kitchen to our bedroom. As I enter the hall, I peek through the door to make sure Eliza is minding me. She leans over the porch rail peering into the rain barrel.

"Be careful, daughter. Don't fall."

I breathe deeply of the fresh air. It smells so good. A mix of wet earth, flowers and grass. The sun hides behind the clouds, and the air is chilly. I draw my shawl around me. Maybe it would do me good to get outside, too. Returning to the kitchen, I grab a bucket of beans and a bowl. *Eliza is right, why should we stay confined? I can work just as well on the porch.* When I return, Eliza lies on her belly, hanging her head over the wood floor, staring under the house.

"Look, Mama. There are sea creatures in the rocks."

"Yes, your father dug them up here on the island. A long time ago, they were under the sea."

Eliza spends several minutes tracing them with her fingers, as I snap beans. The rough, wet stones that form the foundation of our cabin hold secrets from the past. *If someone looked at my heart, would they see the scars?* Eliza rolls over on her back looking at the pattern of the cedar shakes that make the cabin roof. Soon, she is asleep.

I remember the sound of Joseph's ax as he cut those shingles from the many cedar trees growing on the island. Their aroma filled the air when his ax cut the tree trunks. Everything I see makes me miss my husband.

The chickens cluck around the side of the house. The rain drips from the porch. I can hear the seagulls calling out on the bay. Then I hear a familiar whistle from the direction of the shore. Joseph! Joseph is home. My heart beats faster as I stand, scattering beans from my lap onto the porch floor. Eliza wakes as well. Joseph rounds the corner between the trees. Eliza forgets my admonition to stay on the porch. Mud flies around her feet as she races down the path towards him shrieking with delight.

"Papa! Papa! We missed you so!"

I finally feel as though the breath returns to me. My husband is home. He stoops down and swings Eliza onto his shoulders. Her muddy feet bump his chest, and he spins and twirls his way towards the cabin. Barking, Bonaparte dashes in and out between his feet. Even the dog is happy to see him! Oh, I know how he feels!

Laughing Eliza grasps her father's head for balance. Her vantage point must seem very high. Though I am so happy for him to be home, something perverse takes hold of me. Instead of happiness, I feel anger. Where has he been? Why didn't he return sooner? Did he know how much danger we were in? Now, he frolics down the path as though time stands still?

"Joseph, put the girl down! You will make her sick. And look at your shirt. The mud!" I shake my head in frustration. "Where have you been? I've been worried and could only think the worst!"

As though he cannot hear my tone or fear, Joseph swings Eliza down onto the porch and reaches for me. "Jealous my love? I will dance with you as well." Joseph swings me into a waltz around the porch. I push him away.

"Where have you been? Eliza and I have been worried about you."

"I got lost in the storm, Julia. I missed the opening of the bay, and the wind blew me south all the way down to Sarasota Bay. I would have been here days ago if not for the rain. I am very glad to be home. Now look at what I brought my girls."

He hands me a thick packet. How exciting! Three letters! One from Margaret, another from my sister, Monica, and the third from Colonel Belknap, the commander of Fort Brooke! Joseph sits down on the porch floor and draws Eliza beside him.

From a large bag, he pulls out a package wrapped in twine and burlap.

"And for my angel," he says, as he helps Eliza untie the string.

"What is it, Papa?"

"Open and see!"

Eliza pulls away the cloth. Newspapers cover thin sheets of something flat and square.

"Careful, now," Joseph says. "Let me help you. It is breakable." Inside each layer of paper hides a pane of glass! "Now you can have your windows, Eliza. We'll bring the outdoors inside for you. It was pure luck I found them. A ship just arrived from New Orleans when I got to Fort Brooke."

Windows! A gift for me as well. My anger melts a little. "Oh, thank you, Joseph!"

Joseph reaches inside his pocket and pulls out another package. "Another treat for my girl."

"Candy! May I have some now?" Joseph looks at me. *Oh, why not? Didn't he bring me glass windows and letters?* I nod.

"Just one," Joseph tells her. "And why don't you share a piece with your mama. Sweeten her up a little," he laughs.

That man. "I don't need any sweetening up," I say. "Eliza, only one piece. Save the rest until after dinner."

My daughter snuggles next to her father and sucks on a lemon drop, while I eagerly read my letters. Like Eliza's candy, I save the one from Margaret for later when I can savor it. I skim the letters from Monica and from Colonel Belknap. Then, I listen as Joseph tells of the changes taking place in Fort Brooke as more houses are built every day to hold all the new settlers coming into the area. It is good to have him home. I finally let go of all my anger and relax.

"I saw Captain Tresca and he said to tell you hello, Julia. He said he has not forgotten your dinner invitation and will sail down one day soon. What did your sister say in her letter?"

The news in my letters is so exciting!

"Monica says Franz has finally agreed to come to Florida. He cannot find work, and New York is no place to raise children. Little Mary is a year younger than you, Eliza. You don't remember her, but I know you will be friends." *I think of my sister. Like me, she has lost some of her children. Her three oldest girls died from a typhoid outbreak in New York City shortly after they arrived from Bavaria. Little Mary who was born in New York is the only one she has left. Thank God we left the city. It will be good for her to have a fresh start.*

"So, they are coming then?" Joseph asks.

"Yes, I just have to send them the money for their passage," I reply.

Joseph continues, "I visited Colonel Belknap while I was in Fort Brooke. He said he would give you the loan as you had asked. I am not sure that is a good idea. I know how badly you want your sister to come, but Julia, that is a lot of money, and I don't like being in debt to any man."

"Joseph, you said so yourself, there is no other way. I am lonesome in this wilderness you brought me to. You are gone so often and with only Eliza for company I think I will go insane. Besides, with more hands to help, we will be able to expand the farm. More crops mean more money. It won't take us long to pay him back with the extra produce to sell at the fort. Please. I long to see Monica and her little one. She needs the comfort of her family. Colonel Belknap sent the money in his letter. All we need to do now is get it to New York."

"Have you thought about how you will send it to her? Who can we trust to do that? And who will show them how to find us?"

I think back to the last few days alone on the island without my husband to help. I remember the fear and the anxiety. I swallow hard. I so want my sister here with me.

"Well, I thought you would go. Eliza and I will be fine here for a time. We can keep everything just as it is. You will see. Won't you please go to New York and bring Monica to me here?"

"I don't know. I will have to think about it. You ask a lot of me and of yourself and Eliza. Give me time to plan."

Knowing that it would do no good to press him, I change the subject. "In the excitement, I forgot to ask you how your business at the land office went."

Joseph shakes his head. "That is something else I need to think about," he says. "I did not get good news. I just missed the deadline to file for homestead, but the land agent says it is not a problem. The government is eager for new settlers, especially in the coastal lands like ours. Can you believe it? They call this second rate land. How can anyone see such rich soil and call it second rate? Not many people are willing to come here. The agent thinks the papers will be accepted. He promised to forward them to the land office in Newnansville. We just have to wait and see. I want this land to be mine, Julia. I'll do whatever it takes to file this claim. It is good land. I sold all the vegetables for a high price. We can make a fine home here."

Eliza yawns. Her eyes grow heavy, and she rests her head on the table. "Eliza, time for sleep," I say.

Joseph stands. "I'll take her." As I watch him lift our daughter and carry her to bed, I think, how good it is to have my husband home again.

While he is gone, I open the letter from Margaret. It is dated December of 1844. It has taken almost four months to reach us. Margaret begins by telling me all about the Christmas festivities in Hermann. Her daughters were angels in the church play.

She writes, "They looked so sweet and beautiful until Trina said loudly, 'When is Baby Jesus going to come? I want to open presents!' My daughter is much like me. Patience is not my strong suit, either!"

I laugh. It seems like Margaret does have her hands full raising her girls. She tells about activities at the church, her husband's business and her daughters' schoolwork.

She continues, "I am sure it sounds so boring to you, my friend. Not nearly as exotic as the wilds of Florida. Your life seems so much more exciting than mine."

Oh, Margaret, you just don't know. What I wouldn't give for the peace of your town and the friendships and activities there. For people who are kind to us and welcoming.

I read on. My friend understands more than I thought she did.

> "Julia, I know this is not what you planned for your life and every day is a struggle. Be more patient than I am, my friend. You are not on that island by chance. I am confident that God has a great plan for you and that He will use every experience to make you into the woman He wants you to be. Read Romans 8:28. Here, I will save you from looking it up, although I know that your Bible is right at hand! (True?!) 'And we know that all things work together for good to them that love God, to them who are the called according to his purpose.' Keep being obedient to God and following after Him. Read your Bible and pray. Everything will work out in the long run. It is all in God's timing, and He knows best. I miss you and wish we could have a long talk. Write soon! Love, Margaret"

"It is all in God's timing, and He knows best." I wish I were as confident in that as Margaret. The delay in getting our land grant. Uncertainty over Joseph's departure and my sister's arrival. The reception we received in Manatee. How do I know God really is in control? It doesn't seem like it to me. I think again about the verse she shared.

Maybe I just don't love God enough. I should pray more and read my Bible.

I go to bed longing for the confidence of my friend. But instead of praying as she suggested, I plan tomorrow's menu. I think about baking a cake and how good it will taste.

As much as I want my sister here soon, I know there is no point in nagging. Joseph will go when he is ready. With Margaret's words about God's timing fresh in my mind, I do my best to be patient. It is hard because Joseph waits two more months in order to finish the upstairs of the log cabin. He wants to make a place for Monica and her family. As it is, our little cabin cannot stretch to add three more people. He installs stairs on one side of the hallway. They lead to two upstairs rooms. One will be for Monica and her husband and the other for Eliza and her cousin.

I know how happy Eliza is to have a room of her own. I hope she understands it will only be for just a little while and soon she will have another child to share it with. Tucked up under the cozy little space under the cedar shake roof is her bed with a blue and white patchwork quilt I made for her. The mattress is stuffed with Spanish moss and laid down on the floor. Adorned with her baby doll also made of rags, the bed looks very nice. So does the downstairs of our cabin now that Joseph has added the windows letting light into our home.

Surely now, Joseph will make the trip to New York and bring my sister and her family here. Finally, what little patience I have wears out.

"You must make the trip soon. My last letter from Monica told me she is pregnant again. If you don't leave quickly, she will be too far along to travel. Once the baby is born, it will be months before they can come. Please, won't you go? The cabin is complete; the crops are doing well. Eliza and I can manage while you are gone. Please, Joseph."

"I hoped there might be another way to get the money to them so I would not have to leave you, but I cannot find anyone else willing to make the journey. Captain Tresca said his next trip would be to Key West and I could go along. If I help him with the sailing, he will not charge me for the fare. That was several weeks ago, so he should be here any day. From Key West, I will book passage on one of the ocean going schooners. Oh, how I dread that trip! It will take weeks to get to New York and there is no telling how long we will have to wait for a boat coming back this way."

"I know how you hate to leave, and I thank you for going. I agree if there were any other way to get them here, it would be better. I will make sure everything is ready. I know you will have to leave quickly once the captain comes. He will probably want to spend the night don't you think?"

"Yes, and you know how much he loves your cooking, especially your zweibelkuchen. Some of the onions are ready to pull. I still have not gotten used to this country's topsy-turvy growing seasons. Spring should be the time to plant, not harvest! I will get some tomorrow and bring them inside."

"Our French friend does love my onion pie. As soon as you see the Margaret Ann in the bay, let me know and I will start it right away. He is a good friend to us, and he is always willing to help. I wish the other settlers were more like him."

Joseph frowns. "We are lucky to have him as a friend. He has tried to talk to the others. He cannot explain why they are so standoffish to us other than we are not of the same background. They are all from southern states and very cliquish. I don't know what it will take to convince them we are not to be feared despite our strange accents and foreign birth." He sighs, "I'm getting tired. I think I'll go to bed. Are you coming?"

Joseph leaves the kitchen, and I hear him laugh. Then, I hear the sound of little steps going up the stairway. Eliza must have been listening. Joseph winks at me as he reenters the kitchen.

"On second thought, I think I will have a glass of wine before bed. Will you join me, Julia?"

We sit on the porch and look at the stars shining through the trees. The night is so still I can hear waves lapping at the shore. Joseph sighs. *He hates to leave this place.*

I put my hand on his arm. "Joseph, I know you don't want to go, but I want you to know how much I appreciate it. I love you."

"I love you, too. Someday, I just hope to be settled in one place. Come, our daughter should be asleep by now. Let's go to bed as well."

Captain Tresca comes the very next day. I hear his hearty laughter as he greets Joseph down by the bay. I look out the window and see Eliza sitting on the front steps, arms resting on her knees, head propped up on her hands, as he makes his way down the path beside Joseph. His voice booms, "Hello my little Eliza! Don't I get a hug?"

My daughter refuses to answer.

"Eliza! What do you have to say to Captain Tresca?" I ask.

Tears seep from her eyes as she stands. Stomping her bare foot on the porch, she cries, "No! You are taking my Papa away! I hate you!"

Then, she races into the house and up the stairs falling on her bed crying. I greet Captain Tresca and then, excuse myself. I cannot allow such behavior to go unnoticed.

"Eliza." I stand at the top of the stairs. It is all I can do not to kneel down beside her pallet and gently rub her back. *Oh, I know how you feel. I don't want him to leave either, but how else will my sister make her way to us? I must bring her here even if it means we all will suffer, however temporary.*

I stay where I am. "Daughter, have we raised you so poorly you treat our guest that way? Come down and apologize now."

Eliza rolls over and faces me. "I don't want Papa to go. Please don't make Papa go!"

"Eliza, he must go, but he will be home as soon as he can. The time will pass quickly. Daughter, if only I could explain to you how I long to see my sister. You do not know her, but I love her dearly and have missed her every day since we left Bavaria. Now, she is here in America, but I still cannot see her, cannot talk to her or hug her. I cannot wait any longer. Papa will bring you a playmate when he returns. No more tears now. Be a big girl. Dry your eyes. Then, come down and tell Captain Tresca you are sorry and have some supper."

Downstairs, Eliza begins her apology to Captain Tresca. He interrupts her with a tight hug and a pinch on her cheek. "Look at that color!" he teases. "A little spitfire you have here, Joe!"

"Don't encourage her, Captain," I say. "Eliza, if you are finished with your tantrum, set the table, please."

Head down, Eliza gathers the silverware and tin plates and places them on the table. Into bowls, I ladle a thick beef stew from a pot hanging on a hook in the fireplace. I pull the onion pie from where it is nestled in the coals.

At supper, Eliza asks the question I have been wondering, "How long will you be gone, Papa?"

"It depends on the wind and the sea, Eliza. I hope your mother's family will be ready to sail when I arrive in New York, but I may have to wait there for a time as well. I promise you I will be home as soon as I can."

"But, how long, Papa?"

"Two months if all goes well." Tears well up in Eliza's eyes again. I consider the urge to cry as well. *Two months is a long time.*

Instead I say, "No more crying Eliza. Should I send you to your bed?"

Captain Tresca changes the subject. "Julia, this pie is wonderful. I hauled a load of onions to Fort Brooke last week and have been craving your pie ever since. How you can take onions and make them taste so much like apples is a wonder!"

"It is just the sour cream that makes it taste so good," I catch myself blushing with pleasure. How I love to be complimented on my cooking. "This is one of the few recipes from Germany I can make here. Oh, how you would have enjoyed the feasts we cooked back home. Joseph, if you can find any apples in New York, bring some home so I can make Captain Tresca some strudel. Now, that my dear Captain, would be a pleasure to bake for you."

"So, Joe, you are heading for New York?"

"Yes, my wife will not rest until I bring her sister and family here to live with us."

"It is a long journey and not the best time of year to travel. At least you won't have to worry about the cold, but with summer here, we never know when a hurricane might come up at sea."

I try to catch Eliza's eye. She plays with her food as she listens to the Captain.

"What's a hurricane?" she asks.

"A great, big storm," Captain Tresca answers. He tells about a storm he sailed through. I can almost hear the roar of the wind and the creaking of the ship as it plunges through the waves. I remember tossing and rocking. All of a sudden, my head spins and I feel queasy.

I think I will have to excuse myself, but then, Eliza starts to cry. Realizing his mistake, Captain Tresca reaches forward and pulls her into his lap.

"Don't cry, little one. I will make sure your Papa returns safe and sound again." Drawing his harmonica out of his pocket, he plays a happy tune.

Joseph rises, walks around the table, bows and extends his hand to me. I push aside my nausea and smile. Taking his hand, I follow his lead into a quick stepping polka. Tears turn to laughter as Eliza claps and the rhythm of our dance steps fill the cabin. *It will be alright. It has to be alright.*

Chapter Twelve

The next morning, Joseph sails away on Captain Tresca's boat. Wind fills the two sails of the small ship and carries it quickly away from shore. I stand on the bank and hold Eliza's hand. With my free hand, I wave my handkerchief until the boat rounds Rattlesnake Key and disappears from sight. I must be brave for my daughter's sake. Thoughts of hurricanes, wild animals and Indians fill my mind. My sister is so far away.

Quietly, we walk back home. Biscuits! I want some biscuits. That will make us feel better. I leave Eliza to play on her swing, while I go inside to mix up a batch and stoke the fire to the right temperature.

After I push the pan into the fire, I look outside to see what Eliza is doing. She sits idly in her swing with her feet swaying back and forth. *What is that behind her?* Creeping from the direction of the bay is a large alligator. Well over ten foot long, the beast's rough grey skin looks just like the trunk of an oak tree, and its yellow eyes glow brilliantly in the shade. *What is it doing so close to the house? Eliza! Does she see it? I am afraid to call to her. What if she gets down off the swing to come to me? What if Bonaparte sees him?* Though the alligator's legs appear short and stubby, I know alligators can move quickly even on land. I have also heard stories about their hunting skill and know my daughter or dog would be no match for his snapping jaws and sharp teeth. For a moment, I fear it is stalking her. My heart beats as though it would leave my chest. The alligator keeps moving and seems intent upon a patch of sunlight just past the tree. He passes almost underneath my daughter who by now has seen the monster. I wave, catch her attention and gesture for her to be quiet. In the hall, I reach for Joseph's gun. Far more than chickens are at stake here. My daughter's life depends upon an accurate shot.

I step out on the porch, and the alligator's head lifts off the ground as he looked towards the cabin. Obediently, Eliza remains frozen in the swing. I lift the gun just as the enormous reptile decides on his own to move. He lumbers back towards the bay. Tail dragging he leaves an imprint in the sand as he passes. Horrified, I race to the swing and snatch Eliza into my arms. I run in the opposite direction to the cabin. I smell the pan of biscuits burning. *I didn't need them anyway. How will we survive on this island without my husband to protect us?*

Mid summer arrives with its brutal heat. I rise early to complete my work before the sun reaches its full height. I hurry to finish outdoor chores by the noon meal. After dinner, Eliza and I seek the relief of whatever breeze comes off the water. We stay in the shade of the porch or a nearby tree. More than any of my lectures on safety, Eliza's encounter with the alligator teaches her not to stray far from the house alone. She plays in the sand building imaginary farms and gardens with sticks and flowers or daydreams in her swing, while I sew, shell peas or husk corn. Daily thunder storms arrive with such regularity a clock could be set by them. About two o'clock each afternoon, threatening black clouds build in the eastern sky. An hour later, windblown rain drives us back to the house.

I love to watch the storms, but am afraid to venture out on the porch during the times of intense lightning. Many afternoons, I put Eliza down for a nap on a pallet laid in the hallway as we listen to the drum of the rain on the sides of the cabin. High temperatures and humidity encourage mold to grow on the cabin walls. I scrape it off the furniture as well. It even grows on the leather cover of my mother's Bible. I bury it in some fabric in the bottom of my trunk hoping to keep it preserved. Not that it was helping me much anyway. I battle the urge to eat with labor. I cannot gorge myself when my hands are busy.

Though Eliza begs, I dare not bake even a dozen cookies. I will eat them all. I struggle against my desires and hope I have the willpower to win.

The predicted two months pass, and Joseph is still gone. I do not expect any letters as my husband cannot write. Before he left, Joseph made arrangements with Samuel Bishop of Fort Brooke to travel to the island every week to pick up produce for sale to the soldiers and new settlers in that growing community. Whenever Captain Sam appears, Eliza pesters him for information about her father.

"No news, Eliza. Nothing to report," he says.

Then, one day, when Eliza is at play and out of earshot, he quietly tells me of a great storm in the Atlantic. Soldiers recently transferred to Fort Brooke described its fury and how many ships were lost at sea. I try not to let it show, but am worried. At night, when the owl sits on the top of the chimney and his hoots echo into the fireplace or the panthers' screams roar from the woods, I lie awake wondering what I will do if Joseph does not return. The fear is almost more than I can handle.

One day, we escape the house and walk down to the bay. I wipe sweat off the back of my neck and fan my face. Eliza kicks up little stones with her feet as she follows me. Bonaparte races back and forth along the path sniffing out new scents and following the invisible trail of an animal long since passed. *I do not think I can stand one more minute. God, please, please bring my husband home.* When we reached the shore of the bay, I hold my hand above my eyes to cut the glare off the water. *What is that tiny speck in the mouth of the bay? Can it be? After all this time?*

"Look, Eliza! A boat is coming! It doesn't look like Captain Sam's boat. Who do you think it could be?"

"It's Papa, I know it's Papa!" Eliza jumps up and down.

I squint into the sun. Looking closer, I can see Joseph's outline on the bow of the boat as he waves his hat over his head. If I strain my ears in that direction, I think I hear his call dimly drifting across the water. Other figures join him on the deck and soon I recognize my sister, Monica, and brother-in-law, Franz, holding a little girl in his arms.

"That must be Mary! Look Eliza, your cousin is here."

When the boat touches shore, Joseph jumps overboard and wades to the beach. Bonaparte dives in wildly splashing in greeting. I wish I could join him, but instead, I restrain Eliza from getting wet. Upon reaching us, Joseph grabs me in his arms as Eliza presses close to his legs. His pants are wet with saltwater, but I do not care. My husband is home!

"Oh, it is good to be back. There were times, I never thought I would see you again."

I do not realize I am crying. "Don't cry, dear one. I am home now."

He hoists Eliza up into his arms and hugs her tight as well.

"Look who I have brought with me."

He sets Eliza down and wades back out to help the boat captain anchor in the shallow waters. Like Joseph, Franz disembarks straight over the side of the boat, carrying two year old Mary to land before returning for Monica. Joseph and Franz entwine their hands making a seat for her. Already large with child, she climbs out of the boat with difficulty. The captain holds her steady until she can swing her legs over the side and ease herself into their waiting arms.

Once upon shore, I embrace my sister. How I have missed her! We cry more tears, but these are of joy at our now long delayed reunion.

"Oh, how I longed for you to come, Monica. It is so good to see you again." I put my hand on her waist. "How far along are you?"

"Seven months", Monica replies. "I thought I would die before we could get here. The seas almost swallowed us." After watching our tearful reunion and hearing Monica's exclamation, Eliza bursts into tears and is joined by a bewildered Mary.

I address the girls. "No more crying! This is a happy day."

"Monica, come let's go to the house so you can rest. Eliza! Take Mary's hand and help her."

Eliza tries to assist the child, but she rubs her eyes and refuses to come. I lift Mary on my hip leaving Eliza standing on the path halfway between the bay and the house. I feel my daughter's eyes upon me. *She does not know how much her life is going to change!* While the men unload the boat, I settle Monica and Mary down for a nap. Then, I start work on dinner. My stomach growls, but in a healthy way. With Joseph home, I will not have to battle with myself so much. Eliza must be hungry as well. I give her a biscuit left over from breakfast and send her off to help the men.

"Monica and Mary are sleeping. Be quiet now." Her eyes well up with tears. Oh, now I have hurt her feelings. She will have to learn there are others to consider.

Joseph hauls a large crate on his back to the cabin porch. I hear my words echoed when he sets it down with a thud and Eliza runs to him and whispers, "Be quiet or Mama will yell at you. Aunt and Mary are sleeping."

"They are, are they?" replies Joseph in a low growly voice. "Then, I guess you better not be laughing!" In one smooth motion, he swings Eliza upside down and starts to tickle her ribs.

"Papa, Papa, stop," she giggles as he throws her up on his back where just moments before the crate rested. He gallops like a horse, and Eliza holds fast shrieking with joy all the way back to the bay. Oh, my husband will spoil her, but today, I am just grateful to have him back home.

As much as I dreamed of the day my sister would be returned to me, having three more people, particularly my pregnant sister is more difficult than I imagined. From the time she awakes in the morning until she goes to bed at night, Monica grumbles. She complains about the journey to Terra Ceia. Instead of being glad they survived the terrible storm when waves washed over the deck of the schooner and seasickness overcame most of the crew, she talks unceasingly about the misery of the voyage. She finds fault with the size of the second floor room Joseph worked so hard to finish. I suppose Monica expected a house, not a log cabin in the woods. A bed not a pallet on the floor. After the first night, Joseph and I move upstairs giving Monica and Franz our downstairs room and bed, but, Monica does not like the bed or the mattress.

"It sags," she says.

She whines about the food. Nothing tastes right. The mullet so easily found in the bay are too fishy for her taste. The ham too salty. The beef too tough. Why is there no stove? How is she expected to cook in a fireplace? Because she does not even offer to help with cooking, I do not see why it is a problem. Monica also objects to the Florida climate. Such fierce storms. Unbearable heat. Dampness seeps into everything. Despite my joy upon her arrival, Monica hates everything about my home.

I notice Eliza listening to her and take her aside one day to talk. "Be patient with your aunt. Not only is this a new place for her, but pregnant women are often fussy. She doesn't feel well. Give her time until the new baby comes. Then, she will be kinder."

I hug Eliza. "Try to keep Mary entertained and out of the way. There's a good girl."

Eliza does try, but the girls have little in common. Eliza has been raised to work hard on the farm and to enjoy her time outdoors; Mary, to stay indoors, and sew or play. Mary cries when she does not get her way, and Monica always comes to her defense. I do not blame my daughter for avoiding her cousin whenever she can, but still, I expect her to be kind.

Most days, Eliza follows Joseph outside, helping in the garden and with the animals. She loves to sit with him while he milks the cow or help him hunt for the hen's nests and the eggs they hide so well. Joseph teases her that she is a better partner than anyone else. Privately, he compares her to Franz who has no inclination to do farm work. I shush Joseph, afraid Monica might hear, but silently I agree with him.

Franz' skills as a farmer leave much to be desired. A man accustomed to business and not the physical labor the farm requires, he has never cleared land or dug stumps. Nor does he desire to do so. Franz does prove to be an excellent hunter. Because his wife is not satisfied with the meats the farm provides, he volunteers to look for game. Fresh meat supplements our diet, and Franz enlivens mealtimes with outrageous tales of his prowess and aim. As much as Monica complains, Franz brags. I love my sister despite her faults, but her husband is another matter.

Our household is strained and when Joseph announces at supper one night he must make a trip to the land office in Newnansville to settle some problems with his land claim, my temper flares.

"Monica's baby is due in less than a month. I will have much work to do. We will need your help. Can't it wait?"

"No. I have to go now. If I don't get our patent for the land, someone else may take it from us. It is much more valuable now that we have the land cleared and a house built."

Monica interjects, "I don't see anyone else trying to settle in this God forsaken place. You don't have anything to worry about."

I try to ignore her and continue the conversation. "How long will it take you Joseph?"

"It is about one hundred and fifty miles. I will have to walk. Newnansville is inland, and I cannot go by boat. It will take me a week to get there unless I catch a ride with someone in their wagon. At least one day in the land office. I should be home in two weeks or so."

Franz interrupts our discussion. "I want to see more of this territory. I might even find some land to call my own. I think I will go with you."

Monica stands up from the table and knocks her chair over in her haste. "Franz, I forbid you to leave me here alone! You can go another time. The baby will be here soon."

"We'll be home in plenty of time. Besides Joe needs my company. Who knows what might be out there. A man alone is no match for this country. Joe needs a man handy with a gun at his side."

Monica stomps out of the kitchen, but Franz shrugs off her concern and reaches for her plate to finish the dinner she left in anger.

Despite my pleading not to leave us alone, Joseph and Franz leave early the next day for the land office. Monica is no help to me and I must rely on Eliza. I worry, I put too much pressure on her. She is only four, but her assistance is necessary if we are to survive. If only they had left at least one man to help me!

Rising early each morning, I begin my list of chores while everyone else still sleeps. I slip out the back door of the cabin to the small round pen where the cow and her calf live. From that first cow and calf tangled in the bushes, our small herd has grown. They roam free on the island, and Joseph marks each with our brand, the letter "A". There are stiff penalties for taking someone else's cow so it is important that each of ours is marked. Joseph always keeps at least one cow and calf penned near the cabin as a source of fresh milk, butter and cream.

The current cow is a dull copper color with brown smudges on her flanks. As I approach the pen, I see my daughter is here first. *She tries so hard to help, even as young as she is. I must be more patient with her.* I step back to watch as Eliza crawls under the bottom pole of the cow pen and approaches the mother cow. She even remembers the rope which Joseph always uses to tie the cow up while he milks. My husband just walks right to the pen to the cow and swings it over her neck. Amused, I watch as Eliza does the same. At least she tries. The cow eyes her suspiciously and moves between her little grey speckled calf and the approaching threat. When Eliza raises her hand to toss the rope, the cow steps aside and Eliza misses. She pulls the line back, gathers it into her hand and throws it again. Over and over, she swings, but the cow dodges each time. Just as I am about to step in to help, the cow tires of the game. She lowers her head and charges in Eliza's direction. Eliza drops the rope and runs out of the pen. The cow's horns narrowly miss tearing her skirt.

I can no longer stand and watch. Hot and sweaty from the exertion, Eliza crouches outside the edge of the pen frustrated.

"Eliza," I whisper.

Despite my low tone, Eliza starts, so intent is she on figuring out how to catch the cow.

"You forgot one small thing. Put some corn stalks in the pen so she will stop and eat. Then, you can put the rope around her neck and catch her."

When Eliza does as I instruct, she is able to sneak up beside the cow and tie her to the pen.

"Has your papa taught you to milk, then?" I ask.

"No, Mama, but I think I can do it."

"Oh you do, do you? It is not as easy as it looks. A little like catching the cow." Eliza blushes. She has worked so hard and is so determined. *I shouldn't embarrass her.*

I smile. "Come daughter. I don't know if your hands are strong enough, but you certainly have the will to try. I will show you how."

I roll a log close to the side of the cow and sit Eliza upon it. Squatting behind her, I wrap my hands around hers and her hands around the cow's teats. I teach her to grip and pull as she tugs and twists. First a drop, then a stream of milk shoots into the bucket. Together, we rhythmically work the udder to almost fill the container.

"Now you try alone," I say. Eliza coaxes and pulls and adds some milk to the pail on her own. I know her hands must be numb and her shoulders sore, but I can tell she is proud of her work.

"Good job," I say. "Now, how were you planning on carrying that bucket alone back to the house?"

Eliza looks down at the brimming bucket. "Oh, I hadn't thought about it," she confesses.

"I appreciate your help, Eliza, but next time you want to try something new, talk to me about it first, please. You could have gotten hurt or wasted the whole bucket when you dropped it on the way back to the house." I can see the disappointment on her face.

"Eliza," I take her chin in my hand and lift her face up to meet my eyes. "I thank you for your help. This has not been an easy time. I am sorry. Together, we will get through this difficulty."

Eliza wraps her arms around my waist and buries her face in my skirt. I neglect my daughter. I should spend more time with her and not let all these trials get in the way of showing her how much I love her. She will only be little once. Soon, she will have a home of her own. I feel remorse for my sharp tongue as of late.

Then, Eliza's stomach growls. I laugh and say, "My goodness. That was so loud that I believe even the cow heard it!" The mood is lightened.

Joining me in laughter, Eliza says, "I am hungry. Can we have pancakes for breakfast? Can you help me carry this bucket to the house?"

I carry the bucket, and Eliza skips beside me talking nonstop about everything she sees. From flowers to trees to birds, my daughter has something to say about it. I must remember to pay more mind to her. I must remember to treasure these moments.

When we reach the cabin, a sound catches my attention. I reach down and put my hand over Eliza's mouth.

"Hush a minute," I say.

From the direction of the house, I hear a low groan followed by a scream.

"Julia!" The name echoes off the trees surrounding the house. Then, I hear the sound of little Mary's cries.

"Monica!" I exclaim. "The baby must be on its way!"

I begin to run. Half the carefully gained milk sloshes out of the pail onto my skirt, until I reach the back door of the cabin and set it down. I find Monica out of bed. Her nightgown is soaked in blood. I push Eliza outside with Mary. The girls must not see this sight. I help Monica change her gown and get back in bed. She screams and writhes in pain.

"Monica! Calm yourself. You have done this before. In a little while, you will see your baby."

"Never felt like this," she groans. "Not such pain. Not so fast."

Her face is ashen. Her eyes are clouded. Has she lost too much blood? I try to reach between her legs and feel the baby. She screams again and pushes me away. I hold her shoulders down and put my face inches from hers.

"Monica, stop. Breathe. This is not good for you or the baby. Let me help you."

Monica's eyes clear. "The baby."

"Yes, the baby. Think about the baby."

I do not know what I am looking for, but know that when my children were born, the midwives always felt for the baby's head. I feel nothing unusual, just wet, sticky blood. Hours pass as Monica's pain comes in waves. I try to get her to focus on the purpose of the pain, but by noon, fatigue takes a toll on us both. I sit beside her bed, eyes closed and wait for the pains to begin again.

"Julia," I hear her say. "Are you praying for me?"

I am ashamed to admit I was not praying. I might even have been asleep. Instead, I nod my head.

"You have been a good sister to me. I have not always been kind. Forgive me, Julia. I love you. Take care of my children."

I have longed for those words, but instead of pleasure, I feel fear. Is she giving up?

"I will take care of you, Monica. And in turn, you will take care of your children. Now, let's see if this little one is ready to make its entrance into this world."

The pains come faster and stronger. Monica grips my hand and screams as she tries in vain to force the baby from her body. Once again, I check the baby's progress. This time, I feel something, but it is not the head as I expect it to be. Instead, it feels like a shoulder. The baby must be breech! I think about the time I saw Joseph deliver a calf. Reaching inside my sister with one hand, I push on her abdomen with the other. Monica screams and then, faints from the torture.

The child still will not come. Once more, I push for her, hoping to adjust the baby's position. Finally, I feel the baby's head. Reaching around the neck, I find the umbilical cord holding the baby in place. As Monica remains unconscious, I feel the urgency to do something quickly. *Oh, God. I need you, God. Help me!* I unwind the cord from around the child and pull its body out of my sister. Finally, it slips onto the sheets. A girl, but her skin is blue. I slap her and blow her in mouth, but she does not awaken. She is perfectly formed just like a tiny doll, but the baby is dead.

I turn my attention to my sister. Will I also lose Monica? I set the child aside and place thick pieces of cloth between her legs to staunch the bleeding. Finally, the seep of red slows, but my sister still has not opened her eyes. *What will I tell her when she does?* I wash her as gently as I can. She has suffered much. I change the bedding and pull the blankets up around her shoulders. I wrap the baby in one of the tiny wool blankets Monica brought with her from Germany, and place her in the cradle beside the bed. Only then, do I allow myself to cry. *Why? Why do children, innocent as this one, have to die?* I remember my own boys, bright and happy one day, cold and dead the next. I cry for them as much as for this baby.

I do not indulge myself long. There are two other living children who need my attention. Where in the world are they? I leave the cabin in search of them, finally finding Eliza curled beside Mary at the spring. They both have been crying. I gently wipe their tears and help them into the house. I give them something to eat and say, "Eliza, take Mary upstairs and put her to bed. Then, come down and sit with your aunt while I go outside for a while. I have something I need to do."

"Is the baby born, Mama? Is it a boy or a girl?"

I choke on my words, but try to sound as normal as possible. "A little girl. She sleeps. Look here, Mary, Eliza." I point to the cradle. "Now, be good girls. Mary, take a nap. Eliza, watch over your aunt. I will be back soon."

As I exit the house, I pick up a shovel from the back porch. I have to dig a grave.

Chapter Thirteen

Days roll into night and become day again. I am exhausted, but I tend to my sister who still sleeps. Eliza does what she can to help, keeping Mary occupied and out of the room. Mary does not understand why Monica does not wake. Sometimes, I let her come into the room and rest quietly next to her mother. I hope her presence will help Monica remember she has another child that needs her. I try not to think about what may happen to my sister or where the blame lies for her condition. If I had not begged her to come or Joseph to go get her, she would be healthy and holding her new little one in New York. I am responsible for bringing her to this wilderness, and the voyage probably contributed to her distress. The baby's life was in my hands, and I squandered it. Will Monica die as well?

On the fourth day, Joseph and Franz return. Although he is tired and dirty from his travels, I immediately send Joseph to Manatee to find a doctor. As much as I hate to ask for anything from the people of Manatee, we need help.

"I doubt I can convince Dr. Braden to come back with me, but I will try. You know he came here to get away from the practice of medicine."

"Tell him it is life or death. He must come," I urge.

Grief stricken, Franz tries to take the blame for the baby's death from me.

"I should have been here! I never got to see my baby, and now I might lose Monica too."

He wails and grabs his surviving daughter so tightly that Mary screams in fright.

He must stop these hysterics!

"Franz, no! You are scaring her! Calm down. Your wife needs you. There was nothing you could have done. The birth was a long and difficult one. She lost much blood. Now, give your wife a reason to live. Go and talk to her, quietly and gently. She will recognize your voice and hear you. Tell her she must wake up and live!"

Despite my instruction, Franz falls over his wife's body weeping loudly. Mary cries harder as well so I send Eliza to take her on a walk to the spring.

By the time the girls return, Franz has calmed. He sits by his wife's bedside, whispering in her ear and brushing her hair as we wait for the doctor.

When Joseph returns, he shakes his head. "Dr. Braden was not at home. I went to the Gates' and to Mr. Gamble's but no one knows where he is. The doctor's housekeeper said he went hunting. She gave me some medicine that will help to make Monica stronger. I am not sure I trust her, but it is all we have right now."

I open the bottle and sniff the thick black liquid. It smells like whiskey to me, but I cannot think of anything else to try.

"Franz, shall we give her some?"

"Let me try," he replies. Reaching around his wife with one arm, Franz lifts her lifeless body off the pillow. He holds the bottle to her lips, forcing them open and pours a small amount into her mouth. It runs down the side of her chin and leaves dark circles on the bright white sheets.

This man is worthless.

"Not that way," I snap. Pushing him away, I take a teaspoon, fill it with the medicine and dribble one drop at a time in Monica's mouth. Still, she sleeps on.

Through the night, I continue to administer the medicine. Franz sleeps on the floor upstairs in our room. *What kind of man would sleep while his wife is dying?* As hard as that is for me to accept, I know that without a miracle, my sister will surely die.

Though I pray desperate prayers, make promises to God that will be hard to keep and offer my life in her stead, my sister has gone almost a week with no food. She cannot last much longer.

It is easier now that Joseph is home to help with the girls. He makes pancakes the next morning and tries to get me to eat some. I cannot take my eyes off my sister. I feel something is different. Her eyes begin to flicker and open. She is awake! *Is this the miracle I prayed for?*

I call to Joseph. "Get Franz, she is awake."

Taking the stairs two steps at a time, Joseph rouses him. The girls come in as well. Eliza hangs back, but Franz puts Mary on the bed beside Monica. Monica's words are slurred and low, but she manages to say, "Take care of my baby."

Do we tell her the baby is dead? Before I can decide, Monica's eyes close again. She stops breathing.

Franz cries, "Monica, no Monica. How can I live without you?"

Startled, Mary screams.

"Eliza, come get Mary, quickly!" I call. With Joseph's help, I remove Mary from the room as Franz gathers his wife in his arms, sobbing and calling her name.

I rest my hand on his shoulder. "It's over Franz. She is gone. I am sorry."

Another graveside. This one larger than the last. At least I did not have to dig this hole. We do not have a minister, so Joseph attempts to comfort us with a few words. We repeat Psalm 23 together:

> The LORD is my shepherd; I shall not want.
>
> He maketh me to lie down in green pastures: he leadeth me beside the still waters.
>
> He restoreth my soul: he leadeth me in the paths of righteousness for his name's sake.

> Yea, though I walk through the valley of the shadow of death, I will fear no evil: for thou art with me; thy rod and thy staff they comfort me.
>
> Thou preparest a table before me in the presence of mine enemies: thou anointest my head with oil; my cup runneth over.
>
> Surely goodness and mercy shall follow me all the days of my life: and I will dwell in the house of the LORD for ever.

My tongue knows the words, but my heart is dead. Was the Shepherd with her as death took Monica? Was He with me?

As Joseph and I prepare for bed that night, I finally voice aloud what has been in my mind. I choke back sobs.

"If only I had not brought her here, she would still be alive. I was selfish and greedy. I asked for too much. I should have left well enough alone."

"It was not your fault, Julia," Joseph says, but I am too convinced to listen to his reason.

For many days I wrestle with my guilt. Whenever I see Mary crying for her mother, I feel ashamed. Franz, with head down and eyes damp, sits beside the two graves behind the house. That is my fault, too. I brought this loss upon all of us. Joseph says God had a reason for all of this. Well then, if God has a reason, why didn't He save Monica and the baby? Joseph says God loves us. Didn't he love them, too? Where is God and why didn't He do something to stop it? I try to listen, but cannot hear anything but the sound of weeping and the empty wind blowing through the trees.

My sorrow leads me to the kitchen. While I thought I had given up eating to make myself feel better, it seems natural once again to make a batch of cookies or to add a savory sauce to our meat. The girls deserve a treat after all they have been through. But, it is me who most often is comforted by a taste of home. I remember the days when Monica and I were young. Even our life with our uncle, hard as it was, seems like a fond memory. I hate our life here in Florida. If only I could turn back the clock to before the boys died. Before we left Bavaria. My skirt starts to feel too tight again. One day, Joseph comes around the kitchen door just as I cut a large slice of cake.

"Julia, what is wrong?"

What do you think is wrong? My sister is dead and it is my fault. At night I lie awake and listen to the howl of wild animals. I live in fear of being left alone in the wilderness. I owe a debt I cannot repay. We have no claim to this land that takes our every waking moment to keep going. My daughter's world is turned upside down because of the arrival of her cousin who is so needy. I have no friends, no neighbors. I am not even welcome at church. What do you think is wrong? That is what I want to reply, but I don't.

"Nothing, everything is fine."

"No, it is not. I know how you handle difficulties. You are going to make yourself sick as well. Then, what will Eliza and Mary do when you are ill?"

He is right. What is it that makes me act this way?

As though I asked that question aloud, he answers me.

"Julia, your life has not been easy. You manage the best you can and you have been a good wife to me and a mother to our daughter and aunt to Mary. Your sister's death was not your doing. Nor is Franz' despair. I love you, and I cannot stand the way you take so much on your shoulders. I know you worry about what will happen to us. You fret too much. There is a better way. Why don't you let go of your worries? I fear it is too much for you."

Just let it go?

"Joseph, if I don't concern myself with our futures, who will? If I don't work to make things better, who will? If I don't take care of our family, who will?"

My voice gets louder with each question. It is a good thing the girls are outside playing or they would come running to see what is wrong. I try to calm myself.

"I don't see anyone else helping us. If anything I think the people of this region are opposing us. Just look how much trouble we are having over your land claim. And the way they talk behind our backs. What are you going to do the day your daughter asks you what is a 'Dumb Dutchman'? No, Joseph, there is no one else to take care of us. I will do my best not to let my 'fretting', as you call it, interfere with our lives. And I will try to control my eating habits so I don't get sick. At least one of us needs to be able to get this family through the trials life keeps throwing at us."

My husband refuses to meet my words with anger. I think it would make me feel better if we could have a good shouting match. But, he keeps his voice low and steady.

"I did not mean to upset you. Listen to me just for a moment and listen knowing how much I love you. Julia, there is someone who cares. Someone who cares about the girls more than you and I do. Someone who holds this world and each one of us in the palm of His Hand. Julia, it is not me. It is not you that keeps us going. It is God. And you need to learn to trust Him."

I cover my face with my hands. *Did my husband really just say the solution to our problems is for me to trust God?* I lower my hands and push them onto the table.

"I trust God well enough. But do I really believe God will swoop down from Heaven and solve all our problems just because I say, 'Here they are?' God helps those who help themselves. And I intend to help us with all of my might. I've heard enough. I am going back to work."

"Wait, don't go. I don't know who said that about God helping us if we help ourselves, but it isn't in the Bible. God says He wants to help us. That He is the advocate for the poor and needy. Julia, just start small. Promise me something. Choose one thing. One thing to ask Him to help with. Then, let it go. Don't do anything else about it. Watch and see if He intervenes. Who do you think God really is, Julia?"

I just shake my head and return to the kitchen. When my first impulse is to get something to eat, I stop myself. Instead, I set some water on the stove to boil and begin gathering all the pots and pans to wash them. The noise as they bang together makes me feel a little better. I am so angry at my husband I could throw these pots at him. *Who does he think he is? "Just quit worrying so much, Julia." As if that is an easy thing to do.* The process of scrubbing calms me and slows my mind. I understand Joseph loves me and wants what is best for me. I will try to control my eating and give him one less thing to worry about. It is hard to do on my own, and I struggle with the temptation to give into my desires.

Over the coming days, I remember what my husband asked me to do. I can't get his words out of my mind. *Who do you really think God is, Julia?*

Who are you, God?

I decide to test God. Not in the way that I issue a challenge and expect Him to deliver. I don't tell Him some sign I want to see. It occurs to me before I met Joseph I didn't even believe in God, but under his influence, I wanted to believe. My first exposure to God's character was through him. In fact, my husband's kindness teaches me more about God than any sermon I heard preached. He never beats his faith over my head or demands I believe the way he does. He continues to show love and compassion even when I demand my way or impede his plans. He always thinks the best of me and wants the best for me. While he would be the first to admit his imperfections, it is in my husband's character that I finally glimpsed God.

As I work around the farm, I have time to think. Margaret's life and teaching built upon Joseph's example, but my faith will always be weak as long as it is built on theirs. I am too easily influenced by difficult circumstances or people who say they are Christians but do not act like Christ. I say I believe in God, but I do not live like I do. I always want my own way, think I know best and down deep, am afraid to surrender to what God wants for me. Unless I come to know who God is for myself, I will always have trouble trusting Him. I can trust my husband because I know him. Now, it is time for me to know God.

My husband might have thought he was challenging me to ask for something and watch God produce it. Instead, the miracle I ask for is the one thing that will change me. *Show me who you are God. I want to see.*

Not sure how to start, I remember the advice Margaret gave me so long ago. I go back to the beginning. Every day, regardless of what else I have to do, I set aside time first thing in the morning to read my Bible. I don't have a plan in mind, just randomly reading here or there. It does not matter what place I choose, one thing is clear, God is in control. He is always with those who love Him and He has the power to change lives. I find myself talking to Him as I go about my day. Asking for patience with Eliza. Safety for my husband. For help in completing a task. For willpower to stay away from the foods that are harmful to me. For direction in how I should live my life.

I feel calmer, less anxious and eating right is easier, less of a battle and almost natural. Sometimes, a song bubbles up out of me. Songs my mother used to sing. Songs I thought I had long forgotten. One of my favorites is Nun danket alle Gott, Now Thank We All Our God. As I sweep, knead dough or weed the garden, I proclaim:

> Now thank we all our God, with heart and hands and voices,
> Who wondrous things has done, in Whom this world rejoices;

Who from our mothers' arms has blessed us on our way
With countless gifts of love, and still is ours today.

O may this bounteous God through all our life be near us,
With ever joyful hearts and blessed peace to cheer us;
And keep us in His grace, and guide us when perplexed;
And free us from all ills, in this world and the next!
All praise and thanks to God the Father now be given;
The Son and Him Who reigns with Them in highest Heaven;
The one eternal God, Whom earth and Heaven adore;
For thus it was, is now, and shall be evermore.

As I sing, I feel my heart awakening. This closeness to God feels as though I have been here before. As though something that was missing has been returned. I like the change, but wonder if it is real. If it will last.

On a fall night, the moon is full and shines brightly in our window. It is so radiant I cannot sleep. Unlike other times in my life, when I lie awake worrying, I have no troubles on my mind. Instead, I feel compelled to leave the house. It seems ridiculous. Everything I fear most is outside. Especially at night. Snakes, panthers and alligators lurk there. Mosquitoes swarm in the dark and carry diseases. There might even be Indians or someone from the settlement who wants to harm us. Something waits for me. It is urgent that I go.

I ease out of bed. Joseph does not stir. I pull a shawl around my nightdress and slip out the front door. I stand on the porch for a moment while my eyes adjust to the moonlight. I follow its beam and head down the path to the bay. Not even spider webs strung across the path keep me from my goal. A deep need propels me forward. I hold my hand in front of me to brush the webs aside. Near the spring, I smell that same sweet fragrance from that first day when I arrived on the island. I have not smelled it since, but tonight the fragrance, a mix of lemons and flowers, fills the air. I follow it off the path.

Ahead of me, I see another light. I forget about snakes or insects. I want to know what glows so brightly. I gasp as a wall of white comes into view. Upon closer inspection, I see a mass of vines full of flat white flowers. They look like white morning glories. The smell comes from them. I have never seen such flowers in all my time here on the island. I wonder if they only bloom at night.

The perfume, the light, the unexpected beauty combine to make me faint. I collapse to my knees in a place that feels more reverent than any church. The flowers provide the incense. The moon, the candlelight. From within me wells an understanding of who God is. He is the Creator. He is Sovereign. He is Holy. He gives life and breath. He could kill me right now, but instead, He chooses to love me and wants to have a relationship with me. At the same time, I am reminded of my sinfulness.

"I am not worthy," I cry.

Then, I hear a voice. It may have been audible or just in my mind, I do not know. It does not matter. What matters are the words spoken over me.

"In me, you are made whole. Only in me. Not in your husband or your child. Not in your house or your work. Friendships will not make you complete. Neither will church or doing good. I am the only One who can satisfy you. You asked to know who I am. Julia, daughter, this is who I am."

I do not know how long I lie on the ground. I weep in sorrow for time wasted in the past. I weep in gratitude for answers to questions long asked. I weep with hope for what the future will bring. I remember the words of the prayer I repeated so long ago.

"I surrender," I say. "I give my life to you." Then, I make my way back to the cabin eager for a fresh start in my marriage, as a mother and in life.

In the morning, I think it might have been a dream except for the dirt stains on my nightgown. In daylight, I try to find the place where I encountered God the night before, but I cannot find it again. The blooms are not there. The fragrance no longer wafts through the breeze. I wonder if it was a temporary vision, but I vow the impact on me will not be short lived. Starting over is not as easy as I thought it would be that night when I worshipped in the bright moonlight. Though I long to be different, and my heart is indeed changed, there are still my old ways and habits to fight. I am not completely healed.

It is a constant battle in my mind to understand and do what is right. So many times, my own desires get in the way. Though I pray, I am not sure how to separate what God wants me to do from what I want to do. Listening to my husband's opinion sometimes helps. But, not all the time.

Winter comes. The sound of the wind gets stronger as it whips around the cabin and echoes in the chimney. Joseph and I huddle by the fireplace. Franz and the girls sleep upstairs in the attic rooms. Franz snoring wafts down the stairs. Joseph and I continue an argument that has come between us for several weeks. Ever since Monica's death, I have fretted over how to repay the debt to Colonel Belknap. I determined a solution, but my husband opposes me in my plan. The girls and I will go to live in Fort Brooke. I will work off my debt to the Colonel.

"Joseph, I know how this debt worries you. It makes me anxious too. If only I could have predicted Monica's death and how little help Franz would be, I would never have taken the loan from Colonel Belknap. I know you tried to warn me. At the time, it seemed the only way. I do not know how we will repay him except to follow his proposal."

"I do not like the idea of you going to live in Fort Brooke and working for the man, Julia. You are not a housemaid. Soon even our territory will become a state and no longer under the rules of the Federal government. You are a free woman and have a family and land of your own. We came to America for freedom, not so you could go into someone's service. The thought of you working for him like a servant disgusts me."

I cannot bear to hear the contempt in my husband's voice. I do not want to do this, but I must! I stand from my chair pushing it away from me.

"Don't you understand? I am not a free woman until this debt is paid back. The colonel's wife and son will arrive soon. They may already be here. He needs my help and if I go, he will forgive all of what is owed. I don't want to leave either, but I have no choice."

I speak louder than I intend so I soften my voice. It would not do to wake the girls. Joseph must understand.

"The girls will go with me. The move will not be all bad. Eliza can start school in Fort Brooke. It will be good for her to learn to read and write, and she can have some friends her own age. I feel badly she must bear the burden of Mary's loss. Mary clings to her so and it is not right that one so young should be like a mother. It will be alright. It is not forever. A year, maybe less, if the Colonel is transferred again."

I shiver. Is it from the cold or fear?

Joseph stirs the coals in the fireplace with a poker. The light of the fire flickers over the walls. I love our little cabin. We have worked hard to make a home here. But, I will not be gone long. I promise myself as much as Joseph.

"I don't want you to go alone, but I cannot leave the farm untended. Our claim is still tenuous. Until the numbers are corrected and the patent issued, I am afraid someone might take what is ours."

"Why can't we leave Franz here? I know he is not a good farmer, but he needs something to do. I am afraid he will give up and die he is so lonely for Monica. If he felt like he could help, perhaps, he would have a reason to live."

"Julia! He knows nothing about farming. This place would go to ruin in weeks under his care."

"What if he thought he was in charge, but we hired a man to do the work? Would that help?"

In his frustration, Joseph drops the metal poker on the hearth.

"That makes no sense. Spend money on a hired man in order to go and work off a debt to another? I know we must pay what we owe, but you are talking foolishly now. Come let's go to bed. We cannot solve all these problems tonight."

Despite what Joseph says, I see only one way to pay off the debt to Colonel Belknap. I cannot think about anything else until I convince Joseph to agree. Finally, Joseph concedes to taking us to Fort Brooke. He will leave Franz on the farm for the short time it will take to get us settled in the Colonel's house.

I gather what clothes and supplies we will need. I take my father's pocket watch and my mother's Bible. Perhaps they will give me some comfort. The leather of the Bible is stained by mold, and the pocket watch is pitted and worn. Even these things I treasure have been affected by this tropical wilderness.

Joseph loads our bags onto his small sailboat. As the shore slips away from view, I hold fast to Eliza's hand and she holds onto Mary's. I keep my focus on the cabin until the trees obscure my view. *I will be back. It will not be for long and I can come back here truly free.* The January day is cold and the icy wind pushes past my shawl and underneath my petticoat. The clear blue sky seems brighter on the water. I set my face forward and refuse to look back as we round Bird Key and enter Tampa Bay. As the boat cut through the waves, sea birds follow us and dip beneath the wake searching for food. They soar back into the cloudless sky as their shrieks echo over the sound of the wind. *What will Fort Brooke hold? Shops. Soldiers. School for the girls. Maybe a church. It will not be as isolated as the island. Not as much work. The days will go by fast. Perhaps we will like it. What will Mrs. Belknap be like? I know the Colonel. He is kind. I hope his wife is as well.* I shade my eyes from the sun's glare as I wrestle with my fears. Then I spot first one, then another cresting fin and set aside my worries in favor of just enjoying the moment. This day is too beautiful to waste worrying. I tap the girls on the shoulder and point out the approaching school of dolphins.

Chapter Fourteen

Fort Brooke, Florida 1845

The journey is long. It is late in the day when we finally arrive at Fort Brooke. The girls are asleep and wrapped in blankets in the bow of the boat. I am stiff and sore from sitting for so long and bracing myself against the waves. I wake the children, and we all eat some bread and cold ham. It will not do for us to arrive at the Belknap's hungry. Joseph steers the boat into the Hillsborough River and threads among clumps of mangroves and small islands dot the waterway.

I can see the long low barracks, larger homes for officers and small shops serving the settlers and soldiers from all along Florida's west coast. How the fort has changed! So many new buildings! It is so noisy. After our quiet island, the sounds are loud and unexpected. Sailors shout to each other. Somewhere a ship's bell clangs loudly. Creaking and thumping emerge from deep within the ships as workman load cargo from the docks. The sound of hammering drifts from the shore and the many structures under construction. We feel, as well as hear, the blast of the cannons from Fort Brooke where soldiers practice their aim.

Eliza is very interested in the horses. She smiles when one whinnies from the shoreline and eagerly watches a pair of muscular black horses pull a wagon along the riverbank. Upon docking, we discover the team is waiting to take us to the Belknap's home. I have to restrain Eliza from touching their soft noses. She insists if she stands on her tiptoes, she can reach them. I will have to warn my daughter about approaching strange horses, but not now. Mary is tired and cranky so I make Eliza sit with her in the wagon while, along with the wagon driver, Joseph moves our things from the boat to the wagon.

When Mary whines, I tell her to hush, but she continues to sniffle. Eliza sits, arms crossed, and scowls at us both. When Joseph and the driver are finally aboard, the wagon jerks forward. The jolt shocks Mary into silence. With a look of wonder, Eliza uncrosses her arms and grabs the seat to hold on. *Two such different girls. What will they be like when they are grown?*

As the vehicle bumps and lurches over the rutted sand roads, we all crane our necks and gawk. There is so much to see. Soon, we leave the activity of the docks and enter a forest of tall pines. The trees sway in the wind making a humming sound. Mary's head grows heavy, and she stretches out on the wagon bed. Joseph questions the driver, a young yellow-haired soldier named Patrick who speaks with an Irish accent.

"We have Colonel Belknap to thank for this fine road," Patrick says. "He's an engineer and loves to plan and build. What men haven't been sent down to the Everglades to chase ole Billy Bowlegs are put to work everyday clearing land and building roads. I'm sure glad I got this duty though. It is a lot better driving a wagon and taking care of the Colonel's horses than chasing Indians through the swamp or dodging rattlesnakes and clearing stumps." Patrick continues to explain. "You'll see some Indians for sure at Colonel's house. They often come for dinner. He's always entertaining one or the other trying to convince them to pack up and move west."

"Indians!" Eliza interrupts. "There are Indians here? I've never seen an Indian!"

I frown at her, silently reminding her little girls are to keep quiet around strangers. She was too little to remember the Indians we met when we first came to Fort Brooke, but I recall their brightly colored clothes. Patrick describes them to Eliza.

"Oh, wait until you meet Billy Bowlegs. Holata Micco's his real name, but everyone calls him Billy Bowlegs because his legs are so short and squat. He dresses real colorful. Wears a head band with lots of feathers sticking up. A dandy he is. Oh, here we are. Mrs. Belknap's been waiting for you. Whoa now!"

Patrick stops the team and jumps down to help me out of the wagon. Joseph lifts the still sleeping Mary and hands her to me while Eliza prepares to jump down on her own. *I have been neglectful in teaching my daughter manners.*

"Eliza!" I whisper. "Wait for Papa to help you. Smooth your hair and straighten your dress. We want to look proper when we meet Colonel Belknap's wife."

A short, plump woman rushes out of the house. Her head bobs up and down. If I hadn't been so nervous, I might have laughed. She looks just like a sea gull as it rides from one wave to the next.

"Come in, come in! You must be exhausted. Oh, look at the little one, sound asleep. Bring her inside. Your rooms are upstairs. I'm Anna Belknap. Julia I presume? And these are your daughters? Come in, come in! Oh, we are glad you are here."

Addressing Patrick, she says, "Thank you Private. Bring their things in."

Anna Belknap talks in a long steady stream of words. They flow effortlessly. It doesn't even seem like she needs to breathe. Mrs. Belknap races up the stairs with a speed that surprises me. Carrying Mary, I can hardly keep up. I urge Eliza to hurry. I tuck Mary into a cot inside a small room at the back of the house. I expect she will not stir again until morning.

"Eliza, rest a while and stay with Mary while I get our things put away and find out what Mrs. Belknap wants me to do. There's a good girl." Eliza fusses. I can tell she is tired but, knowing my daughter, she does not want to admit it. I help her onto the cot and underneath the sheets that are both soft and crisp at the same time. *Mrs. Belknap is a very good housekeeper. Will my skills meet her standards?* I pull the quilt over Eliza's shoulders and wait for a moment until her eyes close and like Mary, she sleeps.

On my way down the stairs, I hear the sound of men's voices. The conversation comes through a set of large windows at the bottom of the stairs. I see Colonel Belknap. Beside him stands an exact replica of himself only younger. The two are obviously in a heated discussion.

"Father, I want to go south with the other men. They tell me there are many interesting things farther down the coast," the younger man exclaims.

Colonel Belknap shakes his head. "Willie, you have schoolwork to do here. It will not be long before it will be time for you to go to college."

Turning away from the house, he declares, "You may not go."

His son follows him, "Father, I can discover so much more traveling with the soldiers. How will I learn what I will need to know in the military by reading? This is a scouting opportunity. I will learn more engineering and field work than I ever can in my room with a table full of books. I cannot afford to let this chance pass."

I am shocked at the younger man's persistence. He should not talk back to his father, much less a military man. I am sure Colonel Belknap will punish him.

"Willie, I said, no! Go get cleaned up. It is almost time for dinner," Colonel Belknap growls.

Attempting to win his father over one last time, Willie softens his voice. "Please, Father. I will be careful. I long to see something else besides this part of the territory."

In an even, firm voice, Colonel Belknap replies, "Son, do not ask me again."

Colonel Belknap enters the house. The boy's head drops and he walks away.

That will be the end of that. Such boldness from a son. I hope my daughter never speaks to me that way. There is much to learn about this family.

I discover if there is anything to be learned, I only have to listen. Mrs. Belknap talks constantly as we finish preparations for dinner. By the time dinner is ready and on the table, I know the Belknaps have two married daughters and that Willie, their son, is sixteen. Mrs. Belknap worries about him being in the wilderness so far from good schools and tutors. She is not sure he will be able to pass the entrance exams for Princeton College. She is even more concerned about his lack of interest. His father will be so disappointed if he is not accepted.

"All he talks about is Florida. He wants to travel around the peninsula and see it all. He would like to join the military right now, but William is urging him to wait until he finishes college so he can enter as an officer. Willie does not care about position. He only wants adventure."

While the family dines at the big table in the dining room, Joseph and I eat alone in the kitchen. Mrs. Belknap insists we join them at the table, but I refuse her offer. Best to set the ground rules now. I am hired help, not the lady of the house. Joseph senses my unease.

"Julia, are you sure you are doing the right thing? It is not too late. You can come home with me tomorrow."

"As hard as this is, as much as I want to go home with you, I must stay. I will pay off this debt and come home as soon as I can." I try to smile, though it is a little wobbly. "The time will pass quickly. You will see. Mrs. Belknap seems nice enough. I just hope I can keep up with her." At last I can laugh at Mrs. Belknap's mannerisms. Joseph joins me after I tell him how much I think she looks like a sea gull!

Our laughter is interrupted by a knock at the door. I am still not sure of my place, but as housekeeper, I imagine I am expected to open the door.

I step back when I realize an Indian stands upon the stoop. He wears an intricately patterned shirt with silver coins hanging around his neck. There are feathers in his hair! I stifle a scream as Colonel Belknap speaks from behind me.

"Billy Bowlegs! What brings you to my home tonight? I bet you knew it was dinner time, didn't you! Come, come. Willie, get another chair. Anna, set another place at the table. Billy, have some mashed potatoes."

Anna is not the only one who can give orders. I nod to the Indian Chief and make my way back to the kitchen.

After dinner, the Indian Chief asks to speak to Colonel Belknap. I clear the table while they talk. I try to be quiet and stay out of their way. I want to know what the Indian has to say, so hope the Colonel will not ask me to leave.

Billy begins by saying, "You know why I am here, don't you?"

"Now Billy, it will be a better land for your people. There will be more space for each man to have a place of his own. No more crawling through swamps and living in competition for fish and game."

I hear regret in his voice as Billy Bowlegs replies, "This was our land. Once there was enough room for all. No man needed a place of his own. Together, we live and share all we have. My people do not want to leave, but I see we have little choice." He rises to leave.

"Thank you for dinner." He nods to me. I can see the sadness in his eyes.

"Billy, this is Julia Atzeroth. She will be staying with us for a while. She is a fine cook so do not hesitate to come back and join us for dinner anytime."

One thing I do know, food makes everyone feel better. "Yes, please do come again." I smile.

The next day, Joseph returns to the docks to begin his journey home without us. I know he will purchase a few supplies before he leaves. Our parting is bittersweet. He hugs the girls and holds me close whispering in my ear, "I love you. Are you sure you don't want to come with me?" *Oh, I do, but I cannot. Please understand.*

I shake my head, hug him one more time and send him on his way.

I miss my husband very much though the work keeps me busy and occupied. The girls seem happy. Mrs. Belknap pampers Mary, and Eliza makes a friend in Chief Billy who visits frequently, always in time for dinner. He even takes her for a ride on his horse which thrills her. That is all she can talk about for days. Soon, it is time to enroll Eliza in school

Eleven heads swing around to face us as we enter the classroom on Eliza's first day at school. She stops in the doorway and I must pull her by the hand to propel her forward into the room. The teacher, a tall, thin, balding man walks towards us.

"Good morning, Sir," I say. "I would like to enroll my daughter, Elizabeth, in your classroom. Please."

He looks over his glasses and down at Eliza. She leans against my side.

"How old is she?" he says with a nasal tone. Sniffing he adds, "She looks too little for school." Eliza is small, but she is smart. I am sure she will do well if given the chance. Eliza does not help matters by shrinking lower and acting younger. I swear she is trying to make him reject her. Twisting my skirt and pressing her face into the navy cotton, she imitates Mary's babyish habits.

"She is five but will soon be six," I persist. I grip Eliza's shoulder tightly and push her upright. I know it hurts, but I will not tolerate such nonsense. Eliza must go to school! This is America, the land of opportunity! How can a woman, even a little girl, make her way without knowledge?

Eliza stands straight and rubs the bruise. *That's better.*

"Eliza is very quick, and is ready for school. We just arrived and will only be here for a few months. We are staying with the

Belknaps, and Mrs. Belknap speaks highly of you and your teaching."

"Mrs. Belknap?" Suddenly, the teacher seems interested. "I don't often take girls, especially so young, but if Mrs. Belknap recommends Elizabeth, then I accept her as my student." *So Mrs. Belknap will be our ticket to education? I will take whatever help I can get.*

He extends his hand towards me.

"My name is Mr. Harvey. I charge twenty five cents per month. School will be in session until the first of May when we break for the summer. But, I expect Mrs. Belknap told you that already."

Looking around the room, I hope someone will be kind to my daughter.

Mr. Harvey gestures to a vacant seat. An older girl with a long dark braid, twisted in a knot at the nape of her neck, slides over to allow Eliza room. As Eliza squeezes in beside her, I pay the school master and thank him. I wish I could stay with my daughter, but that will make things worse for her. I ignore the impulse to wave at her as I leave. *Please God, let her have a good day. Let her make a friend.*

I stay busy throughout the day, ironing and preparing meals. I have a few minutes to dust and teach Mary, as young as she is, to rub a dust cloth around the baseboards. I might have to do it again, but at least it keeps her out of my way, though I have to fuss at her for whining. At three thirty, I leave her napping with Mrs. Belknap's promise to keep an eye on her. School is dismissed at four o'clock and I don't want to be late picking Eliza up. I am eager to hear all about her day.

I almost weep when I see her come out of the school. I did not realize how much I would miss her! How silly I feel. *Julia, pull yourself together, it was only a few hours!*

The older girl that Eliza was sitting with, introduced herself. "My name is Amy. I know where the Belknaps live. I go right past there on my way home. I can walk Eliza back and forth each day. It will save you some time."

Oh, she's made a friend already. I accept Amy's offer and am grateful Eliza will have companionship.

"That would be kind of you, Amy." I smile. "I appreciate your offer very much." The other girl calls good bye as we leave the schoolhouse.

"So, you have made a friend. That is nice. She seems like a good girl. I told you school would not be so hard."

"I think she only wants to meet Willie," Eliza complains. *I hope that is not true, but perhaps the friendship will grow.*

"Oh Eliza, don't be silly. Be grateful that you have a friend already."

The next morning, Eliza does not want to go back to school. I refuse to listen to her complain she is sick and send her with Amy when the older girl arrives. *Perhaps Eliza was right about her offer to escort my daughter.* Amy peers through the doorway as though she looks for someone.

That afternoon, Eliza confesses school is too hard. I encourage her as best as I can and force her to keep going to class. Oh, how I wish I could keep her at home. Helping my daughter grow is as hard as the day I gave birth to her. I pray as she leaves the next morning her friends will be true and her studies will go well.

The days merge together. I worry about Eliza who gets quieter every day. The schoolwork seems to be a strain on her and even though she is escorted home by Amy and a group of giggling girls every day, she does not seem happy. Finally, I ask her what troubles her.

"I miss Bonaparte."

"Bonaparte?" I ask. "Are you sure that sad face every day is for Bonaparte?" Crying, she tells me about school. Mr. Harvey is strict. The boys are mean, and the girls are nosy.

"I want to go back to the island," she wails. "Please may I go home? I will help with the farm. I don't need to go to school."

I gather her on my lap and hug her tight. "Eliza, I know it is hard but this is something you need so you can grow up to be a fine lady. Your Papa cannot read or write. When he does business, someone else has to read to him because he cannot read. Nor sign his name. Do you know how he longs to have the opportunity you have? Or how embarrassed he is when he places a mark instead of a signature? He never knows if what he is signing is true. You have such an opportunity to learn to read and write. When you do, you can help your Papa with his business dealings."

"If I learn to read and write, can we go back home then?"

"Learn your numbers as well, and I promise we will go home. Now, dry your tears and blow your nose."

From that day on, Eliza set her mind to her tasks. I had not realized how unhappy she was, but I admire my daughter's perseverance. I also learn what motivates her. I did not understand how much she loves the island. *She has a lot of her father's stubbornness in her!*

One Saturday night, Mrs. Belknap invites us to join them for church the next day.

"We do not have a large congregation, but a few of the settlers and some of the soldiers come. The circuit rider is in town, so we should have a good sermon. Some of the men often take a turn, but we will have real preaching tomorrow."

Church! My last encounter with a church did not go well. Reluctant to turn down Mrs. Belknap's offer, I hope things will be different. The next day, I dress the girls in their best calico dresses. I smooth the hems down. They have grown so much; the dresses are almost too short.

"I wish your feet were not so stained," I sigh. "Both of you girls ought to have shoes, but that is a luxury we cannot afford right now."

I tie their bonnets on them. Eliza squirms, she hates to wear a hat, but Mary primps in the mirror when I am done. *Such different girls,* I think again.

Everyone, even Willie and Colonel Belknap, gather at the wagon dressed in their finery. Once again, Patrick drives the wagon, but today, in the presence of his commanding officer, he is quiet. In fact, a solemnity reserved for a day of worship surrounds our entire group. Even Colonel Belknap does not joke and laugh. *I hope people will be kind.*

Church is held in the schoolhouse. The benches are very hard. I understand one reason school makes Eliza so miserable. I am uncomfortable being back among so many Christians, but I remind myself God is not always found in the hearts of His people. I should not base my image of Him on humans and their failings. We do not sing any of the German hymns so familiar to me, but new English ones. One is called, "God Our Help in Ages Past." In particular, I love the final verse, "O God, our help in ages past, Our hope for years to come, Be Thou our guard while troubles last, And our eternal home." Those words are very comforting, and I pray God will continue to be with me during our stay at Fort Brooke.

The preacher uses verses from Romans 12 in his message. "And be not conformed to this world: but be ye transformed by the renewing of your mind, that ye may prove what is that good, and acceptable, and perfect, will of God." I nod as he reads. *Yes, that is what I am trying to do, set aside my old way of thinking and trust God for everything.* He then goes on to explain that as Christians, we should be ready to work together for God's glory. God intends for us to help each other. He gave us each skills to share to build up the church, and weaknesses to keep us dependent upon each other. "For as we have many members in one body, and all members have not the same office: So we, being many, are one body in Christ, and every one members one of another." I feel both convicted for my harsh feelings against the congregation at Manatee and justified in my anger towards them. As if to answer my confusion, the pastor concludes with the following verses:

> If it be possible, as much as lieth in you, live peaceably with all men. Dearly beloved, avenge not yourselves, but rather give place unto wrath: for it is written, Vengeance is mine; I will repay, saith the Lord. Therefore if thine enemy hunger, feed him; if he thirst, give him drink: for in so doing thou shalt heap coals of fire on his head. Be not overcome of evil, but overcome evil with good.

I like the part about heaping coals of fire onto a person's head until the pastor explains it means our kindnesses to someone, even someone we consider our enemy, leads them to repentance not punishment. In my mind, I would prefer to see some people on fire rather than changed by kindness.

That afternoon, Mrs. Belknap and I sit on the front porch of their house. The girls sit quietly at our feet looking at books.

"What did you think of our church service today, Julia?"

"I want to go back and read Romans 12 for myself," I reply.

"There was a lot to take in in those verses," she says. "What impressed you the most?"

I decide to avoid my dilemma over how to treat the people in Manatee. "I liked how direct the Bible is in telling us how to live. Be kind. Do good. Abstain from evil. Love. Work Hard. Serve God. Hope. Be Patient. Pray. Give. Be hospitable. Those are all good ways to live."

Mrs. Belknap smiles. "Yes, they are admirable qualities in anyone, particularly someone who follows Christ. Tell me. Do you find them easy to do?"

I try not to, but a chuckle escapes. "No, I am far from able to follow that list. I start out with good intentions, but most of the time, I fall short. Usually even before breakfast!"

Mrs. Belknap nods in agreement. "Me, too. But, you know what I find that helps?"

I lean forward in my seat. Yes, I want to know.

"Doing it on my own, in my own strength, always results in failure. I might be able to keep it up for a while, but soon, someone will get on my nerves or I will want my own way. I can't do it myself. In another part of the Bible, it says, 'When we are weak, He is strong.' When I confess that I cannot do it alone and ask for God's help, He fills me with the Holy Spirit. Then, I can live as He calls me to live. Not in my power, but in God's power can I do those things."

I think about her words. *Didn't Margaret tell me this, too? Maybe that is what is wrong with me. I am trying to do it in my own strength. Maybe I need to ask God for more help.*

"That is hard for me to do. I need to be strong. That is the only way we survive out in the wilderness."

"No, Julia. You have it backwards. The only way you will survive is if you are weak and you let God do all the work. I don't mean the physical labor, though He can give you the strength to endure that too. But, the ability to act kindly, to be patient, to love and be generous."

I sigh. *Everyone says this, but do they know how hard it is to let go? Especially when I am not really sure God can be trusted? Look what has happened in the past.*

"There's something else you need to remember, Julia. That list is not a to do list you can check off and earn your way into God's favor. God loves you just the way you are, even with your strong temper and opinions. He loves you and calls you His daughter because of grace, not because of anything you have done. He gave you salvation, paid all your debts, as a gift. Don't think you have to earn it because of a list of ways to live. We strive to live that way to say thank you to God for what He already did for us, not because they are part of the deal. And we can ask for help as well."

Eliza and Mary begin arguing over a book, and our conversation is interrupted. I continue to think, not only about the ways we are to live our lives, but the fact that God gives us the ability to do so.

Mrs. Belknap has a chance to show me what she was trying to tell me when Willie does not appear at breakfast the next day. When Mrs. Belknap checks on him, she finds his bed empty and a note on his pillow. It does not say where he had gone; only that he will return in a few weeks and that his parents are not to worry. I suspect he has gone on his journey around Florida. So does Colonel Belknap as he tries to stop his wife's weeping.

"I told that boy he was not to go. I am sure he joined the expedition south. When I get my hands on him, he will be sorry for disobeying me!" *Colonel Belknap could use a lesson on consoling a grieving mother.* I miss Joseph even more right now.

Mrs. Belknap dries her eyes and says, "Husband, we must trust God to protect him and bring him home to us. God knows where He is even if we don't."

Chapter Fifteen

Weeks go by and still no sign of Willie. Although Colonel Belknap sends sailors out along the coastline, south of Fort Brooke, no one knows anything about a red haired boy. Mrs. Belknap misses her son, but says, "God will take care of him. I pray he is safe and will be home soon." I wonder at her strength, then, realize that it is a gift from God.

The Colonel still fumes, but life goes on. On March 3, 1845, Florida becomes a state. Word reaches Fort Brooke a few weeks after the vote in Washington. The soldiers march in a parade to celebrate the news, and Mrs. Belknap hosts a party afterwards. A few of the other settlers and some of the Colonel's officers and their wives attend. I bake several cakes and make sandwiches of ham and chicken spreads. The Colonel is partial to my deviled eggs, and potato salad so I add them to the menu. The party seems to be a success as I check to make sure the food platters stay filled. The women are in the drawing room talking about fashion. I can hear Mrs. Belknap describing a hairdo she saw in a magazine from New York.

The men are on the porch smoking their cigars. Some of them express displeasure that statehood was so long in coming. I listen as one of them describes the vote.

"The law brings Iowa and Florida into the Union and keeps the balance of power between the slave and free states. But, Iowa doesn't even have a constitution yet. How can they govern themselves? Florida could have been a state long before if we hadn't had to wait for them to organize. Mark my words, men, Texas will be a state before Iowa is. No matter that they don't want two slave states admitted at the same time. Everyone wants that land added to the United States even if we have to go to war with Mexico over it. Whether Texas is slave or free won't matter in the long run."

While the men seem eager for war, I hope Florida at least, will stay at peace. The Indians seem content to stay in South Florida. We haven't heard of an attack on settlers in a while. I have enough problems of my own to worry about. Eliza still hates school. She resolutely goes each day, but I know she longs to be back on the island with her father. I miss my husband as well. Some nights, I cannot sleep for wishing I could talk to him again. I would not have pushed so hard to come here if only I had known how much I would long for his company.

Yet, I have a debt to repay. I must keep the Colonel's household neat and food on his table. Unfortunately, with the strain of my new life comes a return to my old habit of comforting myself. Despite my resolve to live like Romans 12 says we should, my concerns about the future and the distance from my husband make me anxious. I fall back into overeating. The Belknaps love my rich cooking and the sweets I prepare for each meal. I keep the cookie jar full, but I am the one most often dipping into the supply. I know I should be more careful of what I eat. I could simply save them for the family and cook my own meals separately, but my daughter's unhappiness, my husband's absence and the sadness in Mrs. Belknaps' eyes are more than I can stand.

I remember what Margaret said about the Apostle Paul doing what he knew he should not and not doing what he should. Margaret said the only way to do right is to ask the Holy Spirit to help you. Mrs. Belknap echoed that belief, but now, I don't want to do what is right. I don't care what God thinks. I feel far away from the woman who encountered God that night in the moonlight. Many things have happened to shake my faith, and it has been so hard to trust God. I take back control of my life, and the emptiness returns. I eat to make myself feel better knowing all the while it will cause problems in the long run.

On April 13, I bake a cake for Eliza's birthday. I know my daughter wishes her father could be there to help celebrate, but it is unlikely he will make the journey or even know what day it is. Because it is a special occasion, Mrs. Belknap invites us to eat in the dining room with them. I warn both the girls to use their best manners and hope they will listen to me. After the meal, I put six little candles into the cake. One for each year of Eliza's life. How fast those years have gone! It seems just yesterday I first held her in my arms.

Everyone wishes Eliza happy birthday as I light the candles. I tell her to try to blow them out with one puff of air.

"If you can," I say, "your wish will come true."

Eliza takes a deep breath and blows as hard as she can. All the candles go out. Just then, a greeting comes from the front door.

"Mother, Father, I am home." Willie! Mrs. Belknap jumps up from the table and runs to greet her son. She holds him close and alternates between crying tears of joy and scolding him.

Colonel Belknap also hugs his son and says gruffly, "Where have you been? Your mother and I have been so worried. You have a lot of explaining to do young man!"

I try to intercede. "Willie, welcome home. Come join us for a piece of cake. It is Eliza's birthday."

"Really?" questions Willie. "Wait. I must get Eliza's present for her. It is outside. Just a minute."

Willie leaves the room and returns quickly. "Here he is! Chief Billy Bowlegs came to call on Miss Eliza Atzeroth just in time for the birthday celebration."

Now it is Eliza's turn to leave the table and race to Chief Billy. In her excitement, her words all run together. "Can I go for a ride on your horse, please may I? For my birthday? I wished two wishes. I wished for my Papa to come home, but I also wished for a ride on your horse!" Everyone laughs including me. *Oh, if only Joseph were here.*

"Now how about some cake," I say. Then, I hear a familiar voice. Will this day continue to bring surprises! It's Joseph!

"Papa, Papa! You're here! I get two wishes!" Eliza exclaims.

"And I get my wish, too," I say.

"Me, too," adds Mrs. Belknap as she hugs Willie. "It looks like we have a lot to celebrate today!"

While we all eat lemon cake with frosting, Willie tells us of his travels. "We went north to Cedar Key and then, overland across the state. We passed close by Fort King on our way to the Atlantic Ocean. The beaches are beautiful on the eastern coast, Father."

From there, the party traveled down to Lake Okeechobee, where Willie met Billy while on a hunting trip in the Everglades. He described how the chief recognized him and asked about his father. When Billy discovered the Belknaps did not know his whereabouts, he scolded Willie for his deception and insisted on accompanying him home right away.

"We rode for several days as fast as we could, Mother. I am sorry to cause you such worry."

Mrs. Belknap cries at her son's confession, but tears turned to laughter again, when Eliza stands up and begins to dance at Willie's next words. "I rode on an Indian pony too, Eliza. So now you have two horses to ride."

"Now, may I go, please Chief Billy? You can finish your cake later!"

In one bite, the Indian gobbles down his cake, scoops Eliza up and carries her outside for a ride on not one, but two Indian ponies. *My daughter could not be happier.* As I stand next to Joseph with his arm around my shoulders, I think. *And I got my wish, too.*

After her ride, I call Eliza into the house.

"You didn't open your presents."

We sit down in the Belknap's parlor to watch Eliza open her gifts. I hand her a package wrapped in brown paper. She carefully unties the string holding it together. It contains some beautiful pink flowered calico.

"It is time to make you a new dress," I say. "I saw this material and thought it would look pretty with your hair and eyes."

Eliza strokes the fabric and smiles. I am happy she is so pleased. She is growing up and becoming more concerned about how she looks. Now that we live in town around other girls, Eliza is learning about clothing and manners. Despite missing my husband, it is good for her to learn how civilized people live.

Mrs. Belknap holds the fabric against Eliza's face and enthusiastically agrees it will look lovely on Eliza. She says, "I have some nice lace around here somewhere that would make a sweet collar. I will see if I can find it. You will look just like a princess, Eliza!"

Joseph steps outside the room and returns holding a small wooden doll cradle. Mary's eyes light up with hope.

"Is that for me?" she asks.

"No, little one," Joseph replies. "This is for the birthday girl."

"Can't it be my birthday, too? I want a little bed just like that one!" Mary exclaims.

"Maybe on your birthday, you can have one, too. Today is Eliza's day," Joseph explains gently.

"How long until my birthday?" Mary whines.

"Five more months. Now let's let Eliza enjoy her new toy." Joseph hands the cradle to Eliza. Neatly made up, the bed is ready for a doll to rest inside. It holds a tiny quilt and pillow. Everyone exclaims over the fine workmanship. "It gave me pleasure to make as I missed my daughter and thought how much it would please her," Joseph explains.

I wonder at Eliza's lack of enthusiasm. I can see she is trying to be grateful, but I know something is wrong. I remember. She gave her doll to Mary when Mary first came to live with us. I will have to make her another doll. Perhaps then, she will appreciate the cradle.

Mrs. Belknap stands. "That cradle is missing something," she says. "And I think I know just what it is."

She reaches behind a chair and hands Eliza another present to open. Nestled in a white box, is a beautiful china doll. Her skin is so white and clean, her hair looks like real yellow hair, and she has pink rosy cheeks. Her little blue gown matches her eyes and she wears tiny black boots. She is perfectly dressed right down to her underwear. She is a little girls dream. I have not seen anything so beautiful since we left New Orleans.

Mrs. Belknap states, "She was my daughter, Clara's. Now that she is grown, I have been looking for a special little girl to give her a new home. I just knew you would love her!"

Chief Billy takes the doll from Eliza. The toy looks odd in the Chief's dark stained hand, but he gently cradles her. "Such a fine baby. It looks real! I want one, too. Where can I find one?"

Everyone is amazed at the Indian's reaction. Is he serious? Does he really want a baby doll?

"I am sorry Chief Billy. She came from New York City and was made a long time ago. I don't think you will find one like her here."

The Chief makes an offer to Eliza. "I will trade you my horse for her." *Oh, I know my daughter. That is exactly the gift she would love.* I catch her attention and shake my head.

Though I know it pains her, she kindly refuses the Indian's offer.

"No, Chief Billy. I love your horse, but this is a special gift I will treasure."

The Chief holds on to the doll tightly and continues his effort to barter for the doll "Two horses, then."

How will my daughter resist? Eliza does what is right. She reaches for the doll and declines.

"No, Chief Billy," she repeats. "Not for a dozen horses would I give up this baby. Perhaps someday you can have one of your own, but this one is mine." With that, she gently puts the doll to bed while Mrs. Belknap smiles and Mary sulks. *I have never been prouder of my daughter.*

Despite her refusal to trade, Chief Billy persists in his efforts to win the doll. We are all puzzled by his attention. The next morning, the doll is gone from its bed, and while we look all over the house, it is nowhere to be seen. Eliza promises me she knows nothing of its disappearance. I think she is secretly pleased it is gone. The mystery of the doll's disappearance consumes much time, energy and discussion as everyone looks and wonders aloud where she might be. Chief Billy has also disappeared. We suspect he took the doll, although Willie stands up for him.

"Chief Billy has a great sense of honor. He would never take something that did not belong to him. There must be another answer."

For a time, the doll cradle remains empty, until Mary begins to use it for the doll Eliza gave her. Joseph returns to the island right after the birthday party. The end of the school year arrives and with it, summer. Eliza is glad to be out of school, and her happiness should be contagious, but I feel listless and tired. At first I think it is the heat. Fort Brooke is much hotter than our island with its salty breezes. My stomach pain gets worse and so does the nausea. I try to continue my housekeeping duties. Sometimes, I double over and press my right side. I try to keep it a secret from the others, but Eliza notices. I am sure it will not be long before Mrs. Belknap discovers my frequent trips to the outhouse. I feel so poorly I am irritable with the girls and snap at them for the least little thing. When I look in the mirror, my face does not look right and my eyes have a tinge of yellow in them. One morning, I cannot get out of bed. I feel hot and feverish. Mrs. Belknap worriedly sends for a soldier to find the post's doctor.

Dr. Cooper sets his big medical bag on the floor beside my bed. Eliza stands in the doorway watching.

Mrs. Belknap speaks gently to Eliza. "Run down the hall and check on Mary. If she is still napping, go downstairs and wait. I promise I will come get you as soon as the doctor is done examining your mother." She pats Eliza's back and pushes her in the direction of the room she shares with Mary. After what she witnessed with Monica's death, I know my daughter is worried.

"Eliza," I call. "Don't fret. I am sure it is nothing to worry about."

Mrs. Belknap shuts the door leaving Eliza in the hall.

Dr. Cooper looks into my eyes and examines my skin. He pushes on my abdomen. I cannot help but cry out, "Oh, that hurts!"

Dr. Cooper shakes his head. "I am afraid it is your liver. Has this ever happened before?"

I think back to Germany before I met Joseph, to New York and New Orleans. Yes, I have had this pain before. I am ashamed to admit I know its cause. After some frank discussion and a lecture on self control, the doctor outlines a course of action to help me regain my strength and eliminate the pain. He warns the medicine might make me sicker in the beginning. I agree to take the medicine, but first I must ease my daughter's mind. I ask Mrs. Belknap to bring her to my room.

As they approach my room, I hear her say, "Eliza, honey, you can see your Mama. The doctor says it is her liver, and with a change in her diet and some medicine, she should get well."

Eliza asks, "What is a liver?"

Mrs. Belknap explains it is a part of the body near the stomach.

"Your Mama is a wonderful cook and has been making a lot of rich foods for us to eat. It has been too much for her. She needs a simpler diet and more exercise. Dr. Cooper will give her some medicine. It will make her sicker for a few days so I thought you might want to see her first."

"Why does she have to get sicker to get better?"

"That is sometimes the way things happen. Come inside and see your Mama and then, she must take Dr. Cooper's medicine."

I can tell the doctor's news makes Eliza feel better. She gives me a gentle hug and smoothes my hair just like I have done to hers so many times.

"Run along and play, my little nurse," I tell her. "I must drink some salty water Dr. Cooper made, and then lie in bed for a while. I hope to be better in a few days. Be a good girl for Mrs. Belknap and take care of Mary."

"I will Mama. Mama?" she whispers low so Dr. Cooper will not hear her from across the room where he is mixing what looks like little white rocks in a glass of water. "If Dr. Cooper can't make you better, Chief Billy can. Willie told me Indians know how to cure people too. I could give him my doll if I knew where she was. I want you to get better, Mama."

Despite my pain, I smile. Willie has been telling stories again and my daughter is desperate enough to believe them.

"I will be better soon. I won't need Chief Billy's help. Now run along."

I feel tears building in my eyes as she scoots out past the doctor and back into the hall. Oh, why do I do this to myself? Why can't I have more restraint! I've worried my daughter so!

The medicine the doctor gives me is punishment for my indiscretion. It makes the pain worse, not better. I curl up with my knees to my chest and moan. The pain increases. *I might reconsider Eliza's offer to find Chief Billy.*

Even if I wanted help from the Indian, he probably would not come. Mrs. Belknap comes to sit with me. While she knits, she talks. I really don't want any company, but I don't know how to tell her to go away without offending her.

"General Worth relieved LeGrand Capers, the Indian Office's removal agent, of his duties. Captain J. T. Sprague is taking his place. They haven't shipped any more of the Indians to the west for over two years now, but now that Sprague is in charge, that will change. William is sure the changes are going to force the Indians to make a move. I do not know what will happen to Chief Billy."

Despite a third dose of the doctor's medicine and a change in my diet, I do not get any better. The Epsom Salts in water is supposed to purge my body of all the poison in my liver, but it makes me even more nauseous and weak. My skin turns a brighter shade of yellow, and Colonel Belknap sends a boat to bring Joseph. He talks to the doctor and Mrs. Belknap. Afterwards, he sits beside my bed holding my hand, but saying little.

"Am I going to die?" I summon the courage to ask.

"I don't know. I pray not."

"Eliza thinks we should find Chief Billy and try some Indian medicine."

"That explains it then."

"Explains what?"

"I found her crawling around the floor of the parlor looking for that doll. She thinks Mary hid it. She thinks if she finds it she can trade Chief Billy the doll for the medicine."

At that moment, Eliza bursts into the room. She holds the doll in her hands, but it is dirty and dusty.

"I found it! I found it! Now Chief Billy can come and make you better."

Eliza explains the doll was stuffed underneath the sofa in the parlor. Upon questioning, Mary finally admits she hid it there to keep it from the Chief. Joseph scolds her and sends her to bed without supper. In my weakened state, I do not intervene, but considering my situation think withholding food might not be an appropriate punishment. When I am better, Joseph and I will have to talk.

Another week goes by. Joseph looks drawn and haggard. I know he is worried. Perhaps it will be better if I just die. I think of the girls. No, I cannot leave them yet. I remember a verse Margaret loved, "All things work together for good for those who love God and are called according to His purposes." *Will God use this to make me into the woman He wants me to be? Only time will tell. If I am given more time. Please God, give me more time. I will learn this time, I will.*

"I'm going to be sick again," I say to Joseph. He holds a basin under my chin as I vomit into it. I have nothing to expel. I am completely empty. As I lie back down, I catch my image in the mirror. I have lost so much weight. Even my hair, once so thick and beautiful, is thin and lifeless.

"It is so hot in here. I can't breathe." *Will this be my end then? Will I leave my daughter as my mother left me?*

I hear a commotion downstairs. Then, quick steps on the stairs. Eliza rushes into the room.

"Chief Billy is here!"

Mrs. Belknap follows behind her twisting her hands together. "I don't think this is a good idea, Julia. A man in your sick room, an Indian at that."

The Chief stands outside the door.

Eliza begs, "Mama. Papa. I think he can help. Will you let him look at you, Mama?"

I cannot speak. I close my eyes.

Joseph does not hesitate. "We have no more options. I will be grateful if you can help."

Chief Billy clarifies, "I am not a medicine man. I cannot heal. I only know some remedies. We will try them if you agree." I open my eyes and see my husband nod in agreement.

The Indian surveys the scene. He walks over to the windows and opens them allowing fresh air into the room.

"Where does it hurt," he asks. I am too weak to respond. Joseph answers for me.

"On her right side. The pain is great."

Turning to Mrs. Belknap, Chief Billy asks, "Please bring me a tea kettle full of hot water and a cup."

Mrs. Belknap hurries to do his bidding. We watch the chief pull a leather pouch from under his shirt. Inside are several different compartments filled with dried leaves and flowers.

Confident in the Chief's powers, Eliza pesters him with questions. "What are those?"

"Plants my people use for medicine."

"What plants?" she asks again.

"Beautyberry, Button Brush, Prickly Pear and Queen's Delight." Eliza repeats the names softly to herself.

"Where did you get them?"

"From the land. A gift from the Creator. To help his people."

Mrs. Belknap arrives with the hot water. Chief Billy mixes some of the plants into the kettle and lets them steep. Placing his arm around my back, he lifts me off the pillow.

Offering me a cup of the brew, he says, "This will calm your stomach and strengthen your body. The real cure is within you, not these medicines. You must get up and go back to work. Get out of this bed. Do not lie here any longer."

In melodious tones, he continues almost as though offering a blessing upon me, "You are a strong woman. This illness will not defeat you. You have much to live for. Be well and live."

I drain the cup and he gently places me back onto the bed. Turning to Joseph, the Chief says, "I will leave you more herbs. Make her a strong cup of tea and give it to her each hour. Soon, she will want to eat. Do not let her eat rich foods. Simple meals are best. An egg, some toast. Then, add vegetables and fruit. Take her out of this room and into the sunshine. She is not a woman to live like a weakling."

My breathing feels easier. I don't feel as feverish. For the first time in weeks, I feel hope rise. The Chief knows what will make me well.

Over the next several days, he comes regularly, always waving away my family's exuberant thanks. Eliza shyly offers her doll in exchange for the herbs, but the chief only smiles and looks down at her fondly. Taking the baby gently in his arms, he laughs and returns the toy to her.

"A beautiful gift, but I cannot take payment for the cure. I told you, I am not a healer." He continues in serious tones. "If you want to offer thanks, give it to the Creator who grew the plants and gave your Mama a will to fight the disease. Now, I must find Colonel Belknap. We must discuss the fate of my people."

Yes, I give thanks to God, and vow not to forget His help. In the moments when I have the least control is when He takes over. I must not let life get so dire before coming to Him for help.

Chapter Sixteen

The next day, I am able to go down for dinner. Leaning on Joseph's arm, I slowly make my way into the room. Mrs. Belknap flutters around me as Colonel Belknap and Willie rise out of respect. Eliza claps with excitement and Mary begs to be held.

Once I settle into a chair, Joseph picks up Mary and announces, "I have been talking to Colonel Belknap. As soon as your Mama is ready to travel, Eliza, we will be going back to our island. Once before, working the land made her strong. It will again."

Back to the little cabin and the spring. To Bonaparte and gardening chores. To the bay and the cows.

Eliza jumps up and down and shouts, "Hooray!"

What about the debt? I have not repaid the debt. In fact, I probably owe the Belknaps more for their care during my illness. I cannot go home no matter how much I want to go.

As if he reads my mind, Colonel Belknap shares news of his own. "I am being sent to Texas. Between the Indians and the Mexicans, there is much turmoil there. The settlers need the protection of the army. I will leave next month."

Frustration shows in his voice as Willie continues the tale. "I cannot go to Texas with father. Instead, I am to be sent back to New York like a baby until time to start college."

"Willie," Colonel Belknap warns, "We have been through this before. Let's not start it again. This is a happy day. Julia is getting better. The Atzeroths are going back to their island. Julia, the debt is forgiven. Come let's celebrate."

The next few weeks fly by. I grow stronger each day. Soon I am back to work, overseeing the packing for both my family and the Belknaps. Everything must be sorted as some of their things will go to Texas with the colonel and the rest will be sent to the Belknaps' home in New York.

I fret over what to do about Eliza's schooling. One morning, after breakfast, Mrs. Belknap gives me an answer.

"She is a smart girl and learns quickly," Mrs. Belknap says. "She has a good foundation. If you encourage her, she should be able to continue on her own for a while. I will give you some books to use. Someday, you may want to send her back to the Village of Tampa for school, but for now, these will do."

Perhaps that will work. I know Eliza will be happier if she does not have to go to school.

When Mrs. Belknap calls her to come and select some books to take home, Eliza reluctantly follows her. I don't think it will be as easy as Mrs. Belknap predicts to continue Eliza's education once we are on the island again.

Mrs. Belknap hosts a party to say good bye to all their friends at the fort and in the village. Though I cook huge quantities of food to feed the guests, I carefully restrain myself. *I cannot get sick again. It could interfere with our return home.* The guest list is a mix of ages, social status, and position. Patrick comes, though he is reluctant to enter an officer's home, and stays out on the porch and visits with the men.

I wonder if we will see Chief Billy again before we leave. As though I conjure him up in my thoughts, the Indian appears before me in the kitchen one night before dinner. I speak my question aloud. "Will I ever see you again, Chief Billy?"

"I know where you and the little miss live. Your island was once the home of my forefathers. You will see me again. I promise." He smiles, "You never know when I will appear. Now, would your daughter like one more ride on my pony?"

Eliza shouts with pleasure as he swings her up over the horse's back and leads her around the yard.

A few days later, we celebrate Mary's fourth birthday. Her real birth date was over a month earlier, but it was ignored during my illness. *Even she had to suffer for my mistakes*. As promised, Joseph presents Mary with a doll cradle of her own. Mrs. Belknap produces a tiny china doll Mary adores and names Pat, much to Patrick's chagrin. The big man blushes every time the little girl appears with her doll.

Terra Ceia, Florida 1846

Finally, the day comes to return home. It seems like longer than eight months have passed since our arrival at Fort Brooke. We wave farewell to Patrick and his team of black horses. Mrs. Belknap cries and places a handkerchief to her eyes. Joseph helps me into the boat and the winds carry us away as we leave the confines of the river and move into Hillsborough Bay. From there, we will follow the eastern shore of Tampa Bay, south to Terra Ceia. It will be good to be home again. I settle back against the bow of the boat and enjoy the ride.

In our absence, Joseph made many improvements around the cabin. A small dock now extends out into the bay so we do not have to climb overboard and wade ashore. Franz reaches eagerly for Mary but the little girl views him as a stranger. Cranky and tired from the long trip, she cries until I take her and carry her back to the cabin. Disappointed, Franz concentrates on unloading the boat. I feel sorry for Franz. Mary does not even know her own father. Maybe now we are home again, the two can get to know each other again.

The cabin looks the same but it is not clean. I sniff with disapproval. After Mary goes down for her nap, I start cleaning. Franz is not much of a housekeeper. When I go out back to shake the rugs, I see at least work has been done here. The vegetable garden has doubled in size! There will be plenty for us to eat and even more to sell in Fort Brooke.

Christmas arrives and brings my thirty-fifth birthday. How long ago it seems when I enjoyed my own mother's preparations. I follow her traditions and, despite being in hot, muggy Florida, try to make it as close to a German holiday as I can. Joseph cuts a cedar tree and brings it into the house where it stands in the corner of the room. Eliza and Mary place tiny white candles among its branches. On Christmas Eve, I light them and the room glows. The girls hang stockings above the fireplace and in the morning, they are magically full of treats, candy, hair ribbons, a top and a whistle Joseph carved.

Joseph gives me two gifts.

"One for your birthday and one for Christmas," he says with a flourish as he bows before me. I think we are both relieved to have the last year behind us. I open my gifts to find a tea pot in one package and a matching sugar and creamer set in the other. Made of white china, decorated with lavender violets and tiny green leaves, the pretty set brightens up the kitchen table. I skip over to him like a schoolgirl, kiss him on the lips and say, "Why thank you, sir! I love them."

Franz watches quietly from the corner of the room. Since our return, Mary refuses to bond with her father. In fact, despite efforts to teach her otherwise, she mimics Eliza calling Joseph, "Papa," and me, "Mama." Over time, Franz withdraws from family activities and spends more and more time away from home. He improves his skills as a sailor and takes on the job of delivering produce to Fort Brooke. I understand how lonely he must be here on the island, surrounded by memories of the deaths of his wife and baby and his surviving daughter's rejection, but am helpless to do anything about it.

On the first day of 1846, winter arrives. The cold wind and the grey sky keep us indoors. Franz retreats upstairs from where we can hear bumping and scrapping sounds as though someone is rearranging the furniture. I ask Joseph if he knows what Franz is doing.

"He is packing, Julia. Now, don't get angry. He is determined to go," Joseph says. "He wants me to take him to Fort Brooke as soon as the wind eases. He says he is tired of farming and wants to move back to the city."

"Will he stay in Fort Brooke, then?" I ask.

"No," Joseph states. "He plans to find a job in New Orleans. He wants to find a wife, Julia. It has been over a year since Monica's death. There is nothing here for him."

"What do you mean?" I snap. "He has a daughter here. We are his family."

"Really?" Joseph replies thoughtfully. "Think of it from his perspective, Julia. He sees how happy we are. His own daughter calls us Papa and Mama. What is there for him here? You must let him go. He is pining away and it is not good for him. He needs to feel like a man again and not be dependent on the handouts of relatives."

"Will he take her then? How can he care for her?"

"No, Julia. He will not take her. She is our daughter now."

Mary doesn't even seem to notice his departure. Time passes, and no word comes from Franz. One day, in midsummer, Joseph returns from Fort Brooke with disturbing news.

"I was talking to a sailor on the docks. He said there is an outbreak of Yellow Fever in New Orleans. Hundreds and hundreds of people have died. I fear for Franz, Julia."

When months pass and still no word arrives, I weep in sorrow, as much from the uncertainty of what happened to Franz, as from the loss of my sister. We once had such hopes for the future. I resolve to make it up to my niece who is now my daughter, and make every moment count. I want to be the woman God calls me to be. Yet, I am so busy with chores and taking care of the girls I often forget to read my Bible and pray. I remember what Margaret and Mrs. Belknap said about trying to live life on my own and how it can only result in failure when I strive to be good in my own strength, but taking the time to build the relationship with God is easier said than done. I am not a lady with servants to help take care of me. Who else do I have to depend upon but myself?

It does not help that 1846 brings so many problems. In addition to Franz' death, we have concerns about the other residents of the Manatee lands. Though we focus on making friendships in Tampa, we still hear things that make us uneasy. Several times, someone from the Manatee settlement drops by on their travels north, but we do not think that they come to pay a friendly visit. Instead, we feel like they are looking over our claim and the progress we have made. Though we do not hear about any Indian problems from the people in Tampa, the settlers of Manatee are quick to warn us about the possibility of attack.

"Rumors," Joseph says. "Only rumors."

"Why would they come here to spread them? Are they trying to scare us?"

Joseph just shrugs and keeps on with his work.

One of our visitors tells us of the death of little Ella Gates. She was only two and it is unfair she was taken so young. No one knows what killed Ella. She took sick and, without warning, died. Despite my distaste for the other settlers in our area, I feel sympathy for her mother, Mary. I hear she is out of her mind with grief. Her husband, Josiah, is concerned for her safety. I know what that feels like. I consider traveling to Manatee to try and console her, but decide it will do no good. I doubt Mary would listen to me even if her husband would let me in the house. *What does a "Dumb Dutchwoman" know?*

Two weeks after Ella's death, tragedy strikes our own home leaving me to wonder if I am being punished for my callous attitude. That morning, Joseph senses something is not right with the weather. A huge storm blows in without warning. We take refuge in the center of our house after Joseph shutters the windows and bolts the doors. One minute we sit in the hallway singing a hymn to drown out the sound of the winds and rain beating against our house and the next minute, we huddle under the limbs of a fallen oak watching our house crash into pieces. A tornado spawned by the storm blows our house down. All I remember is Joseph forcing us out of the house and under the tree.

"Julia, I do not know what prompted me to seek shelter there. It was as though I could not stay in the house. It seemed like danger was right upon us. I know it sounds strange, but I felt like a huge hand pushed me out and under the tree. I think it might have been an angel. God was protecting us."

I stand under the tree, soaked to the skin, shivering from fear as much as cold, as I look at the ruins of our house. *If God could warn us, He could also have stopped the house from falling down.* Still, I must be grateful. We would have died had we stayed inside.

Eliza cries beside me and rubs her forehead. Joseph explains as he rushed through the doorway, he knocked her into the frame. For once, Mary keeps still. I think she might be in shock.

In the wake of the hurricane, silence creeps over the island. The tornado sucked all the wind out of the sky and left a quiet emptiness. What about the animals? Not even a cricket or bird breaks the stillness. After the roar, the unnatural calm seems odd. Joseph gathers us all into his arms and holds us fast. My head is to his chest. I can hear the racing of his heart. I do not know how long we stay huddled together there. I wish this was all a bad dream. *If I close my eyes and then open them again, will I be back inside our house listening to the rain?*

I rub my eyes, but my mind refuses to comprehend the loss. It wasn't a dream. The wind finally dies. Joseph climbs on top of the tree before going down to the bay to check on our boat. The storm washed it on shore, but it is not damaged. He retrieves the canvas sails from the boat and stretches the fabric over the limbs, tying it in place to give us some shelter for the night. He finds a tin of crackers on the boat, and after a supper of crackers and rain water, there is nothing left to do but try to sleep. Joseph leans against a tree limb with Eliza and Mary in his lap and snores softly.

I cannot sleep. *What will we do now?* I feel Bonaparte's head as he pushes against my side trying to get comfortable. The moon begins to glow through the tree limbs. I see what once was our cabin.

What was that? I look closer. Something flutters high above my head. *A ghost?* I do not believe the tales of haunted spirits, but that scrap of white looks real and alive. I'm cold. Bonaparte draws closer. *Can he see it too? Is it a sign of what will become of us?* For a time, I watch the apparition until finally, with the dog huddled beside me for comfort and warmth, I sleep.

Bright sunlight casts shadows on the ground when I wake. I hear a bang and flinch at the sound. Then, a muffled curse. What is Joseph doing? Peeking out from under the tree, I watch as he lifts boards and stacks them neatly together. I move slowly and methodically across what was once our home.

"Be careful," Joseph calls. "Watch out for the nails and pieces of glass. Don't step on them."

I do not want to think about what happened yesterday. Maybe if I work hard enough, I will forget. I know the memory will not fade with this mess surrounding me. Every time Joseph drops a board into the growing lumber pile, I jump. As we lift the wood and move it out of the way, we ask Eliza to look for what might be hidden underneath. Soon, she has a small pile of metal utensils, pots and pans, a few crocks and some of her school books gathered. We pull quilts, sheets and clothing from the chaos as well. Looking up into the trees around the clearing, I see towels and clothing strewn in their branches like laundry hung out to dry. I laugh out loud. My ghost!

Joseph turns and smiles. "What are you laughing at?"

I point upwards and tell him of my fear. In the daylight, it seems so silly when we have so many other concerns. The storm was random in its destruction. Our bed stands upright, exposed to the sunlight, sheets and covers still intact. Yet the cabin is open to the sky, its second floor and roof completely gone, walls broken and the chimney in pieces. The kitchen table is split in two but my rocking chair rests unscathed beside it.

Despite our loss, there are no tears. We are numb and beyond weeping. Even Mary sits unusually still in the shade of a large oak. She clutches her rag doll, wide eyed, watching us work. As Joseph pries a log up and out of the way with a bar, Eliza gasps. Reaching gingerly behind a crushed chair, she lifts my still intact teapot into the air.

"Mama, look!" she calls.

I reach for the teapot and stroke its sides tenderly. I remember the day Joseph gave this to me. Who knew then what we would suffer today? Eliza rummages back into the mess and finds the sugar bowl and creamer. With its lid cracked in two, the bowl still holds a small amount of sugar. The cup is missing its handle, but perhaps at the end of the day, I will make some tea and be grateful the storm spared this reminder of our life before its attack.

Eliza asks, "Where will we sleep tonight, Papa? Will we have to be under the tree again?"

Looking around our homestead, Joseph says, "I think we have only one choice. There is only one building still standing." He points to the chicken coop. "Eliza, that will be your home for a while until I can rebuild our house."

I shake my head. "Joseph, it is nasty in there. The birds have made such a mess. How can I take two children inside? It is a wonder we are not sick already. We cannot sleep in there!"

"We can clean it up. We will stop looking for what we can salvage right now and make it alright. The day will get away from us. We have weeks of work ahead, and Eliza is right, we must think about where we will sleep tonight. I don't think we can spend another night under the tree. What if it should rain? Fall is here. It could turn cold soon. At least the coop will be warm and dry."

What Joseph says is true, but I am not happy about our situation. *What kind of God lets this happen to us? To leave the chicken coop and take our home? What have we done wrong to deserve this?*

Eliza finds the broom and a shovel in the pile of things she has salvaged. While she scrapes out the straw and droppings, I scrub the walls. Joseph makes a ladder and climbs on the roof to check for leaks.

"It looks like no harm was done. I can't see any damage," he calls down from above.

As I work, I try to make sense of our situation. Why did the tornado destroy the cabin, but leave the tiny little chicken coop standing erect?

While he is on the ladder, Joseph climbs up in the trees as high as he can go and pulls down the linens hanging there.

"The sun has dried them nicely," he says as he makes a pallet underneath the tree for Mary whose eyes droop in exhaustion. *I need to take a break and try to comfort her. Poor thing. If it is hard for me to understand, how much harder must it be for her? She has suffered so much already. We all have.*

"We need to be thinking of something to eat. Are there any crackers left? Eliza, did you find any food in your search?"

Eliza produces a tin of flour, one of coffee, another of tea and a jar of pickles. I add a dozen eggs hidden in the nest boxes.

"We had better enjoy these while we can," I say. "The chickens are giving up their home for us and will be left to roost in the trees for a while. It will be hard to find their nests now."

Joseph gathers some broken pieces of chairs and a portion of the porch rail that was crushed under the tree. He builds a small fire, and I fry the eggs in a pan Eliza uncovered in what had been the kitchen. Smelling the eggs cooking, I am suddenly hungry. Odd that I would not have felt the need to eat before now.

"Take a bucket and go get some water from the spring," I tell Eliza. Bonaparte follows her down the path.

The eggs are cooked and we are ready to eat, but our daughter still has not returned. *Probably stopped to play.* Irritated, I walk towards the spring after her. Things look so different. Trees that once stood straight and tall are bent and twisted in gruesome shapes. When I reach the spring, Eliza sits beside it crying.

"What is the matter?"

Between sobs, Eliza says, "It tastes bad."

I cup my hands and lean down to drink. I did not realize how thirsty I was until I suck in the water deeply. But, I spit it out. *What happened to our spring?* The water tastes bitter! Even Bonaparte will not drink it.

I remember water covered the yard during the storm. The bay washed inland and must have polluted the spring. What will we do for drinking water? This is the last straw. Finally I weep for what we have lost. I hold Eliza and we cry together. Tears flow from our eyes and mix with the salty water of the spring.

"Julia. Eliza. What is taking so long? Dinner is ready. Come let's eat."

Through my tears, I manage to say, "The water does not taste good. What will we drink?"

Kneeling beside us, Joseph samples the water.

"You are right. The bay water must have mixed in the pool. Well, no use crying over it. We will just have to wait. In a few days, it will probably be alright to drink again. Let's go see if we can find some rain water."

Ever calm, Joseph locates the rain barrel. Though tipped on its side, it still holds enough water for a day or two if we are careful. That night, after an emotional day of hard work, I hold my cup in both hands and drink tea before bed.

"Thank you for finding my teapot, Eliza. I am glad to have it. Doesn't it brighten up the place?"

It took effort, but I have done my best to make even the chicken coop a home and the tea pot sits atop one of the old nesting boxes nailed to the wall. From her pallet on the floor next to Mary, Eliza smiles.

"Night, night, Mama," she says drowsily.

"Did you say your prayers?" Joseph asks.

"No, Papa. I can't think of anything we have to be thankful for tonight. I miss our house."

Oh, daughter, you say exactly what I feel!

Joseph says, "Yes, Eliza, you have a lot to thank God for. Be sure to thank God for keeping us safe in the storm. And for this roof over our heads and food in our stomachs. And thank Him for leading you to your Mama's pretty little teapot."

Eliza sighs and does as she is told.

I listen to her prayer, but do not join in. What I really want to do is ask God why He let the tornado destroy the cabin and made us move into this chicken coop. Despite our efforts, it still smells like manure. Couldn't he have saved the cabin and knocked the henhouse down? I have some other questions I would ask God if I could. Why was the spring full of salt water when we need it to drink? How will we ever rebuild our cabin? Or replace all our things? With my head full of confusion, despite my fatigue, it is a long time before I can sleep. Even though I am in my own bed, I toss and turn for a long time as I breathe the scent of chicken dung.

Chapter Seventeen

We spend the next few days salvaging what we can. I do not see any hope we will be able to rebuild our house unless Joseph goes to Tampa to seek assistance. Before he can leave, surveyor, John Jackson, and some other men sail into the bay and anchor in front of what used to be our home. The waves during the storm washed away the dock, but the men do not seem to mind wading ashore. They greet Joseph with much backslapping and handshaking.

"Joe, I am so glad to see you," John says. "We have been hearing from other settlers that it was a terrible storm. I was worried about you. I am sorry about your cabin, but am glad you and your family are alright."

"Yes," agrees Joseph. "We are very lucky to be alive. If we had not gotten out when we did, I hate to think what might have happened."

I feel chilled again as I remember being huddled under the tree in the cold and rain. *What might have happened if we had stayed in the cabin instead of taking shelter outside? What if the tree had not fallen on our porch providing us a safe place to hide? Could Joseph be right? Was God in the storm after all?*

With the help of the men, we continue to clean up the remnants of the cabin and salvage what we can. The men also help chop the big oak that fell on the porch and set up a temporary kitchen under the sails strung between three trees.

At the end of the week, John says, "Joe, I need to move farther south. I have work to do and there are others I should see about. I will be back soon and we will help you rebuild. I have the contract to survey this island and the surrounding lands. I could use a chainman who knows these parts. If you want it, the job is yours."

Joseph looks at me for approval. Though I don't want him to go, I know that he is worried about how we will pay for the repairs. We can reuse some of the wood, but the glass windows, nails, and other materials will have to be replaced. I nod.

Joseph accepts John's offer.

"I'll be glad for the extra cash right now," he confides. "I don't want to get back into debt again, but it is going to take some cash to rebuild. In the meantime, we can stay in the chicken coop a little longer."

Leaving supplies and food, John promises to return soon. That night, before she goes to sleep, Eliza says her prayers without prompting. "God bless Mr. Jackson and help him to return soon so we can get out of this hen house!" she prays. *Amen,* I think.

True to his word, John and his survey crew return and bring with them nails, window glass, and other building supplies. He also brings a surprise for me, a stove!

"Julia, a good cook like you deserves a stove to prepare meals upon. I hope you won't mind taking on the task of cooking meals for my men while we are here. We'll sleep on the boat, but it is hard to cook a good dinner there. I went ahead and picked all this up while I was in Fort Brooke," he explains. "Joe, you can work it off and then, you don't have to waste time on another trip to town."

The men divide their time between surveying and construction. Some days, they leave early in the morning and are gone all day or overnight. At other times, they stay on the island and work on the new cabin. Joseph enjoys his new job and the chance to explore the areas around our home. Eliza and Mary like playing with the metal links that make up the chain Joseph uses to measure the land. It is good for Mary to have something to do. She is still very quiet since the storm. I work hard to reassure her everything will be alright. Playing alongside Eliza as they pretend to build their own houses, laying the chain on the ground in "rooms" marked on the ground, seems to bring her some comfort.

So does seeing our house rebuilt. With so much help, the new cabin takes shape quickly. It is an improvement over our old cabin with a chimney constructed of rocks instead of sticks. The kitchen boasts a wood stove in addition to the fireplace. Always the optimist, at our first meal in the new house, Joseph thanks God for sending the storm so we could have a stove. I am just glad to leave the chicken coop to the chickens that seem happy to have their nesting boxes back as well.

Even though the cabin is rebuilt, Joseph continues to work for John as a surveyor's chainman. He says it will be good for us to save some money for the future. "You just don't know what tomorrow will hold." *Oh, how I know that!* It seems odd my husband, who tells me to trust God, is so eager to fill our bank account. The reality is he enjoys travelling around our state seeing new places. Their job includes completing the survey of our area and one of the new Town of Tampa.

I do not mind when Joseph does work close to home, but in early 1847, Surveyor General Robert Butler assigns John Jackson to survey a private land grant given to a former United States Consul to Mexico, Dr. Henry Perrine. Dr. Perrine was not only a diplomat, but a doctor who experimented in finding cures for diseases using tropical plants. He asked for and received a grant of more than thirty-six square miles in southeast Florida to establish a tropical plant nursery. Dr. Perrine never got to realize that dream. He was killed by the Seminole Indians in the Florida Keys in 1840. His widow petitioned the Federal Government to allow her to assume her husband's claim. It is no surprise to me to hear that their paperwork moves slowly through the Federal Government, but finally, a survey crew is being sent to map the

Perrine Land Grant on the shore of Biscayne Bay. Jackson asks Joseph to join the group. They will be gone at least six months.

At this news, I put my foot down and insist Joseph stay home. We have had enough difficulties. How am I to run the farm alone? Joseph will be gone during harvest season. Our crops will rot before someone can take them to market. What about the safety of the girls and myself? No, my husband must stay with us and care for this place we still do not even own. While I sympathize with the Perrine family and their need for a survey that could provide the solution to their problems, I don't see anyone making an effort to help us get our land claim.

We don't hear from John for more than half a year. When Joseph finally talks to him, I think he is relieved I refused to let him go. John confides, "It was a very different terrain than what we are used to. There were many rocks, and each of us wore out two pairs of shoes every week! The country is so rough and so wet it took us much longer to complete the survey than I planned. Plus, the original work done by another surveyor, George Mackay, was not well marked. We could not rely on his findings to prepare our maps." Jackson shook his head. "It is a beautiful country, but you have much finer land here, Joe. Be glad for your island. It is heaven compared to the Perrine tract!"

After John leaves, Joseph and I talk about what he said. We only wish this land was truly ours. It has been five years since we first settled here. We have done everything that was required of us; cleared five acres, built a house, built two houses actually and fulfilled the time length required. Yet, we do not have a deed to our land and are still unclear as to whether a permit has even been filed. John says we should be patient and he offers to see what he can do when he returns to the land office the next time.

Sometimes, I wonder if we should just pack up and go somewhere else. It is obvious we are not welcome here.

That becomes clear to me one day when Joseph is away in Tampa. John needs his assistance with some survey work as the Town of Tampa received 160 acres of land from the Federal Government to build a county seat. Joseph promises to come home as soon as possible. Though there is some comfort in knowing he is only a day's sail away, I am still uneasy about being left alone. Especially when I see a small boat anchoring off shore. It is not a boat I am familiar with, but I recognize the man it carries. Mr. O'Connell from Manatee! *What does he want with us?*

I watch as he comes up the path towards the house. *Should I meet him on the porch or stand inside the doorway? Should I shut the door and refuse to talk to him? What if he has a message from Joseph?* I whisper to the girls to stay in the house and step outside. Maybe if I stand on the steps, I can keep him off the porch. Eliza disobeys and follows me. Instinctively, I push her behind me. If the man means to bring us harm, he will have to go past me to get to my daughter. Mary does as she is told, but I know she watches from the window. Once again, I revert to talking to God when I am desperate. *Please. Don't let it be bad news.*

"Greetings, ma'am." he says. "May I speak to your husband?" His hat is pulled low over his eyes. I wish I could see his face. I might be able to read his intent there. He stands on the ground while I try to stand tall and block him from coming up the steps. *At least I know Joseph did not send him. Should I tell him the truth?* I decide to be careful.

"My husband is not here. I expect him back any moment though. May I give him a message?"

"If you expect him back soon, I can wait. I just wanted to tell him some news he might be interested in."

I try to remain calm. It is hard not to gather up my apron and twist it into a knot, I am so anxious. I take a deep breath. "What news would that be?"

Mr. O'Connell tries to look around me into the house. He pauses and says, "Indians are getting ready to revolt. They ain't happy about the Federal Government telling them they gotta move. Some folks in the middle part of the state were murdered while they slept. This is not a time to be careless. You did say your husband would be back soon?"

Indians! Attacking! I fold my hands to keep from fidgeting. It would not do for him to see I am nervous.

"Oh, yes. Any moment. I will be happy to give him your message. Thank you for the warning."

Mr. O'Connell takes a step towards me. I reach behind and push Eliza back into the house. Could I get inside as well and have time to shut the door if he comes after me?

"Looks to me like you are all alone. What kind of a husband goes off and leaves his wife and little ones to fend for themselves when the Indians are about?" I take a step back.

He continues, "I think you'd be better off to go live somewhere else. I don't think you have what it takes to live here anymore. Do you?"

Mr. O'Connell puts one foot on the bottom step. *Why didn't I bring the gun out with me?* As he moves to the next step, I see a flash of brown coming around the house. In one leap, Bonaparte is on the porch between me and the man. He growls a low threat. The hair rises on the back of his neck.

"Call your dog, Ma'am. I don't mean you harm."

"I am not so sure of that, sir. And I don't think I can control this dog. It is you who had better go." To emphasize my point, Bonaparte growls again and steps to the edge of the porch. He utters one sharp bark and lunges at the man who pulls out his gun.

"No!" I scream and grab for the dog's collar. "Get out of here or I will let him loose. Can you shoot faster than he can run?"

"Yeah, I probably could shoot him and you too, but I didn't come here for no trouble. Just trying to warn you is all. Better give the message to your man." O'Connell turns to go. As he walks away, he calls, "Trouble's coming. You don't know when, but troubles coming. Better get before it catches up with you."

I stand as still as possible holding on to Bonaparte's collar. The dog wants to chase after him. Only when he is on his boat with sails carrying him away and I am sure he is out of sight, do I collapse on the porch steps and cry. I hug Bonaparte. *Thank God for the dog. When will Joseph be home?*

It is two days before Joseph returns. I have not been able to sleep since O'Connell left and am exhausted from fatigue and fear. Eliza sees Joseph first and tells him all about the man's visit.

"You should have seen Boney, Papa! He would not let the bad man on the porch. He growled and protected Mama. I think the man was afraid. I would have been afraid if it was me. The man didn't know Boney is just a good ole dog. He saved us!"

I repeat the conversation with O'Connell and share his warning. "I don't know if he intended to hurt us, but he did succeed in scaring us. Oh, Joseph, you must not leave us here alone again. I don't know what he would do!" Once more tears fall as I think about what could have happened.

Joseph holds me and lets me cry. He strokes my back. The girls huddle around us, disturbed by my weeping.

"But, Mama, Boney was a good ole dog wasn't he?" Eliza tries to comfort me.

I whisper into Joseph's ear hoping the girls will not hear me, "I thought he was going to shoot my dog."

"It will be alright, Julia. Don't cry," Joseph says.

Later that night, after we are in bed, we talk some more. "Is what he said about the Indians true? Do I need to worry about attacks from the Indians as well as the settlers?"

"You don't need to worry. God will take care of us. Yes, there are stories about Indian attacks beginning again. I am not sure if they are true. I think there is more concern about slaves running away to be part of the Seminoles. The Federal Government is sending in more troops to take control of the situation. Billy Bowlegs has disappeared into the Everglades and peace will come again soon."

"What about O'Connell? What did he mean about trouble coming soon?"

"That I do not know. Maybe he really was just trying to warn us about the Indians."

"Joseph, you were not here. The menace in his voice frightened me. Have you ever known Bonaparte to go after a man? He knew we were being threatened."

"Julia, he's just a dog. He probably sensed your fear is all."

I roll over in disgust. "I know what I know. O'Connell is trying to run us off this land."

Joseph replies, "Well, I need to talk to you about that. John thinks we should move." When I sit up in surprise, he rests his hand on my arm. "Not permanently. Just until our claim is better established. There is a lot of work available in Tampa right now. The town is really growing. John is even going to open a store. He is tired of surveying and wants to spend more time with his wife. After hearing what O'Connell told you, I think it might be safer for us to move to Tampa. Just for a little while."

I can hardly believe what I am hearing. Joseph works so hard to keep the farm prosperous. We have a steady trade with Tampa. The town is growing as more settlers arrive. With demand for our produce high, Joseph develops a reputation for providing quality farm goods. More importantly, I am healthy again. It is easier to eat well on the island where there are less choices and hard work keeps me from thinking too much. And now, when we are finally doing well, Joseph wants to move again?

I say as much to Joseph and finish with, "I think you are out of your mind if you are going to let O'Connell run us off our land."

"He's not running us off our land. We are just going to go somewhere a little safer where I can work and keep better track of our land claim. I still cannot figure out why it is taking so long. Perhaps it has something to do with the lack of communication. Think of the girls. If we move to Tampa, they can go to school. Eliza had a chance, but needs to learn more. Mary should have started school a long time ago."

Joseph knows how much I worry about schooling for the girls. We still do not have a school nearby. Eliza works everyday on her reading and arithmetic, but it is not enough. Eliza skips her lessons whenever she can and would give up her school books forever if she had a choice. I want her to have more opportunities than Joseph and I did, but even with her reluctance to sit still and learn, she has already surpassed what I can teach her. Mary is another story altogether. While Eliza hates her books, Mary is intrigued by them. Whenever Eliza sits to study, Mary joins her pretending to read and write on the little slate Joseph purchased in Fort Brooke.

"Maybe a stay in Tampa would not be so bad, but you must give me time to think about it. Let's wait to see if anything comes from O'Connell's threats or the Indian rumors. Promise me you will give me some time."

"A little time," Joseph says. "Now let's get some sleep." I think I will never sleep with so much to think about, but now my husband is home to protect us, I cannot keep my eyes open a minute longer.

I am amazed at how quickly time passes. Word reaches us the Indians are on the attack. Two men, Captain Payne and a Mr. Whidden, who live near Payne's Creek in the middle part of the state are murdered.

John Jackson comes to visit and says, "The Indians have set the whole country in an uproar. People are gathering together in every large home or building they can find to protect themselves while the Indians are allowed free rein throughout the country. I do not know how this state can be settled if something is not done about the Indians." He urges us to consider moving to Tampa. "That is the only place you can be truly safe once war begins."

The latest news is enough to force my husband to make a decision. I no longer have an argument to keep us on the island. I ask Joseph to wait until after Mary's birthday. This is the home she remembers best. I do not want to spoil her special day.

"Make a wish, Mary!" Mary closes her eyes, sucks in her breath and blows as hard as she can. The six little candles on her cake flicker and waver and then, go out.

"I did it! See Liza, I told you I could. Now I get my wish, I'm going to," Mary does not finish as Eliza claps her hand over her cousin's mouth.

"Mary! Don't say your wish out loud!" Shaking her head, Eliza corrects her. "If you tell anyone, it won't come true."

Looking at me, Eliza rolls her eyes and I laugh.

"Don't make fun, Eliza. When you turned six you were just as excited."

It is hard to believe my girls are now eight and six. Eliza, though small in size, is a big help around the house and farm. Joseph swears he could not do it without her. Mary stays in the house with me. Eliza grumbles that I expect less of Mary and treat her with more kindness. Maybe I do, but only because of her past. If I spoil her, it is because she suffered so much as a child. Because of my protection, Mary seems like more of a baby at six than Eliza did, but she still has plenty of time to grow up.

"I'm a big girl now, right Mama?" Mary asks as she eagerly eats her dessert. "When can I learn to read and write like Liza did?"

Well, at least one of my daughters will be happy with our news. Perhaps it is time to tell the girls our plans.

"Well, Mary," I glance at Joseph and he nods in agreement.

"Papa and I have been meaning to talk to you girls. We are going to be moving back to Fort Brooke for a while. You both need to go to school, and we think it will be best if we go in time for the winter term. Papa has gathered wood to build a house for us there, and we are going to go next week to look at our land."

"I don't want to leave the island. I don't need to go to school. I can learn everything I need to know here!" Eliza's face turns red. "This is our home. We don't need another one!"

She stands up from the table and speaks as forcefully as she can. "I don't want to go! I am going to stay here!"

"Eliza! Sit down and mind your manners. Do not talk to us that way!"

I cannot believe my daughter's anger. "It is not only your need for schooling that takes us to Fort Brooke. Papa still has not received his homestead papers. The land office refuses to acknowledge our claim. The same number was issued for two different sites, and we cannot prove this land is ours."

I try to reason with her. "Mr. Jackson is helping Papa as best as he can and we hired an attorney to represent us. They think it will be best if we move off the island for a time until the problem is resolved. This is not something we choose to do, but we will make the best of it."

Mary interrupts, "I want to go to Fort Brooke. I want to go to school. Don't you know that was my wish! I want to read and write like Liza."

I smile at Mary. "Well, birthday girl, you will get your wish. Now finish your cake and let's get ready for bed."

Eliza opens her mouth to speak again, but I reprimand her. "No more Eliza. The matter is settled. We are moving to Fort Brooke. Get used to the idea."

After the girls are in bed, I walk out on the porch. Through the big oaks that surround the house, I look up at the evening sky full of stars. I hear the frogs as they begin their nightly song.

Somewhere, a mourning dove coos in the eaves of the house. I smell the salt air and the rich scent of earth. Terra Ceia is my home. We have put so much work into the house and farm. Will it all be a waste? A tear trickles down my cheek. Why must we leave?

Joseph follows me to the edge of the porch. His hand rubs circles on my back. "I'm sorry Julia. I know you've finally come to love it here. So do I." He lights his pipe. Tangy grey smoke swirls around us. "I have done everything I can to keep this land as our own. It doesn't seem right to be leaving it behind." He sighs.

"John talked to the land agent. I cannot make any sense of the rules, but he knows how these matters work. He says this is for the best. He knows how much we value this land and how hard we have worked to make it our own. I trust him to do what is right for us. We must go."

I lean against my husband. "At least I will not go alone. I need you with me, Joseph. I could not bear it to be apart from you again."

Joseph smells of tobacco and leather. He turns me around and kisses me. "I am glad we will be together. Julia, I fear you put too much faith in me. You must trust God as well."

Trusting God again. Why does it always come back to that? It seems so much easier to trust God here in my own little home where I can control the routine and know what each day will hold.

"I will try. I promise, but I will look forward to our return. Now, let's go get ready for bed. I fear Eliza will be difficult to deal with tomorrow!" I turn to go and Joseph's pipe smoke follows me inside the cabin. *As long as my husband is with me, I can face anything.*

I spend the next several days packing. In wooden crates, I place our possessions which have accumulated since our arrival five years ago. I decide to leave some dishes and pots and pans for Joseph to use when he visits the farm to oversee plantings and harvest. The land is too rich and valuable to leave fallow. We will pay the Petersen brothers, Danish immigrants who lived across the bay, to take care of the farm, but Joseph will return periodically to check on their work. Joseph disassembles the wood stove so we can take it with us to Fort Brooke. Eliza is still sullen, so I give her the job of gathering books and toys. As I help her pack the china doll that Billy Bowlegs loved, I wonder where he is. Will we see him again in Fort Brooke? No more Indians have been sent west, so I assume he is safe and sound in the Everglades with his people.

Packing is hard work and emotional too. Who knows when we will be able to return? As moving day approaches, everyone's nerves are stretched thin. I fuss at Eliza for getting in my way and at Joseph when he moves some boxes out of the kitchen before I am finished loading them. It is unlike him to snap back, but he responds.

"You're packing them too heavy. I cannot lift them onto the boat by myself. We are not going forever," he added. "You don't have to take everything."

"Don't tell me how to pack. Don't you know I have done more packing in my life since I married you than I did the whole time before I met you?" I frown. "Wouldn't it be nice to stay in one place for a while instead of always being on the move?"

Joseph glares at me, but says no more and continues to relocate the cartons to the front porch. I can feel the tension in the room. Joseph and I hardly ever fight. Something else is not quite right either. The air seems oppressive and heavy. Maybe that is the problem. Everyone is jumpy because of the weather. Though the overcast sky promises rain, the clouds hold in the late September heat. I fan myself. My skin feels sticky and damp. *Isn't it time for some cooler weather to arrive?* I think about Bavaria and its cool autumns. *What are we doing here in Florida?*

Chapter Eighteen

That evening after supper, Joseph, the children and I walk down to the bay. I hope getting us all out of the house will improve our dispositions. Joseph whistles for Bonaparte who follows us until he catches the scent of an animal and races away. As we walk along the shoreline, Eliza squints at the western horizon.

Taking her father's hand, she asks, "What is that light, Papa?"

The sun has been down for a while now, but a strange glow, resembling a sunset, lights up the night sky.

"I don't know," Joseph says. "I have never seen anything like it. It looks like a fire, but it is out at sea." He shakes his head puzzled. We watch the sky for a while as the colors flicker and burn before turning back to the house.

"It is so hot, Papa," Mary says. "When will winter come?"

"Not for a while."

"I'm hot," she complains again. Joseph just sighs and keeps walking.

The next evening, the same glimmering appears in the sky after dark. We walk back down to the bay and face west. Despite the heat, I feel cold and ask, "What is it? Is it a fire?"

"Unless the sea is burning, I can't imagine what it might be," Joseph says. "A ship would have sunk by now."

I echo Mary's complaints from the night past. "This heat," I say. "I can hardly catch my breath. Something doesn't feel right."

"I know," Joseph agrees. "I just can't put my finger on it. I hope it's not another storm, but it could be." We stand quietly and watch the sky for a long time.

Joseph is right. The hurricane breaks the next day. We wake to high winds which push the bay closer and closer to the house. Joseph moves all the crates and boxes up to the second floor. Even the pieces of the cook stove line the floor of the girls' bedroom. The wind blows as palm trees lose their grip on the earth and fall to the ground. Their fronds break free and soar through the air. Memories of the last hurricane and tornado fill my mind as I watch from the porch. I remember the winds that blew our house down as we took shelter under a fallen oak. *That storm left our house in ruins. Will it happen again?*

Pushed by the wind and rising tide, the bay covers the yard. By mid day, water laps at the top step of the porch. An hour later, it creeps under the cabin's doors. We take refuge on the second floor with most of our belongings. Despite my protests, Joseph decides to open the front and back doors, hoping the water will flow through the cabin rather than push against it.

"The house was not designed to withstand such pressure," he explains. "I think this is for the best."

When he opens the doors, the water rushes through the hallway. He wades through the water to the stairs. Several inches fill the bottom floor of the cabin and continue to increase. I keep watch down the stairs and see a chair float across the hall. It bumps against the walls before slipping out the back door.

Another hour passes. Rain pounds on the roof. The water now reaches halfway up the stairs.

"Joseph," I whisper, hoping the girls will not hear. "What will we do if it fills the house? There are no windows up here. How will we escape?"

I remember the chair and imagine being carried higher and higher on top of the water until my head hits the ceiling and there is no more air to breath. Mary starts to cry.

"It will be alright," Papa consoles her. "I don't think the water will get that high. See, look closely. It hasn't moved beyond that same step for several minutes. In fact, I think it might be getting lower."

I stare at the step. Yes, it does appear to be stopping.

"What time is it, Joseph?" He reaches into his pants pocket and pulls out my father's pocket watch. Seeing it reminds me of the frailty of life. "Four o'clock. Listen, the wind seems to be dying as well."

We know from experience the worst of the storm might not be over. I still remember watching the cabin collapse in the second half of the last storm. We are lucky. Other than water damage, our house is spared.

Weeks later, comparing stories with other settlers, Joseph learns the storm waters indeed reached their peak at four o'clock in the afternoon. The next day, when the water recedes, a thick sticky mud covers the downstairs of the cabin. It smells rank like rotten vegetation and dead fish.

"It could have been worse," I tell the girls as they help me sweep and clean the floors and walls. "At least we still have a roof over our heads. Thank God the cabin still stands."

That night as we prepare for bed, I apologize to my husband. "I am sorry I argued with you about opening the doors. You were right, Joseph."

"It is alright Julia. I am just glad we are all safe." Joseph gathers me in a tight hug. I wilt in his arms and begin to cry.

"Joseph, I am not sure I can go through another storm like that again. When will they stop? Will we always live in fear of the next hurricane?"

Joseph does not answer my question, but holds me close and pats my back in reassurance. I lie in bed and talk to God. *I know you are there. Margaret and Joseph tell me I should trust you. How can I do that when so many bad things happen? You seem so far away.* That night when I worshipped God in front of the wall of white flowers seems far away as well.

In Eliza's opinion, one good thing comes from the flood. She does not have to move from the island right away. Joseph returns to Fort Brooke to check on our property and his substantial lumber pile. I am grateful all our belongings were already packed and easy to move above the flood waters. Others did not fare as well. Joseph brings back word Fort Brooke has extensive damage. The storm destroyed the wharves along the riverfront and washed some of the large sailing vessels into the town streets. Waves fifteen feet high demolished the public storehouses and ruined their contents. Although miraculously, no one died, many of the townspeople have only the clothes on their backs. The only available food is beef from the cattle who roam the woods farther inland.

Two weeks later, a second storm surge floods the north side of Tampa Bay. Just as the people of Fort Brooke start to recover, the military outpost and the little village growing around it are underwater again. Despite high tides, farther to the south, we are spared. When a third storm follows in early December, the logs and shingles Joseph stockpiled are scattered all up and down the Hillsborough River. The storms change Fort Brooke forever.

"They are calling them the "Equinoctials," Josephs tells us. "Many of the buildings are beyond repair. The village is leveled. I hired a man to watch our lumber. There is a shortage of building materials now. I am afraid someone will steal ours. We started work, but I know you wanted to see the house while it is under construction. If you still do, we need to go right away. It will be done soon."

Yes, I do want to see the house before Joseph finishes it. I cannot leave all the decisions about my home up to him!

Village of Tampa, Florida 1849

A few days later, we sail back into the Hillsborough River. Joseph is right! Things are completely different! Where are the docks and the barracks? The stables where Patrick once kept his horses are gone, too. Trees lean, all in the same direction, as though a giant brushed his hand along their tops. All the familiar landmarks have disappeared. As Joseph sails the boat up the river, he stops on the west side across from where soldiers busily work to restore Fort Brooke. He gestures proudly to the frame of a small two story house.

"Here we are," he says.

"This can't be it!" I exclaim. "Why are you stopping here? This is the wrong bank of the river. The town is on the other side! How can the girls cross the river each day for school? Joseph, what have you done?"

I am so angry at my husband I do not speak to him for two days. We camp at the home site while Joseph continues his work. With every blow of the hammer, I am more and more upset. Eliza acts as intermediary carrying messages back and forth between Joseph and me. Neither of us will give in, least of all me. I am right. Joseph tries to convince me the village will eventually come to us and until then, Fort Brooke is just a row or a sail across the wide river. He wants to stay away from town life as long as possible desiring the peace and quiet he enjoys on Terra Ceia. I contend it is foolish to live so far from the school, shops and other residents.

"We came to live in town, Joseph. We will earn our living there and the girls will go to school. If we have to depend on you to take us to town all the time, you will never get any work done here. If we wanted isolation, we could have stayed on the island."

Finally, I insist he take me across the river to Fort Brooke. Worn down by my silence, he agrees. It does not take me long to find another settler, disgusted by the weather, who plans to leave the state. I purchase his lot near the fort and announce I am moving and if Joseph wants to come with me, he is welcome.

Defeated, Joseph builds a raft of logs and floats the building's frame across the river. Eliza giggles when she sees her future home in the middle of the river.

"Look, a house boat!" she calls to Mary. Once the decision is made and I have my way, it does not take long to finish the house in its new location. I refuse to wait any longer and we move in on December 18, the very day the last nail is in place.

A week later, we celebrate Christmas in the new house. Once again, a cedar tree decorates our parlor. The traditional candles burn, the girls hang their stockings by the new fireplace, and I bake Christmas cookies. Some of the tension between us eases. He is still touchy about my insistence on moving the house. I think some of the other settlers tease him and call him henpecked. *I don't want to be known as the one who runs our family, but Joseph cannot expect me to just be quiet while he makes a mistake either.* I sigh when I wonder what Margaret would think about my attitude. *It has been a long time since I heard from my friend. I should write to her soon. How surprised she will be to find us living in Tampa!*

We join others in the village for a Christmas Eve service. I try to act like the obedient wife, but cannot miss the looks of the other settlers.

I try to explain myself to my husband. On the way back from church, I ask, "Joseph, do you understand now why I wanted to live on this side of the river? Think how hard it would be to attend church if we had to load the girls in the boat every time we wanted to go!"

"Julia, I admit you were right, but sometimes, I wish you were not so headstrong and demanding. Just once, I would like to make a decision without you arguing with me about it. Why do you even bother to keep me around, I wonder?"

Teasing, I link my arm in his, then, poke him in the ribs and try to make him smile, "Oh, I can think of a few reasons." He just shakes his head.

Christmas morning arrives, and St. Nicholas leaves some packages under the tree for the girls. While Eliza seems subdued and I suspect she misses the island, Mary is beside herself with excitement. As soon as Christmas passes, she begins asking when classes start. She begs me to show her the school and one day, we walk over to see it. This is a different building than the one that Eliza first attended. The old school at Fort Brooke collapsed in one of the storms. The new hastily built school stands in the growing Village of Tampa. The doors are locked as winter term will not begin until after the New Year, but we peek in the windows.

"I see a little desk just my size!" Mary exclaims. "Do you think that is where I will sit? What is the teacher's name, Mama?" She talks constantly about school while Eliza grows quieter and quieter. I wish my daughter would develop a love for learning. Why can't she see how much it will benefit her in the future?

Mary loves school from the moment she enters the classroom. She soaks up everything Miss Amelia Jones teaches her and quickly becomes the teacher's pet. Eliza, on the other hand, finds school just as tedious as before. I cannot believe how different my girls are. I would have given anything to have the education she hates. She is behind the other children her age, and I insist she study at home. Miss Jones tells me she is a daydreamer and lazy. I am not sure with whom to be more angry, Miss Jones or Eliza.

In spite of my concern over Eliza's attitude towards school, I am content with our life in Tampa. I worry the move to town might be too difficult for me and my old eating habits will return, but I stay busy and carefully watch what I eat, limiting the amounts. It helps that Joseph seems to have forgiven me for my bossiness. I also take in boarders to add to our finances, our old friend, Captain Sam Bishop, pilots a schooner that travels up and down the west coast of Florida. He is one of only four men issued a license as a Tampa Bay pilot. Our second boarder, Nicholas Wilson, works on Captain Sam's ship.

In 1850, a man comes around asking questions. He says he is the Census taker and we are to be included in the United States Census! Everyone is very excited. This is the first census since Florida became a state. It is important that everyone be counted so we get the proper representation in Washington. I feel proud to have my name recorded. Even the girls are mentioned as well as Captain Sam and Mr. Wilson.

Every night after supper, pipes in hand, the two men join Joseph out in the yard or in front of the fire to tell stories about the land of Florida and the people who live here. Had they told no tales at all, Nicholas's lilting Swedish inflection, mixed with Captain Sam's New York accent, would keep my attention. The girls and I listen closely as they tell about the amazing sights they have seen. Flocks of pink birds so thick they block out the sun. "Flamingoes," Captain Sam called them. Eliza enjoys saying the word aloud and repeats it over and over. She takes my hand as he describes storms at sea, so strong the waves toss their ship high in the air like a child playing with a ball. Nicholas describes huge sea animals called manatees some sailors think are beautiful mermaids in disguise. When Captain Sam recalls herds of wild cattle and horses roaming free on coastal islands, I know Eliza goes to bed each night dreaming of horses and mermaids.

One evening, Joseph does not join the men at their usual spot. He complains he does not feel well and goes to bed early. Days before, while cutting timber to sell to the military for the rebuilding effort, he cut his foot deeply with a saw. Despite my doctoring, it swells to three times its size and grows hot and angry red in color. The infection spreads, and Joseph shakes with cold; then, thrashes about in bed with a fever. I am more frightened than I have been in a very long time. *I remember the boys. How quickly they died. What will I do if something happens to my husband?* I regret being so harsh to him about the location of the house.

Captain Sam fetches the doctor from the village who prescribes a poultice made of stewed pumpkin to draw out the fever. I do not have confidence in his remedy, and wish for some of Billy Bowleg's wisdom and medicine instead. With Joseph so ill, I am not sure how we will afford to live. To supplement the loss of Joseph's income, I open a beer and cake shop in our home. Many of the soldiers and some of the villagers came to buy my wares. Though she cannot stand the smell of the brewing beer, Eliza offers to quit school and help me in the store. I try to laugh off her concern and send her to school each day as though nothing were wrong.

We still wait to hear something about the Terra Ceia homestead. Despite the fact that both Judge Simon Turman and Captain Sam Bishop send letters to the land office witnessing that Joseph settled upon his claim and occupied it for the required five year period required by the Armed Occupation Act, we hear no word from the Land Office about the mix up in permit numbers. *For all we know, someone else owns our land and will seize our house and farm. After all the work we have done. For all we know, we could live out the rest of our lives here in Tampa.* I have to shrug when I realize I have just admitted I cannot change the future.

There you go, God. It's all yours. See if you can influence the land office. I cannot fix this. I cannot make the papers come.

I don't know what I expect. I know I did not anticipate feeling a weight removed from my shoulders, but that is how I feel. And I certainly did not expect to get a letter from a Treasury

Department Agent the very next day ruling that Permit Number 949 belongs to Joseph. Weeks maybe, but not the next day.

I can't help but wonder if my husband wasn't sick from worry. Once he receives the letter informing him of the land agent's decision, he begins to get better. While his foot heals, he continues to suffer from alternating chills and fever for more than a year and he walks with a limp. I do not think it would be good for him to go back into the woods where he might take ill again and be so far from home, so he takes a job at John Jackson's store. Selling goods to the settlers, he can sit and rest when he needs to do so.

Despite the resolution of the permit number, under advice from Judge Turman, we stay in Tampa for three more years. The girls have their school and the doctor is nearby. Even Bonaparte adjusts to living in the village. Each day, Joseph walks Eliza and Mary to school, and then goes to work at the fort. At home, I bake, make beer and cook for the guests who stay with us. I thought it would be a struggle to not indulge in the treats I make, but surprisingly it is not. I don't know if it is constantly working with the smell of baking sweets and fermenting beer or that I have finally learned my lesson, but I am not tempted to eat more than I need to live. *Maybe it is simply I have learned to rely on God to satisfy me.*

Instead of eating them myself, I give any leftover baked goods away at the end of the day. It feels good to help some of the people in our community who don't have as much as I do.

Eliza longs for the island and hates being confined to her desk, but I think she has finally resolved herself to learn as much as she can. One day, she asks me if I think we will ever leave Tampa.

What should I say? God did provide the papers from the land office. His Hand was certainly in that.

"I don't know daughter. I am learning not to plan too far ahead. Only God knows what the future holds. I do know God wants me to do everything to the best of my abilities so that is what I am focused on right now."

Eliza sighs and returns to her homework when she realizes I am talking to her too. Not very subtle, but at least effective!

One day in early August of 1850, a tall thin young man accompanies Joseph home from the store. They arrive almost at supper time. With Captain Sam and Nicholas away on a voyage, I tell Mary to set the table on the porch. The stove warms the kitchen to an unbearable level on an already hot day in the late afternoon August sun. The men enter the kitchen just as I take a pan of biscuits from the oven. Eliza gingerly pours a pot of beans into a bowl.

"Julia, I have brought a guest," Joseph introduces us. "This is Thomas Reese. He just came from the Manatee lands."

"Welcome, Mr. Reese. You men go wash up. Supper will be ready in a minute."

Turning back to my work, I order, "Mary, set an extra place. Eliza, get a jar of honey and put it on the table."

As they approach the porch, the younger man holds back. Clasping one hand, then the other, he cracks his knuckles. Head bent, with his chin tucked into his chest, his eyes peer over thick glasses as Eliza places the rest of the food on the table. His forehead wrinkles together. Is he worried or just nearsighted?

"Sit, sit," I urge. Joseph gestures to a chair, and Thomas sits down knocking his knees into the table leg. Water glasses rock and gravy sloshes out of the bowl onto the tablecloth. Mr. Reese turns red and looks down at the table.

I study him. I know the girls do, too. In fact, I frown at Eliza and Mary as they look as though they might erupt into a fit of giggles. I know why they are amused. His arms and legs don't quite go with his body. Eliza has a toy one of the soldiers gave her. "Dancing Dan" the soldier called him as he showed Eliza how to make its wooden arms and legs swing around. I wonder if Mr. Reese could polka. No, maybe he looks more like a scarecrow than a dancer. Now, I must turn to keep from laughing.

Despite Joseph's efforts to make conversation, Mr. Reese eats quietly replying with yes and no answers that stifle further talk. *Is he shy or starving?* What he lacks in chatter, Mr. Reese makes up for in the amount he consumes. *Maybe he is like the toy man with a hollow leg to pack the food into!* Joseph reaches for another biscuit but his fingers meet an empty basket. He looks at me, and I shrug. I want to say, "I wasn't expecting guests," but don't want to embarrass Mr. Reese. The ham disappears off the plate. I rise and fry more which Mr. Reese gobbles down as well. When the last crumb disappears into his mouth, he sighs and pats his stomach.

"Thank you Ma'am," he says simply. "It has been a long time since I ate so well."

Though he still appears jumpy, now that the plates are bare, Mr. Reese appears finally ready to talk. Motioning to the girls to begin clearing the table, I ask him, "What brings you to Fort Brooke, Mr. Reese?"

He hesitates and looks away. "I am embarrassed to say, Ma'am, but perhaps you can help me find a way out of my predicament." Rubbing his forehead as though to smooth out the wrinkles, he explains, "A year ago, I bought forty six acres on the north shore of the Manatee River." He clears his throat and pushes his chair back. Standing, he paces the porch as he continues, "I built a cabin and tried to open a store. I thought I could make a profit from it quickly as it is several miles from Clark's store in Manatee." His voice grows more agitated. "I did not realize people were used to buying from their friend. I miscalculated the demand. Last week, Henry Clark died."

"We had not heard," I say. "His poor wife. But, surely now, they will need your store?"

"No, Mrs. Clark sent her employee, Charles Macy, to see me. They plan on keeping things just as they are. Even those who did not buy from her before, will now. Sympathy you know." *Threats, you know,* I think. *I know how that feels.*

Stopping, he turns to face me. "My real problem is I used credit to buy my land and build my cabin. The note is now due. I have no money to pay my debts. Tomorrow, everything I own will be sold by the sheriff at auction." As though all the stuffing comes out of him at once, he abruptly sits back down again. Shoulders slumped, head down and arms limp, he was once more the same defeated man who first arrived at the table.

"How much do you owe?" I ask.

"$300."

Joseph sits quietly smoking his pipe. He looks at me and frowns.

Standing up to take the last of the dishes off the table, I say, "We will talk about it and see if there is anything we can do to help."

After the house settles down, Joseph and I lie in bed and talk about Mr. Reese's predicament.

I turn to Joseph. "Such a young man to face losing it all. What if that had been you? Wouldn't you have wanted help? We have saved a great deal from our work here. We could loan him the money to redeem his land."

"Julia, he has no way to pay you back. He already said his business has failed. Think of it. He is no shopkeeper. You know how much work it is to be successful at a store. He will just end up in debt to us and then, how will we collect what we are owed?"

"Well, what if we buy the land and give him a chance to buy it back from us? We could go to the auction. We might even get a bargain price on it. Hardly anyone here at the fort even knows where the Manatee lands are anyway. I wonder if anyone will even bid on it. What do we have to lose?"

"Julia, we have our place on the island. Surely it won't be much longer before the title is clear and it is ours free and clear.

We have this house as well. We don't need any more. How do you even know what you are buying? You have never even been to his property."

"We can never go wrong with land, Joseph. Storms will come and go, money will be hard to find, but the land, it will always be there. Let's at least go to the auction. We don't have to make any promises to him."

"I don't know, Julia. Let me sleep on it."

I know better than to push my husband to make a decision tonight. For a long time, I think about the land and the money. How could we make it work? My stomach starts to ache. I close my eyes. Joseph would say God cares about all the details. I suppose he would tell me to pray about it.

All right God, here's another one I cannot work out. You take it. With that settled, I fall asleep.

Chapter Nineteen

The next morning, I know what to do. I rush everyone through breakfast. Joseph has agreed we can bid on the property, but he has set a limit on what we can spend. I leave the dishes to soak and urge Joseph, the girls and Mr. Reese to the riverbank and into the boat.

"Stay," I call to Bonaparte. He will guard the house.

"Bye, Boney," the girls echo and wave to him as we board the boat.

"Mr. Reese, we do not know if we can help you, but we will go with you to the courthouse. Come girls. Let me tie your bonnets. We don't want to be late."

As we sail, Mr. Reese sits still as a statue in the bow of the boat. *Poor man, if it were my land being sold, I would be terribly sad.*

Though it is cooler on the water, I know it will be another scorching day. Joseph teases Mary by telling her today will be a dog day. Mary thinks that means we will see a dog and asks excitedly what kind it will be.

"I like black dogs!" she chatters. "With white spots and a shiny nose."

Joseph laughs and explains, "No Mary. These are the dog days of summer when the sun is high and hot and the dog star shines at night."

"Dog star?" asks Mary. "How do you know it is a dog? Does it bark?"

Joseph loves to tease. "Yes, you listen carefully tonight and see if you don't hear it yelping." When we arrive down river, Joseph maneuvers the little boat towards the docks.

"Lots of people here today, Julia. Maybe others have heard about the sale."

I think of the young man's concern for his investment. "Don't worry, Mr. Reese. Let's just see what happens, shall we?"

I accept Mr. Reese's hand and climb from the boat onto the dock. We walk to the courthouse. The two story white frame building is only three years old. Captain James McKay built it strong enough and far enough away from the river it managed to survive the storms of 1848. It is twenty feet long and forty five feet deep and has a double porch across the front. A cupola projects from the roof mid center of the courthouse. As we cross under the wooden arch that spans the opening in the white picket fence around the courthouse lawn, I see a large crowd already gathered in front of the courthouse. A group of men stand on the second floor of the porch so everyone could see and hear them.

We move closer to the courthouse. Joseph places one hand on Mary's shoulder and another on Eliza's.

"Girls, stay close. I don't want to lose you in this mob," he says.

I fan myself with my hand. "Goodness, it is warm today. I hope they start soon. Mr. Reese, see that heavy set man to the left? That is Benjamin Hagler, the sheriff. He is the one who will conduct the sale."

"Are all these people here to buy my land?" Mr. Reese asks.

"No," Joseph replies. "They must have several parcels for sale today. Listen. I think they are going to start."

At that moment, Sheriff Hagler begins to speak. "Welcome, everyone! We will start the sale in a moment, but first let me say how good it is to see everyone here today."

"Politicians," I whisper as the sheriff launched into a rousing speech.

Mr. Reese's face grows more and more pale. In a minute, he is going to faint, I think, but he manages to stay on his feet as the rules are read and the sale finally begins.

Several other pieces of land are auctioned first. I listen carefully and watch how bidders proceed to either buy back their own land or purchase that of others. Finally, Mr. Reese's land is described. The sheriff makes it sound like a delightful place right on the Manatee River. The bidding start slowly. Joseph and I do not participate. Mr. Reese's face is tense. He looks at us and expects us to help him. The bidding grows to one hundred dollars.

Finally, I nudge Joseph and nod. He holds up his hand and calls out, "One hundred seventy five."

The amount increases as other bidders continue to raise the price. Finally, he shouts, "Two hundred thirty."

This time, no one counters, and the sheriff says, "Sold!"

Joseph keeps one hand on Mary and another on Eliza as he pushes his way through the crowd to the courthouse steps. Mr. Reese and I follow him closely. He finds a clear space on the edge of the porch and sits Mary and Eliza down.

"Girls, stay here. Don't move. If we get separated, I will come back for you. Eliza, keep an eye on Mary."

We join the line in front of the desk outside the courthouse where post auction transactions take place. It takes more time than I thought it would to get all the signatures we need, pay the fees and make sure that the deed is recorded properly. With all the trouble we have had over the Terra Ceia homestead, I want to make sure everything is done according to the rules. By the time we are done, my stomach is growling. I am sure the girls are hungry, too.

When we return to the place where we left them, Eliza and Mary are gone. Mr. Reese has already left the courthouse so Joseph and I split up. I go inside the courthouse calling their names and looking behind every open door. Joseph searches the porches and courthouse lawn. With so many people, it is hard to see through the crowds. I look through people's legs and over their heads, but see no sign of the girls. When I join Joseph outside, I immediately see he has not found them either. By now, I am frantic. *What if they were run over by a wagon? Someone might have taken them, or they could have wandered off to the river looking for the boat. What if one of them falls in the water and the other tries to get her out? They could both drown. Oh, I know we should have taught them to swim!*

Our search catches the attention of some of the crowd. Word goes from one group to another the girls are missing. Surely someone will find them! An hour goes by with no word of their whereabouts. I know they both must be hungry and thirsty. Thirsty! That's it!

"Joseph, didn't we pass a water trough on the way to the courthouse? I bet they are there! Come on!"

I run as fast as I can with my skirts getting in the way. Joseph passes me. Sometimes, I wish I were a man so I could wear pants! Ahead, I see the crowd part as he races down the street.

Panting with exertion, I finally get close enough to see the water trough. In between the horses that are gathered there, I see Mary on Joseph's shoulders and Eliza holding his hand. I don't know whether to be relieved or angry. The stitch in my side from running pushes me towards anger.

"Eliza! Mary, why did you leave? Papa told you to stay on the porch. We were so worried!"

"I was thirsty, Mama. Liza told me we were in trouble. I am sorry. I was coming right back as soon as I got a drink. Look at the pretty horsies! They are thirsty too." On Joseph's shoulders, Mary can reach their big heads. They drip water from their mouths onto her hair.

"I am sorry, too, Mama. I tried to catch her, but she got away from me. Oh, aren't you the most beautiful things," distracted, Eliza croons to the horses.

"Are these the two who were lost at the courthouse?" The wagon driver asks us. "I heard about them. I am glad you found them safe. I am sure you are all worn out. Let me give you a ride. Where would you like to go?"

I am too exhausted and emotionally wrought to say anything. Joseph just nods. The wagon driver swings Mary, and then Eliza up into the wagon then takes his seat beside them. Joseph helps me in as well. The driver cracks his whip on the horses' backs and they step smartly down the street.

"Oh, Liza, isn't this fun?" Mary calls over the rattle of the wagon. Eliza laughs in agreement.

I shake my head in disbelief. I know two little girls who ought to be in trouble, but for some reason, they are getting a reward instead. When the wagon stops in front of the boat dock, the girls are sad to see the ride end. I think they also know they are going to be punished. Joseph reaches for Eliza and sets her down beside him so he can pull Mary from the wagon as well. He thanks the driver for returning us safely, but neither Joseph nor I say anything else. I hold tightly to Eliza's hand as I help her board the boat.

When we get home, I send the girls out to cut a switch off the willow tree. The delay allows time for my anger to cool. Besides, I think it just to gives them an opportunity to think about what they have done wrong before they receive their punishment. I rarely spank my girls but if anyone deserves a spanking, it is these two for running away. I do not get pleasure from it, but I hope they will remember their disobedience the next time they are tempted to stray. Mary cries for a long time after her switching, but Eliza takes hers without complaint. I think she is more worried about upsetting Joseph. At bedtime, I stand outside the girls' bedroom and hear Joseph and Eliza talking.

"I'm sorry, Papa. I didn't mean to worry you. I tried to take care of Mary, but I was watching the horses and didn't see her run off. I will do better next time. Please don't be angry with me."

"Eliza, I know you were distracted, but that is what worries me the most. What if something terrible had happened to Mary? How would you have felt? When I tell you to do something, it is not because I want to deny you pleasure. Daughter, I need you to understand I will never give you a task that is not for your good. You must trust me that I know what is best and be obedient."

"I know that Papa."

"I wonder, how do you know?"

Eliza hesitates and then, says, "I know because you love me. Because you are my father and because you always look out for me."

"That's my girl. Just remember, I do love you. Even when you are naughty! All is forgiven. Now, go to sleep."

"Will you tell me a story, Papa?"

"Hmm, let's see. Once upon a time, there was a girl who loved horses…"

As I go to my own room to prepare for bed, I do not listen to the bedtime story Joseph weaves. Instead, I think about the conversation I just heard. As a child, Eliza grasps a concept it has taken me years to understand. *Why can't I trust God the way Eliza trusts Joseph? Do I struggle with trusting my Heavenly Father because I am putting Him into human terms? Perhaps God seems distant because I hardly remember my own father, and my uncle was both neglectful and malicious. Do I think of God that way? Do I think of God as someone far away who occasionally checks on me and most often finds me disobedient? Do I think of Him as someone who delights in punishing me? Maybe I do. No, I know that I do. How do I get to the place where, like Eliza, I can be assured of God's love for me? How can I become so comfortable with God that I could think of Him as my Father?*

Maybe it comes from spending time with Him. Eliza trusts Joseph because she has a relationship with him. She trusts him because she knows from experience that she can. And she knows he loves her even when she disobeys. I have a lot to think about, but I am so exhausted from the day I fall asleep quickly, but not before I realize that, despite all the commotion of the day, I did not turn to food to relieve my anxiety. Maybe I have learned at least one lesson for my good.

Six months come and go. I spend more time in prayer and start reading my Bible every day. No matter what or where I read, I see God will provide and He cares about me. He gives me a list of instructions to live my life, care for the poor and needy, seek justice, and be humble. It is not easy to do, but not as hard as trying to do things on my own all the time. I read in Matthew 11:29, "Take my yoke upon you and learn of me; for I am meek and lowly in heart: and ye shall find rest unto your souls."

Rest. That is what I desire. If following God can bring me rest, then, I am willing to do so. I also keep a list of reasons I have to be thankful. I feel a change happening in me. I think back to the first prayer I prayed with Margaret. And to the night I felt God's presence so strongly as I fell on my face before God, worshipping in my nightgown. While those were magnificent, emotional moments for me, they did not last. I find I am more changed by the simple daily walk with God than by those intensely moving encounters.

I begin to see God at work in everything around me. In conversations with others. In opportunities to help people that God sends on my path. In the choices to do what is right and act Christlike even when others do not do the same for me. I am not as anxious and not as demanding of my way. I am willing to wait and see what the future holds instead of trying to manipulate things to go my way. Yes, I am changing.

I decide to write a letter to Margaret to tell her. I have not heard from my friend in a while and hope she is alright. Perhaps our frequent moves keep her letters from reaching me.

"Dear Margaret," I begin.

I hope all is well with you and your family. I miss you and think of you often. Life certainly did not follow the path that you and I planned so long ago. I remember the day you said to me, "God is in control." You said if I would just let God be in charge, everything would work out for the best. I confess I did not believe you when you said that. Who else but me could know what was best for me and for my family? Can you see me smiling as I write? It has taken a lot of hardship for me to see you were right. I guess it just takes me a long time to learn. When I look back, I can see God's Hand at work in the decisions that were made, the lessons that were learned and the choices that propelled us to turn one way or another. Sometimes, I wish I had given in sooner, but then, maybe I would not be so appreciative of what I have now. The girls are doing well. We have a good business in Tampa. We have not given up on the land on Terra Ceia, but until I wrote this, I did not realize that maybe it is God Who keeps sending us in a different direction. We will have to wait to see what the future holds, but I can finally say I am content to wait on God to show us what we need to do. Thank you, my friend, for teaching me that, even if I was not a willing student. Someday, I hope to tell you all that has happened in person. But, for that day, I will wait as well.

I don't know if Joseph notices the changes in me or not. I hope he does, but I am grateful he does not tell me "I told you so," about his suggestion to trust God or about the fact he correctly predicted Thomas Reese's inability to pay us back for the land we purchased for him. Not only does he fail to make even one installment on the loan, but Mr. Reese disappears from the county without a trace. Now Joseph must travel not only back and forth between our Tampa home and the Terra Ceia farm but also to the Manatee River land.

I dare not tell Joseph about the plans I have been making. I must wait for the right opportunity to speak up. I want to leave Tampa, but not to go back to the island. *As much trouble as we have had with the land claim, I feel our next home should be on the Manatee River, on the property we purchased from Mr. Reese. I am not sure if it is God's leading though. More than anything I want to be obedient to God. If He wants us to stay in Tampa, then, we should stay here. If He can use us more on Terra Ceia, then we should go there. But, oh, I hope I am right it is to the Manatee River we should go.*

We celebrate Eliza's eleventh birthday in Tampa. She argues eleven is old enough to quit school. I might be more willing to compromise on some things, but I will not listen to her when it comes to school. I still insist she go each day.

"As long as we are here, Eliza, you will go. Someday, if we go back to the island, there will not be a school. Take advantage of the opportunity to learn while you can." Joseph agrees. Eliza offers to teach him some of what she has learned. Whenever they can find the time, Eliza becomes the teacher as Joseph sits beside her and learns to sign his name. "Joseph Atzeroth," he pens over and over again until finally, both he and Eliza are satisfied with his penmanship.

"See daughter? There has been some benefit to the time you spent in school," he smiles. Getting up from the table, he leans over and hugs Eliza. "Perhaps someday, you will be a teacher yourself. If you can train this old German farmer to write his name, surely you can teach anyone."

"Oh, Papa. I would like to be a teacher. Let me teach you how to count!" Mary chimes in. "One, two, three."

Joseph laughs, reaches down and swings Mary around by her arms in a circle.

"Oh, I am getting dizzy!' she giggles.

"I already know how to count, thank you very much missy." He sets Mary down and spanks her gently on the bottom. "Go show me how to wash the dishes." Joseph pretends to chase her, and Mary shrieks and hides behind the chair.

"Tomorrow, I go to the Manatee lands, Julia," Joseph says as he bends down to remove his boots.

Now is the time for me to share my surprise. "I have been thinking."

Joseph stops pulling at his boots and looks up. Eliza watches me from the table and Mary comes out from behind her chair.

I continue, "We should move to the Manatee River cabin and reopen Thomas Reese's store. I heard General Twigs is trying to close the fort here. He already sent many of the soldiers down to Port Charlotte. I have half as many customers as I used to. I think we could make a better living down there."

Joseph nods. "I have heard the same thing. One of the men told me the general would rather place a fort at Manatee instead of here. He is tired of the civilians engaging him in their petty squabbles and wants to be nearer to the Indian villages. He caters to that Manatee crowd with their big homes and plantations. Gates, Braden and Gamble are more his class, I think."

Good! He is thinking the same thing I am. Maybe this is God's leading after all.

"While you are gone, why don't I see if I can find someone who will rent this house? We could always return if we can't make it down there and business gets better here. What improvements would need to be made for Reese's cabin to suit us?"

Joseph laughs, "It already suits me. As for you, now, I will have a lot of work to do to bring it up to your standards."

He gets up from his chair and walks over to me. Taking me by the hand, he spins me around and draws me into his arms. "Are you sure?"

I nod my head.

He smiles, "I confess, the thought of moving out of this crowded town makes me want to dance."

He leads me into a polka around the kitchen table. Eliza and Mary clap along in time. At the end of our dance, I curtsey, and then push him away.

Breathless, I manage to gasp, "Joseph, get on now. The day is creeping away. It is time for the girls to go to bed. We have much to do tomorrow if we are going to move."

Still laughing, Joseph kisses me on the cheek. He turns and with a flourish, bows low over Eliza's hand and kisses it. "Good night, princess. I will be gone when you wake in the morning, but I will be back soon." He repeats the same to Mary, and then exits the kitchen.

By Joseph's return, I find a new arrival to the Tampa community who agrees to rent our house. They wish to move in immediately, so I keep the girls home from school to help prepare for the move. Eliza is happy and eager to help, but Mary cries when she realizes she will not be going back to her books and friends.

As I pack, I pick up my father's pocket watch. Joseph no longer carries it as it does not work, but I cannot bear to throw it away. In some ways, it is hard to believe that it is 1851, but in others, it seems like a century has passed since I remember my father caressing this watch in the same way I do now. I rub the back and think of the times this watch represents, both good and bad. Though I remember the inscription, the words are no longer legible. The island's salt air left pits in the metal. The glass front is scratched, and the chain is bent and frail. This watch has outlived its usefulness. It is broken and worn, but I still treasure it.

Is this how God thinks of me? Weak. Unstable. Stongwilled. Frequently disobedient. But still beloved? Oh, God, how can you love me so much? Though I don't understand, I know now it is true.

Joseph loads all of our belongings onto Captain Tresca's sailboat for the journey to the Manatee River. The Captain's big schooner will travel much faster than our little boat, and we have acquired so many things including some new furniture during our stay in Tampa that it will not fit onto our vessel.

As we sail around the western shore of Terra Ceia and past the opening to Terra Ceia Bay, I wonder if we will ever own the land there that was our first Florida home. The captain continues on south towards Shaw's Point and the entrance to the Manatee River. Eliza looks longingly back towards the island.

Joseph goes to her. Placing one hand on her shoulder, he says, "It is not so far from our new home to our old one. I promise you will go with me on my next trip to the farm. Look ahead little one, not behind." He escorts Eliza to the bow of the ship and points out landmarks as we enter the Manatee River. They hang over the rail to watch the water as Captain Tresca slows the boat to make his way past some sandbars.

In the clear river, we can see almost all the way to the sandy bottom.

Tugging on Joseph's coat, Eliza points. "Papa! Papa! What is that?"

Several grey animals bigger than a man drift slowly along beside the boat. Two little flippers protrude from where their arms should be and a great flat tail arches and waves propelling them gracefully through the water. Periodically, they float to the surface, take a breath and sink below the water again. Their eyes look like tiny black buttons in their wrinkled faces and fuzzy whiskers extend from their snouts. Bonaparte utters a low growl at the shapes floating in the water.

"Look, look," Eliza says again. "A baby."

One miniature sea creature nuzzles close to its mother.

"What are they Papa?" she asks again.

"Those are manatees, Eliza. Remember Captain Sam telling you about them? They gave their name to this river. Some say the word means Big Beaver in the Indian tongue. Their tail does resemble the tail of a beaver. They are also called sea cows."

"They don't look like cows!" scoffs Eliza, "but they do have a beaver's tail."

Mary calls from the other side of the boat. "There are more over here. They are all around us! Will they hurt us Papa?"

"No, Mary. They won't hurt us. They are very gentle creatures. They say at one time you could walk across the river on their backs. People have been killing them for their oil and blubber like whales. I don't know how good it is though."

"Someone kills them?" Mary begins to cry.

Seeking to distract her, Joseph says, "We are here! Mary, dry your eyes. Come help me put down the anchor. Look there, Eliza. We are home."

Joseph points in the direction of an oak grove. I count six large trees and under their spreading limbs sits a small log cabin.

"Joseph, what have you gotten us into?" I ask. "The cabin is so small! How can we live there and make a store, too?"

Joseph holds both hands up in frustration.

"We? There was no 'we' about this, Julia! This is your land. You purchased it. You made the decision to leave Tampa and come here. I am not a magician. I did the best I could with what you gave me. In time, we will build a bigger house and use the cabin for a store. But, for now, this is all there is!"

Frowning, he abruptly turns around to join Captain Tresca at the wheel. The two men debate where to anchor the ship.

I hurt his feelings. I am going to have to learn to be gentler with my husband! Maybe I should keep my opinions to myself. God will have to work a miracle if that is going to happen. At least I have learned Joseph, like God, is forgiving.

"It is my land, isn't it?" No, not quite my land. I think about Billy Bowlegs.

"A gift from the Creator," I say aloud to no one in particular. Bonaparte must think I am talking to him. He wags his tail and nudges my hand so I will pet his head.

I laugh. We've come right back to where we started. A new beginning. A chance at a new life. I am different than I was when I first arrived. I have learned some things since we first made Florida home eight years ago. Margaret was right. I've been through the wilderness, but all things have worked together for good. The bad times made me stronger, but also forced me to depend upon God. The good times taught me to love and to enjoy life. There has been joy even in the darkest of days. I can see it clearly now, though I doubted then. Margaret taught me everything starts with asking God for help, trusting Him and being grateful. Now, as we begin this fresh start, that is what I need to do.

I whisper, though no one could probably hear me over the wind in the sails. I want this moment to be just between me and God. "What do you want to do with this land? What do you want to do with me? I'm willing. Take this place. Take me." Then, I begin to count the things I have to be thankful for. *Let's see. Number one, we won't have to live in a tent…*

Author's Notes

The second book is harder than the first! I heard that from someone, I can't remember who, but they were right. Eliza's Story was an experiment to see if I could write a novel. Once I proved I could and more importantly that it would be well received, my next task was to prove that the first book was not a fluke! It surprised me how much more difficult Julia's Story was to write.

Some of my problem in writing this book was I was more conscious of you, my readers, than I was with Eliza's Story. With Eliza's Story, you didn't exist. Now, I want to please you and reread your compliments (and criticisms) in an effort to make this story even better than the first. At times, that left me anxious and afraid to write until I finally realized the only critic I truly care about is the One who gave me the gift of writing. When I gave the story over to Him, it went much easier.

Julia's Story is a different tale though, and that led to my second difficulty. Julia's Story, out of necessity, had to be much more invented than Eliza's Story was. Eliza's Story is basically hung on a predetermined framework. The Atzeroth family history is well documented from their arrival on Terra Ceia in Manatee County, Florida. I had the facts, all I had to do was add the conversations and some of the reasoning for why they made the decisions they did.

In going back in time to write Julia's Story, I also had to answer the questions of how they got to Florida and why they came. Those facts are not recorded. The need to know why led me to do research in German history, immigration history and the history of the cities of New York City, Philadelphia, New Orleans and Tampa. I have to apologize to the countless History Fair students who I lectured about the evils of doing research on the Internet. While I urged them to go to the library and wade through microfilm, I now know there are millions of documents available on the Internet and set aside for public use by thoughtful historians and archivists across our country. I am appreciative of the people, many of them volunteers, who took the time to index those documents. Who knew how much could be found sitting on your own couch in your pajamas!

I spent hours upon hours scouring ship records for the arrival of the Atzeroths. I found Joseph listed on the Ship Sully thanks to an arrival date on naturalization papers found by a fellow historian, but he is listed as a single man and Julia's and Eliza's arrival records are nowhere to be found. Believe me, I have looked and the best family historian I know, Cindy Russell, also looked. It is as though Julia did not exist until she arrived with Joseph in what became Manatee County.

Once I found the facts about why people were leaving Bavaria and how they travelled to America, I had to make some decisions about what motivated the Atzeroths, why Julia and Joseph might have been separated and why they ended up in Florida. Just as in Eliza's Story, I put myself in their shoes and imagined what it must have been like. I was struck by how many people were willing to completely uproot their families and start over in America for opportunity to freely worship God. As modern Americans, we do not understand what a privilege we possess to have that right today.

As Floridians, we also must be grateful for the people who were willing to risk their lives to lay the foundation for our present day state. This beautiful tropical land was not an easy place to possess with its diseases, weather, wild animals and the same mixed up politics we still endure.

As with Eliza's Story, I have many people to thank. Most importantly is my friend, Patty Armstrong and her mother, Claire Rhoades, who prayed with me on the phone one day so that a two month period of being stuck in one part of the book miraculously resolved itself that very day. Other friends prayed me through difficult sections of the writing including Bethany Ford, Di Bennett, Julie Vogel, Karen Eason, Penny Hedrick and Vera Jo Strickland. Some of the spiritual discoveries Julia makes were inspired by the sermons of Pastor Philip Hamm of First Baptist Church of Palmetto, Florida and Rick Hedrick's Sunday School lessons on Job. I also want to give credit to authors Chip Ingram (True Spirituality: Becoming a Romans 12 Christian), Lysa TerKeust (Made to Crave) and Craig Groeschel (The Christian Atheist).

Cindy Russell and Lu Rupert helped me greatly with the research as did Joe Knetsch, who documented the life of John Jackson and continues to provide information on the Atzeroth family. Ron Prouty is a great encouragement to me. If he has his way, someday, you will read Henry's Story (but first, I have to finish Eliza's Story as told through the eyes of her daughter-in-law, Caroline).

The four supervisors in the Manatee County Clerk of Circuit Court's Historical Resources Department, Diane Ingram, Mandy Polson, Amara Nash and Phaedra Rehorn are an inspiration. Their creativity, professionalism and commitment to making history come alive for the residents and visitors of Manatee County makes our organizations unique among local history museums. I am confident our county's heritage is in good hands with these four women in charge. As always, my boss, Chips Shore, Manatee County Clerk of Circuit Court, is supportive in my quest to preserve Manatee County's past. He always knows just who to call and how to gain the influence we need to do that work.

My husband who frequently says, "I told you so," as he first suggested self publishing Eliza's Story continues to push me to do more as do you my readers. Put your name here in the blank. Thank you, ________________. I could not do this without you!

Thanks also to Cherie Hill who makes the books come alive with her beautiful covers and layout. A special group of people read the first and second drafts, caught a lot of typos and misspellings and corrected my punctuation. Thanks so much to Cindy, Bethany, Elizabeth, Genni, Sarah, Cathy, Norma, Miranda, Julee, Bob, Emily, Kay, Ben, Vera, Ola, Peggy, Amy, Valerie, Stephanie A., Stephanie L. and Tari and my parents, Bob and Emily. Special thanks to my niece, Emily Lenart, English and French major extraordinaire who read the proof and made some corrections.

And as always, I give praise to God who provides the Holy Spirit and the gift of imagination. To Him be the Glory forever and ever. Amen.

What's True?

Julia's Story is more fiction than Eliza's Story, but it is still based upon historical research and true events. For those of you who want to separate fact from fiction, here is a list of what's true.

Introduction

The Owl Story comes from Atzeroth family history

Beds were stuffed with Spanish moss

Armed Occupation Act gave 160 acres of land to new settlers in exchange for defending their property from the Indians.

Chapter 1

German Christmas traditions and food

1816 famine and weather in Germany

Julia's parents died and she moved in with her uncle, but his treatment of her is imagined as is how she met Joseph

Julia's sister married a man with the last name of Nichols, but there is no record of her first name or her husband's

Julia was later diagnosed with a torpid liver but the cause was unknown; the doctors said the cure was hard work

German Politics, hymns and crops

Chapter 2

Description of their house is based upon a painting of a house in Bavaria in that time period

Julia was known as a good businesswoman

They had two boys who died before they left Bavaria; cause of death unknown

Persecution of Prussian Lutherans

Gomfried Duden's book describes America as a land of plenty

The letter is a quote from a letter sent from America to Germany during this time period

German politics and the Ultramontaines

The quotes from Martin Luther are true

Scarlet Fever's symptoms and treatment

Chapter 3

Route and method of transportation from Bavaria to America via LaHavre

Description of LaHavre

Joseph travels on the Sully

Julia's travels and arrival date are unknown

Eliza was born in France

Margaret and Ada are not real

Chapter 4

Description of travel in steerage

Story of woman who commits suicide on a ship is true

Meta and her family are real names of people who traveled about the time period Julia would have been immigrating

Description of Little Germany in New York City

St Matthews Lutheran Church was established in this time period to be an English church

Chapter 5

Travel to Philadelphia was along this route and up the Delaware River

Race Relations were tense in Philadelphia at this time

There was an earthquake and rogue wave in this time period

Settlement of Hermann, Missouri by the German Settlement Society of Philadelphia

The Ohio was a real ship during this time period

Chapter 6

Route of the Ohio from Philadelphia to New Orleans. There were some overland travels at this time, but I chose to take them by sea so that they would go past Florida's west coast

Passage Key is a real island, but it disappears and reappears depending on the shift of sand. At one time, it was large enough to have a fresh water lake used for supplying drinking water to ships.

Cedar Keys were an army depot, at one time headquarters of the Army of the South, and place for meeting the Florida Indians to negotiate treaties

The Mikasuki under Coosa Tustanugge did surrender and were sent to Western Reservations

Mr. Lewis, who is imaginary, expresses commonly held beliefs from this time period

Michaela Ingraham is real

German Settlements at New Orleans had more influence on that city's culture than is commonly known

The scene where the slaves are working on the riverbank comes from a painting of New Orleans from that time period.

The advertisement for the slave auction is also real

German baked goods and Christmas traditions

Treatments for a torpid liver come from medical books of that period

Hahn means rooster

Chapter 7

The crops Joseph grows are common to Louisiana and Florida

Armed Occupation Act regulations

The Essex was an army ship that patrolled Florida's west coast

The wall of water that destroyed Cedar Keys really happened. The Seminoles refused to meet there with the army any more after that.

The passage between Egmont Key and Mullet Key can still be tricky today

Description of Fort Brooke and the Hillsborough River

The Indians came and went freely at the fort during this time period.

Palmetto bugs are real. Ask any Florida homemaker.

The settlers called Julia and Joseph, Madam Joe and Mr. Joe because of difficulties pronouncing their last name.

Chapter 8

Colonel Belknap was the commander at the fort for several years

Their dog was named Bonaparte for the reasons given

The *Margaret Ann* was a real ship.

The details about Captain Tresca's life are commonly held, but have recently been debated

Julia's reaction to living in a tent is from family records

The spring was a freshwater spring but it had a sulphur taste and odor

Song, One More Day, was a seafarer song from this time period

The Golden Orb or Banana Spider is a common spider in Florida

Julia wove a roof of palm fronds which leaked

The Yellow Rat Snake or Eastern Rat Snake (also called the Chicken Snake) is common. There are still water moccasins and rattlesnakes on the island.

Chapter 9

Cattle, descendants of the ones brought to Florida from Spain by the explorers, were rounded up by settlers branded and then, set free to run wild again. They were often called Cracker Cattle.

Ponce DeLeon named Florida, La Florida, after Feast of Flowers, when he landed on Easter Sunday, 1513.

Delay in statehood was due to the Missouri Compromise and the need for a free state to be admitted at the same time.

Bull Sharks have been known to swim in shallow waters during mating season

Chapter 10

Foundation stones of the log cabin can still be seen on Terra Ceia

Shell mounds at the mouth of the Manatee River were at present day Emerson Point and DeSoto National Memorial

The spelling of the river was originally Manitee

There was discord between the Atzeroths and the settlers of Manatee, but no record of why.

Ezekiel Glazier was a Presbyterian minister.

During this time period, throughout America, there was a great distrust of Catholics

Description of the house and chimney is from family records and is a typical construction for the area accurate

Chapter 11

Joseph gets lost in the storm and is blown to Sarasota Bay

He brings glass windows from New Orleans

Nicholas Family is Julia's sister and brother in-law, but the first names of parents are unknown

Homestead issues

Surveyor's reference to "Second rate land"

Captain Tresca talks to settlers on Atzeroths behalf

Onion Pie is a real German dish

Spring on bay bank

Chapter 12

Sam Bishop was a real ship captain

There was a storm while Joseph was bringing the Nicholas family home

Mrs. Nicholas' pregnancy

Trip to Newnansville

Cracker cow

Baby dies

Chapter 13

Mrs. Nicholas dies

Dr. Braden, Gates and Gamble were real people

Burial behind house

The flower is Night Blooming Moon Flower
Debt to Belknaps

Chapter 14

Move to Tampa
Description of Fort Brooke
Belknaps family including Willie, (There were also two older daughters)
Billy Bowlegs visits Belknaps and Madam Joe cooks for him
Willie's education
Joseph cannot read and write

Chapter 15

Statehood
Eliza's birthdate
Billy Bowlegs fascination with the doll
Julia's illness
Epsom salts cure was used in that time
Herbal remedies
Belknaps transfer to Texas

Chapter 16

Return to Terra Ceia
Julia's birthday
Mr. Nicholas leaves, dies in New Orleans
Ella Gates' death and her mother's reaction
Hurricane
Collapse of the cabin
Move to hen house

Chapter 17

Cabin rebuilt after the storm
Joseph works as surveyor
Description of Perrine Land Grant is by John Jackson
John Jackson hires him and writes in his support
Homestead issues
Indian uprising begins
Petersen brothers were their neighbors across Terra Ceia Bay

Chapter 18

Return to Fort Brooke
Phosphorescent light before storm
Second hurricane
Flood
Third storm
Lumber scattered
Lot on wrong side of river
Move house
Move in date
Samuel Bishop and Nicholas Wilson
Mama's beer and cake shop
Papa worked at fort, but not Fort Brooke
Two men vouch for Papa
Ruling in his favor
Papa's illness
Henry Clark's death
Charles Macy was shopkeeper for Clarks

Chapter 19

Description of courthouse
Name of sheriff
Mr. Reese's property purchased

Joseph learns to write his name, whether Eliza teaches him is not known

Attempts to move fort to Manatee

Economic problems in Tampa

Description of manatees also known as the "sea cow"

There were six oak trees at location of cabin which was at the present day site of Regatta Point Condominiums on the corner of 11th Avenue and Riverside Drive in Palmetto, Florida

Preview of
From A Heavenly Land:
Caroline's Story

Where is she? The boat will be here any minute. I see the steam rising from its smokestack in the distance. It will not take it long to reach the dock. *Where could she have gone? Wasn't she just here?* I stopped to show the children the location of the foundation for the old cabin, but we didn't linger long. She was there one moment and gone the next! *How could she have gotten so far away in such a short time?*

"Eliza! Mother Eliza!"

The children echo my calls, "Grandmother Fogarty! Where are you?"

We walk through orange groves. I tilt back my head so the light peeks around the brim of my hat and feel the warmth of the autumn sun upon my face. "Ladies always wear a hat," Mother Eliza says. I suppose her mother said it to her, as well.

They planted this grove of trees. Lush with round globes of fruit not quite orange, but no longer green, they flank the path before me. They were brought as tiny seedlings from across the bay. Who knew that Terra Ceia would be such a good place for citrus trees? My mother-in-law, I am sure. I sigh. She seems to know everything.

Just beyond the trees, I catch a glimmer of light reflecting off the waves of the bay. I love fall. In some parts of the country, autumn and the encroaching cold and dark it heralds brings fear and sadness, but here on the west coast of Florida, fall means an end to the mosquito infested season of rain and dreaded storms. Fall brings a break from the oppressive summer heat. It's time to plant the garden and net the gathering schools of mullet that fill the bay's shallow inlets. I breathe deeply and glance at the sky again. It should be another beautiful day.

Or it will be if I can find my mother-in-law in time to catch the boat whose whistle I now hear. It must be at the dock. *How long will it wait for us?* I send the children back to meet it. Perhaps they can hold the captain a little while longer.

"Hurry now. Go straight there, and don't wander off. We don't need anyone else to get lost. Stay together. I will be there as soon as I find Grandmother."

I walk alone towards Terra Ceia Bay. They say Terra Ceia means Heavenly Land. From the tales I hear, this island was not so heavenly.

"Mother Eliza," I shout. *She must be here somewhere.* I squash the rise of panic that wells up inside me. Maybe she fell. The image of her lying helpless unable to get up again presses me forward.

Behind me, men work in the groves and fields. Mixed with the bray of a mule and clank of the plow, I hear their laughter. There is always laughter in my life these days. Once upon a time, it wasn't so. I shudder when I think of those lonely years. The times I thought life was not worth living. Yes, even then, my mother-in-law was right. I survived. Well, most of us did.

There! I see her now. *What is she doing? Can't she hear me? Doesn't she know how worried I was?*

Her back is braced against a rough gray palm tree. She has always been tiny, but today, against the tree, she seems shorter than I remember. She used to be so vigorous, so full of life. I thought she would live forever. Today, I am not so sure.

I hurry towards her. "Mother Eliza, I was worried. Come, the boat is here. The children are waiting for us."

She turns to smile at me. I see the woman I first met so long ago hidden in the wrinkles. How long has it been since I was the nervous girl afraid to meet the mother of the boy I loved? Are there tears in her eyes?

"The children. I remembered another story for them."

"Come, you can tell them on the boat. It is time to go. We must hurry."

"Caroline, I want you to write down my stories. I am the only one left who recalls the story of this land's taming. I was only three, but I can remember. If you don't keep my stories alive, no one in the future will know what it was like to live in the wilderness."

"Yes, Mother. I will. But, now, we have to go. Come, the boat will leave without us. We don't want to have to spend the night here."

I take her arm and help her over the sandy path. I wish I could hurry, but slow my pace to match hers. If I can just get her to focus on walking, we might make it to the boat before it leaves. Are the children already on board? Why did she have to walk so far?

"I loved this place," she murmurs. "This has always been home to me." I just nod. We don't have time for stories. We have to get to the boat.

ABOUT THE AUTHOR

Cathy Slusser is a second generation Floridian who grew up in St. Petersburg, but spent holidays and vacations with her grandparents who lived in Manatee County. She moved to Terra Ceia Island in northwest Manatee County in 1979. Cathy fell in love with history upon reading Eugenia Price novels in Middle School. When she traveled to St. Simons Island, Georgia and saw the places those characters lived, she knew that the subject of history could be alive and exciting. Ever since that time, she has made it her goal to share that message with others.

She has a bachelor's degree in history from Furman University and a master's degree in history from the University of South Florida. She has worked for the Manatee County Clerk of Circuit Court's Office for thirty years and is Director of Historical Resource. In this role, she supervises five historical sites, the Manatee Village Historical Park, the Manatee County Historical Records Library, the Florida Maritime Museum at Cortez, the Palmetto Historical Park, and the Manatee County Agricultural Museum, as well as Manatee County Teen Court. Cathy has two grown sons, Rob and Tim, a fabulous daughter in law, Miranda, and a daughter of the heart, Christina. She married her husband, Glen, a third generation Floridian in 1981. She enjoys horseback riding, fusing glass, felting and writing. Cathy is passionate about preserving Manatee County's past and telling its stories to residents and visitors of all ages.

Made in the USA
Charleston, SC
23 May 2014